St. Louis Noir

ST. LOUIS NOIR

EDITED BY SCOTT PHILLIPS

Published by Akashic Books
©2016 Akashic Books

Series concept by Tim McLoughlin and Johnny Temple
St. Louis map by Sohrab Habibion

Front cover photo: *A Hobo "Jungle" Along Riverfront. Saint Louis, Missouri.* Library of Congress, Prints & Photographs Division, FSA/OWI Collection, LC-USF34-001830-E.

ISBN: 978-1-61775-298-8
Library of Congress Control Number: 2015954064
First printing

Akashic Books
Twitter: @AkashicBooks
Facebook: AkashicBooks
E-mail: info@akashicbooks.com
Website: www.akashicbooks.com

ALSO IN THE AKASHIC NOIR SERIES

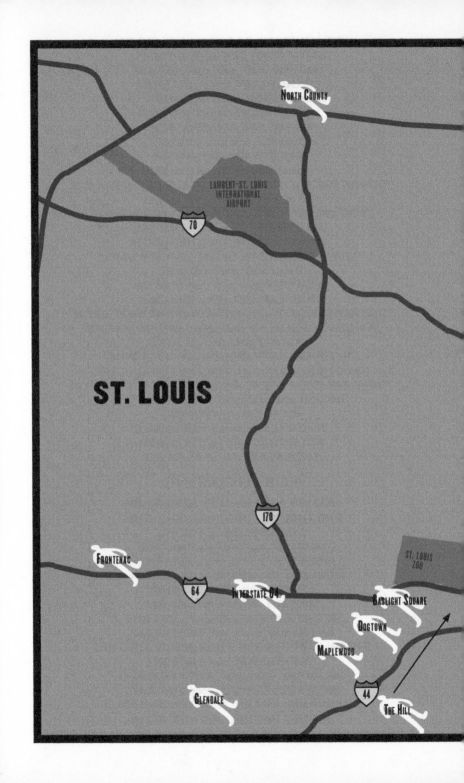

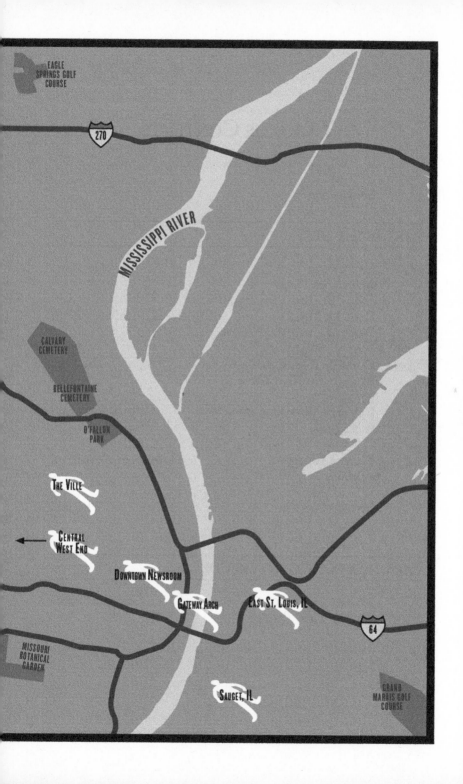

TABLE OF CONTENTS

INTRODUCTION
HIGH AND LOW COLLIDE

The St. Louis region has had a rough time over the past few years. A number of our school districts are unaccredited. A large section of a North St. Louis County landfill is burning uncontrolled—yes, it's on fire—and said fire is only yards away from a World War II–era radioactive waste dump. There's the matter of the region's de facto segregation, a persistent pox on the city and county decades after the explicit, institutional variety became illegal. A number of our suburban municipalities have lately been exposed in the act of strong-arming their poorest citizens, running what amount to debtors' prisons. In recent years one of those cities, Ferguson, has become a national synonym for police misconduct and institutional racism. At the same time we are preparing to build a billion-dollar football stadium (40 percent of that sum taxpayer-funded) in an attempt to try and hold on to our hapless and unloved Rams, who may have already decamped for Los Angeles by the time you read these lines.

The region can seem closed off to outsiders. The inevitable question locals ask upon meeting a stranger is, "Where'd you go to high school?" It took me years to understand the geographical, ethnic, and religious subtexts hidden in that question, but I realized early on that responding "Wichita, Kansas" was a quick way to lose my interlocutor's sympathy and attention. Side streets tend to be haphazardly marked, so much so that my wife and I used to joke that this grew out of a stubborn philosophy that *if you're not from here, you don't need to know.* This was proven a few years back when the federal government demanded that the route to Lambert–St. Louis International Airport be better indicated on area freeways. The classic response in the media from the spokesman for the local agency responsible for the missing airport signage was something along the lines of: "We just figured everybody knew where the airport was."

Amid all this is a rich, multicultural history of art and literature both high and low, stemming from conflict and passions running hot. The ballads "Stagger Lee" and "Frankie and Johnny" are each based on actual murder cases from St. Louis in the 1890s, a far cry from the wholesome turn-of-the-century version depicted in *Meet Me in St. Louis*. But the highbrow and low meeting head-on are part and parcel of the St. Louis experience. Tennessee Williams got his ass out of here as soon as he was able, but Chuck Berry still lives down the road in Wentzville, and until he turned eighty-eight in 2014 he still played a monthly gig at Blueberry Hill in the Delmar Loop.

Maybe the quintessential yin/yang St. Louisan in the arts was Lee Falk, who created the comic strips *The Phantom* and *Mandrake the Magician* (both of which still run today); in a loftier vein he was also a theatrical director who worked with Marlon Brando, Paul Newman, and Basil Rathbone on the New York stage.

This collection strives for some of that same energy that the collision of high and low can produce. From L.J. Smith's smoky ballad "Tell Them Your Name Is Barbara" to S.L. Coney's brutal "Abandoned Places," these writers have staked out the far ends of the noir spectrum and hit most of the key points between them. The first story I requested for the anthology was "Fool's Luck" by LaVelle Wilkins-Chinn. I'd read an early draft of the story and loved it, but when I asked if she'd be willing to include it here she wasn't sure it qualified as noir, since, though its central character is certainly criminal, it isn't a crime story in the most obvious sense. But one of the definitions of noir (and I hesitate to open that particular debate here, so please don't write to tell me the proper definition) is that it traffics in fatality and doom and bad luck and characters who persistently, knowingly, act against their own best interests. And that's what "Fool's Luck" is all about.

Some of the writers included here will be new to you, at least in this context, though you may be familiar with them from their day jobs. Umar Lee is a prominent local activist and has become a fixture in the national media since the tragic death of Michael Brown in Ferguson. Jason Makansi wears many hats but I first knew him as a publisher; we have not one but two accomplished film critics providing stories: Calvin Wilson (who is also a jazz deejay) and Chris Barsanti.

Some of the other writers in the book are well known nationally. Laura Benedict and John Lutz, both of whom produced fine stories with good humor, need no introduction here. I hadn't realized, though, that Colleen J. McElroy had lived in St. Louis until Akashic Books publisher Johnny Temple suggested we approach her about submitting. Jedidiah Ayres is recognized by aficionados of noir fiction as one of the originators (along with Peter Rozovsky and my own bad self) of the now-ubiquitous reading series Noir at the Bar. Paul D. Marks is fast becoming a major force in crime fiction. And I'm very proud to be able to include four poems by St. Louis's Poet Laureate, Michael Castro.

All these writers come at their work with different perspectives and styles but all with a connection to and a passion for our troubled city and its surroundings. I am immensely pleased to have been able to collect them in this volume.

Scott Phillips
St. Louis, Missouri
May 2016

PART I

THE CITY

ABANDONED PLACES

BY S.L. CONEY

Dogtown

"Your dad's a bastard, kid. You should be mad. Hell, you should be madder than me. The fucker ran off and left you with someone you hardly know. You know what I think?"

He knew what Vickie thought. He'd heard it over and over the past couple of days. Tuning her out, he pressed his forehead into the window, the dust along the edge tickling his nose as he watched the cars pass through, hoping to catch a glimpse of curly blond hair and his dad's wide, wide smile; the one he called his "fuck me" smile. He'd never seen it fail to bring a girl to her knees. Sometimes he locked himself in the bathroom and practiced that smile, trying to make it reach his eyes so they crinkled at the corners and blue shined.

She slammed the door on the washer, the vibration tugging at him through his hip. He turned, studying her short black hair spiked like porcupine quills, her eyes squinted against the cigarette smoke as she flapped one of her shirts. He didn't understand why she bothered to wash them. They stank like smoke before they even made it to the closet.

Vickie was only seven years older than Ian and had been married to his dad for two. She hadn't been thrilled with him before his dad left; now he kept waiting for her to call social services and have him taken to a home.

"Everybody needs a vice. Val could've had the decency to

leave me some damn money." Dropping her cigarette to the concrete floor, she ground it under her heel, hand digging her pack out of her pocket. "Are you listening to me?"

"Yes." He didn't call her *ma'am* because that usually pissed her off.

She paused long enough to light her new cigarette, cheeks hollowing as she sucked against the filter. "I saw that look you gave me."

He turned back to the window, staring through the grime to the world outside, wondering how it could keep functioning when everything in his life had turned upside down.

Vickie stopped hiding her smoking the day Valentine left, moving from behind the shed to lighting up inside the house, and every day since then she kept accusing Ian of giving her looks. Maybe she just felt guilty for ruining her lungs, but every time he saw her light up, the pit in his stomach opened just a little wider. Either she'd stopped caring if his dad found out, or she knew he wasn't coming back.

"I take good care of you. I feed you, make sure you're clean. Fuck, I'm damn good to you, considering you're not my kid."

Ian supposed she was right; she did feed him, and so far she hadn't called anyone about him, but he wished she'd stop making him feel like he owed her something for being there.

"I need a vice, and mine left, walked right out the door while you were at school. Didn't even tell me where he was going."

Ian bunched his hands in the sleeves of his shirt, the back of his head tight. He knew this part of the story too. She kept repeating the same things over and over, until the more she said the less he believed her. Vickie reminded him of Sandy Robinson, the girl at school who kept saying Justin Bieber was her brother. She kept repeating it as if it would make it true, as if they'd start believing if she said it enough. Even he was a better liar than Vickie was, and she had seven years on him. It was a little shameful.

"It's such fucking bullshit. At first I was sort of relieved. No offense, kid, but do you know how much foundation I was using to cover the bruises from your daddy's fists? There's vice and then there's vice. Shit, it's sick. I know it's sick." She paused to take a draw off her cigarette, the tip of her tongue poking out between her lips as she picked off a stray piece of tobacco. "It's odd what you can get used to. When I look in the mirror, my face seems empty without the occasional black eye."

He wondered if she stood in front of that mirror and rehearsed the things she said. It was like seeing the same play over and over again. That was one thing about lying: you never wanted it to sound rehearsed.

She stood, pulling an armful of clothes from the dryer and dropping them in the basket. He couldn't tell if she was using any less makeup. It still looked like a painted mask, the edge of it not quite meeting her hairline. Sometimes he thought about seeing if he could peel it back to reveal what lay underneath.

"Mean fists or not, the bed gets lonely without someone in it. Shit, I haven't been alone in bed since your daddy came and I crawled out my window." She dumped ash on the floor before sticking the cigarette back into her mouth, one side clenched down around the filter, making her face uneven, like old Mrs. Ashworth after she'd had her stroke. "I didn't know I was trading one bad man for another, but at least your daddy was better in bed than mine."

He didn't want to hear this. Rolling his eyes, he pushed off the washer and started up the stairs, palm skimming the handrail.

"Hey, runt, you're supposed to be helping me. Get your ass back down here."

Ignoring her, he yanked his dad's old union jacket from the chifforobe in the entryway and pulled it over his shoulders, the sleeves hanging to his fingertips, shoulders still too wide. He closed the door on her—"Ungrateful bastard"—and loped off the porch, body all right angles, his joints loose as if he wasn't securely put together yet. The wind blew up the street, ruffling his hair as he stared at the redbrick duplexes across Tamm Avenue, satellite dishes sticking out like malignancies. He kept his eyes trained on Cindy McClellan's upstairs window, hoping to catch sight of her moving behind the glass. At night he sat in the dark, watching as she changed without pulling the blinds. He liked it best when she raised her arms, her breasts jutting out in small peaks, her nipples perfect exclamation points. One of these days he was going to try out his "fuck me" smile on her.

The sun was just starting to go down, highlighting the tower on the old Forest Park Hospital along the east side of the neighborhood. Soon they would gut it, tearing it down to build another parking lot. It was what happened to abandoned places.

He walked past green, white, and orange, the Irish flag painted on the curb and flying high, down past the faded shamrocks on Tamm Avenue. Concentrating on taking deep, burning breaths, he walked through the fog of each exhale, pretending it made everything new.

There were still kids climbing on the giant stone turtles poised midcrawl over Turtle Playground, arms out as they walked along the back of the long stone snake, moms and dads watching, laughing. The constant hum of traffic on 64 edging Dogtown followed him as he turned from their laughter and made his way up to the swings at the end of the park. At this time of day it was mostly grown-ups in this part of the park. It was his favorite time to swing. With them here he didn't feel too old to be playing. Maybe growing up wouldn't be so bad if he could still swing.

He closed his eyes, pumping his legs and thinking about his dad as he listened to the squeak of the chain. It wasn't unusual for Val to leave on business, but he always said goodbye, and he always let Ian know when he was coming back. Ian knew better than to think his dad was a saint. He'd overheard Mrs. Donovan say Valentine had a quick smile and an even quicker zipper. He'd never knocked Ian around, but he knew his dad had quick fists as well. He was loud and boisterous, and life seemed to bend itself to his will.

The thought of going back to a house filled with Vickie's practiced monologue and the choking haze of cigarette smoke twisted his stomach up. Pulling his dad's coat closer around himself, he watched as the sun set, the children's laughter disappearing as they made their way home.

That night he could hear Vickie laughing through the wall, her high, fragile cackle scattered by a deeper rumble. For all she talked about her bed being lonely, she hadn't spent much time alone since his dad disappeared. Ian couldn't figure out if she thought he was deaf or just stupid.

He curled up on his side, listening to the squeak of the bed and her grunting moans, his stomach tight, face hot. Tension coiled in his belly, cock hard whether he wanted it or not. Reaching down into his pajamas, he touched himself, the warnings of Sister Theresa running through his head. He didn't want to think of Vickie, of her makeup mask and ashtray stench, so he turned his thoughts to Cindy. Cindy Mc-

Clellan's tits, Vickie's moans, and his hand, and he was coming over his fingers, eyes closed against the tears, the heat in his stomach burning to ash as he pressed his face against the pillow to soothe the sharp sting in his eyes.

Benny had violin practice on Tuesdays so Ian was walking home alone. He tucked his hands into the pockets of his dad's jacket as he walked, the smell of fried food following him down Tamm. It was a straight shot from St. James the Greater once he crested the small hill. He could see Vickie sitting out on the stoop, her long legs stretched out until the tops of her shoes lit up in the sun. The cafeteria macaroni and cheese turned to a hard lump in his stomach. Staring at her was like looking at a black hole.

Letting his pack slip to the ground, he sat down on the bench outside the Happy Medium Barbershop and focused on the people walking back and forth. He closed his eyes, listening to the sounds of the neighborhood as he tried to find the familiarity in its daily routine. The traffic hummed along 64 and the radio droned from the patio behind Seamus McDaniel's farther up the avenue. It was the same as every other day, except it felt empty, a vital piece of Dogtown missing.

"Your daddy is still gone, huh?"

Mr. Allen settled on the bench next to him, cane propped between his legs, wrinkled face hidden under the brim of his hat. Ian glanced at the squashed slope of his driving cap and away, staring up the street toward the gazebo. "Yes sir."

"It was bound to happen." He tapped his cane on the sidewalk, snorting and then spitting into the flowerpot by the bench. "You can't run with the types of people he did and not get into trouble." Mr. Allen glanced at him and then down the road toward the house. Ian wondered if he was staring at

Vickie's long legs. "She taking good care of you? You're looking a little peaked."

"Yes sir." He'd found it was best to stick to yes and no when you weren't sure what to say. Glancing at the rheumy paleness of his eyes, Ian wondered what Mr. Allen would say if he told him how he woke up in the middle of the night, sure the world had ended because the house felt so empty. What if he told him he sometimes thought Vickie had killed his dad? He opened his mouth, unsure of what was about to pour out, and then caught Vickie with her head turned, watching him.

Swallowing the grit in his mouth, he dropped his gaze. "She feeds me, does the laundry, sometimes she cleans."

"She feeds you, huh?"

"Yes sir."

"Guess you can't ask for much more than that." He patted Ian across the back and stood, pulling himself up by his cane and walking back into the barbershop.

Someone drove by in a golf cart and Ian settled into the seat to wait Vickie out. Closing his eyes, he listened to Mr. Allen's voice through the open door of the shop.

"Poor kid. You know Valentine started running with the Miller boys. They knew he was part of the hit on the Pulaski Bank last year, they just couldn't prove it. Now it's come back to bite him on the ass."

"Richard, shut your mouth. Door's open. You keep that up and you'll be neighboring with Valentine at the bottom of the Mississippi."

There was a rustle and then Mr. Beech, low and urgent: "The kid's still out there, you big oaf."

The door closed and he was left with a crushing hollow-ness in his chest, his arms and legs numb as reality receded, taking the air with it and leaving him alone in the still, discarded world. He sat there, blind and unfeeling, until a passing car blew its horn, shattering the bubble he was caught in. Pulling in a deep, shuddering breath, he folded over his knees, the flood of sight and sound making his stomach cramp until he gagged, nose running and eyes burning.

When he was five his Grandma Shone had died, leaving his world a little more gray, a little more empty. It'd been one of the few times Valentine allowed him to cling and Ian anchored his world to his dad. It wasn't always a steady anchor, but it'd always been there, whether it was in the raised echo of his voice or the rumble of his engine as he pulled out of the drive. Now that anchor had been ripped from him.

What am I supposed to do?

The question was present in every beat of his heart. Each time it ripped through him, pulling dry heaves from the depth of his guts. The vague feeling of wrongness solidified until it was too heavy to breathe around. He sat there, bent over his knees, waiting for the profound weakness to pass.

The question wouldn't leave. The constant knowledge of his father gone and his own uncertain future darkened his world. Cars passed on the street and Vickie watched, and nothing changed except for the dropping temperature, the cold solidifying his legs.

Wiping his mouth with the back of his hand, he stood and hefted his pack over his shoulder and continued down Tamm. Ian stopped on the street, staring at Vickie squatting on the stoop of the house he'd lived in his whole life. She stared back, eyes hard and sullen as she flicked her butt into the yard. Dropping his gaze, he crossed to the house, cheeks and head hot, eyes burning.

"What's wrong with you?"

He tried to step around her, but she reached out and snagged the sleeve of his jacket.

"Hey, kid, I was talking to you."

The last week had grown too big for him. All he could think about was her heavy moans and the banging on the wall every night. The shadow of his missing father was a vise, squeezing his chest until he couldn't breathe. Dropping his bag, he jerked out of her grasp, and using the momentum of his turn, he smacked her across the face, a fingernail raising a welt under her eye.

She stared at him, mouth opening and closing in a perfect purple O, and then she stood, catching him across the cheek with her knuckles. The punch sat him down on his ass, the shock reverberating up his spine to ring against his head like he'd stuck it inside the church bells.

"You little shit. I may have taken that from your daddy, but I'll be damned if I let a little runt like you hit me." She ran a hand through her hair, spikes popping right back into place, and glanced around as she tugged at the hem of her shirt. Bending, she hauled him up by the lapels of his daddy's coat and leaned close, her hot breath stinking of cigarettes and mint. "Keep that up and maybe I'll look real hard, make sure you end up with your daddy, you understand?"

He still couldn't think, the world gone plastic and shiny around him. Shoving her off, he left his bag on the porch and stumbled up to his room. He wiped at the warm trickle from his nose and stared at the red smear across his fingers. It looked like they'd both learned something from his dad.

That night he couldn't sleep, his chest tight and aching as he thought about his dad tangled in the murky current of the Mississippi. The swollen side of his face throbbed with every beat of his heart, a constant echo of Vickie's knuckles across his face.

He'd climbed into bed in his school uniform and now his pants were twisted around his legs, his shoes dirtying the sheet. Across the room his Iron Man action figure threw its shadow at the wall, the outside light catching the childhood guilty pleasure. The house was silent in a way it never was when Vickie was there. Even at night she left the TV or radio on, as if she was afraid of what she'd hear in the quiet.

Maybe I'll look real hard, make sure you end up with your daddy, you understand?

Sitting up in bed, he shoved the covers off and pulled on his dad's jacket, the nylon slick in his hands. The house was cold against his belly, the brick scraping his shirt up as he lowered himself from the window. The world was lit by scattered streetlights, their jaundiced light spreading along the sidewalk like watercolor. The low hum of conversation floated down the street from Seamus McDaniel's, sprinkled with the rise and fall of laughter that colored his idea of adulthood.

Ian started down Tamm, away from the noise and laughter, past the empty lot with its foundation rising from the ground, lost and haunted. Wind blew down the street, trapped from spreading by the buildings along either side, rattling the broken fence with its overgrown lot and crooked *Beware of Dog* sign. Pausing, he turned and looked back, expecting to see Vickie standing in the door, laughing as she locked him out, but the small brick house was still and dark, empty.

The barking of the big red mutt down the street pulled him forward toward the swings, the miserable squeak of the chain floating over the neighborhood. Cutting across the street, he stopped in the shadows by the house on the corner of Graham and watched the woman as she arced out over the highway. The light caught her hair at the apogee, shining blue black and unmoved as she hung suspended above the river of lights along the freeway. Vickie crested again, legs out as if she would fly off the swing right into the traffic along 64.

Up the street, people spilled out of Pat's Bar and Grill onto the sidewalk, heading toward their cars. A man broke off from the crowd and started down Oakland toward Vickie, passing the silent stone turtles, their shapes rising from the playground like burial mounds.

Shifting closer, Ian tried to catch a glimpse of his face, wondering if it was the man in his dad's bed. Vickie started across the avenue, away from the light. She was so close Ian could hear the click of her mint against her teeth. The man looked both ways and crossed, the light catching him full in the face. He had long stringy hair, the brown shot through with silver, his tall, lanky frame stretched too thin.

Tucked in the shadows, Ian held his breath as they passed, studying the man's doughy face. When they were a good ten feet past, he turned and followed, staying along the edges of the light.

He didn't remember his mother much, just the fuzzy picture his dad kept in his wallet. Her name had been Barbara, and Valentine used to say she was an angel. Ian wondered if his mom had made his dad happy though. She'd been blond and fair, and in that faded picture she'd laughed with her mouth open and eyes crinkled. Sometimes he liked to pretend he could hear that laugh. He bet it was a good one, high and wild, and not at all like Vickie. Vickie was lucky if she could wash the stink of brimstone off in the morning.

When Vickie and the man reached the corner they turned away from the house, toward Hampton and the abandoned Forest Park Hospital. Ian stopped in the last of the shadows and watched as they paused between the hospital and the empty parking garage. The man swung his doughy face about, looking around before he pulled the fence back, letting Vickie climb through and following after.

He could feel his heartbeat through his teeth. They'd come here sometimes, after school, smoke cigarettes and dare each other to go inside while they remained safely on the opposite side of the street. They'd tell each other stories about the horrible disfigurements and deaths, about the ghosts that wandered the halls and the gray lady who Stevie swore he'd seen in the tower.

No one ever took the dare. They would tease and taunt, but nobody was stupid enough to go inside.

Ian sunk to the concrete and watched as they walked along the other side of the fence. His bed was calling, safe and warm, even if his life had turned upside down. It would smell like him, and the blanket would scratch just as it did every night. He wanted to turn back, bandage the crack in his world, but he had to know what Vickie was up to, if she really knew where his dad was.

He slipped in after them, something catching him by his jacket, biting into his skin. He froze, a terrible pressure squeezing his heart and filling his head until he couldn't hear past the trembling rush of his blood. Jerking forward, he ripped the collar of his dad's jacket, sharp pain filling his mouth as he bit his tongue. Gravel gouged into his hands as he sprawled across the pavement, head turned back to stare at the jagged edge of the metal fence. The emptiness of the night behind him left him shaking and he collapsed forward, taking deep, aching breaths.

Remembering Vickie, he craned his head up, staring at the hospital rising in front of him, jutting out in odd, painful angles, the tower pointing to a black sky. A shiver gripped him, cold settling into his insides like ice had frozen over his bones, locking him in place. He stared at that building with its brick the color of skin and waited to hear it breathe, the lumbering beast to move, to pulse, creaking on its misshapen joints.

Vickie and the man had disappeared into an alcove on the south side, fading into the dark. Making himself move, Ian followed, head down so he didn't have to see the building. He reached the corner just as they climbed through a broken window into the black behind the brick. Waiting until the flare from their flashlight faded, he boosted himself through the window, stopping just inside. The room reeked of rotting blood and old disinfectant, fetid and sour.

Little light trickled through the window behind him, the dark in front deep and alive. Somewhere ahead he caught the ineffectual sweep of a flashlight and pushed forward. He tried to breathe through his mouth, but the taste of stale sickness settled on his tongue. Starting through the debris, his foot caught, hand bracing against something warm and soft. He jerked back and stumbled forward into the hall. Outside light spilled through the windows and into the empty rooms, creating islands of safety in the hungry dark. Ian knelt behind an old bed, watching as something blacker than the rest moved at the end of the hall.

"Damnit, Vickie."

There was a meaty smack and then silence.

He licked the dust off his lips and watched as they disappeared through a door, the metal clang reverberating through the hall. He hadn't realized how noisy they'd been until they were gone. Now it was quiet, and the light spilling into the hall didn't seem so bright, the silence thickening the shadows.

Starting down the hall, he passed room after room, not wanting to look, but unable to turn away. He catalogued the oddities: the dark rusty stains pooled in one room, tiles from the ceiling missing and broken, a giant light hanging like something from a space movie, a pile of phones, cords twisted and grimy, and in one what looked like the hips of a man. Ian froze, staring as he tried to make sense of it. It was chopped off at the knees and just above the stomach. There was no blood, no bone, just rubber and plastic, and the taste of his pulse on his tongue.

Turning from the sight, he ran, ears straining for the quiet whisper of pursuit.

The door at the end of the hall was heavy, his breath loud in his ears as he leaned against it, easing it shut. Stairs stretched before him, light flickering through the metal grating like hellfire below. Their voices rose, cadences sharp and brutal. Everything he'd learned in chapel escaped him, leaving him stuck with the beginning of an Our Father and the end of a Hail Mary.

Our Father who art in heaven, hallowed be thy name. Blessed art Thou amongst women and blessed is the fruit of Thy womb, Jesus. Pray for us sinners.

Pray for us.

Their voices bounced off the metal pipes and tanks, spreading and overlapping until it was like listening to the crazy people at his Aunt Marsh's church as they knelt at the pulpit. The bottom of the stairs spread out before him, filled with tile and plastic ghosts, the showers ragged with their curtains partially ripped from their rings. Squatting next to a bank of metal lockers, he stared at the poster fixed to one of the doors, the woman's legs spread, her fingers opening her pussy as he listened to the voices around the corner.

"Tell me where you hid the money, brother."

The man's voice was deeper than he thought it'd be, bouncing off the tile. It was followed by another one of those meaty thuds. The rapid beating of Ian's heart stilled as he stared at the blonde on the poster and listened to his dad grunt through the half-light.

"Val, don't be a fool. Tell us where you hid the money and we'll leave you alone. We'll even call the cops when we get out of the city, tell them you're here. You can go back to Ian." Vickie's voice wavered like the dying battery in their flashlight.

Ian closed his eyes, listening to his dad's thin laugh. "Vickie, sweetheart," he paused for air, "I tell you and Brady Miller'll be after me. Between the two of ya, I'll take my chances with you and Spastic Shortcake over here."

His dad screamed. He screamed until his voice broke, freezing Ian's insides as it repeated over and over, caught against the tile. The cold locker pressed against his cheek as he watched the man cut off his father's pinky with a pair of shears. Vickie kept her back turned, like she couldn't bear to watch.

The man leaned close, his mongrel face pressed against his dad's. "You'll tell me, or I'll bring your little runt down here and gut him in front of you. Shit, brother, I'll hoist him up right overhead and let his insides rest against the top of your head while he screams your name."

There was blood on his dad's chin, painting it red like he'd been eating strawberry pie. His dad closed his eyes and let his head fall forward, a thin line of drool stretching from chin to chest. "It's in the basement coal chute," Valentine said.

Ian huddled in his corner, watching as the flashlight trembled in Vickie's hand, throwing shadows around the walls with their grungy caulking and bloody tile. His father's skin was gray, hair matted dark. He didn't look like Valentine anymore. His father was big and strong and when he walked into a room you knew it, felt it, because he brought life with him. The man in the chair was hollow, broken. Ian shoved his fingers into his mouth, biting as the world went soft and watery.

He couldn't hear, everything echoed in his head like he'd been stuffed into a drum. He sat there, watching the man beat his father while Vickie trembled on the sidelines. He sat there, tucked safe in his corner, his insides shaking and trembling, the world far away as he watched the man put away his shears and pull out his knife. He sat there, piss warming the crotch of his pants, the world roaring around him as the man slid that knife over his father's throat, unzipping his neck.

The skin gaped on either side of that opening, giving his dad a second smile.

He tried to make himself crawl forward, to press his hands against that hot grin, but he couldn't. He tried, but he'd lost his sense of direction, crawling the other way and tucking himself into one of the showers, face pressed against the tile, cooling his heated cheek. The iron-rich scent of blood and the darker scent of mold touched his nose; death and hunger. The world devoured them.

After a while, the tile was no longer cold under his cheek, the world gone dark, as if it had started with its tail and just kept swallowing, a giant ouroboros. The seat of his pants was cold and wet, the denim rough against his legs. His body ached as he crawled forward, head loose on his shoulders. The metal of the stairs felt distant under his numb fingers while he crawled out of the hospital.

Outside it had grown cooler, as quiet and dark as that

basement. It was as empty as he was, an abandoned place. Nothing worked right. He wasn't sure he was feeling the ground under his feet, the asphalt giving with every step. He walked up the middle of Graham, passing in and out of the pooled streetlight until he overshot Berthold and had to turn back down Clayton toward his house. He could still hear his father scream.

It sounded like the swings down at the park. (It sounded like the squeak of his dad's bed.)

Slipping into his open window, he stood in the middle of the room, listening to the squeak of the bed next door. Ian pulled off his jacket and folded it on the bed, running his hand along the too-long sleeves. Moving down the hall, down the stairs, down to the basement, he found his dad's ball-peen hammer and hefted it a couple times, the wooden handle cold in his hand. He dragged his feet back up the stairs until he stood on the other side of his dad's door, listening to that monotonous squeak, a machine that needed oiling. He pushed open the door, the light streaming through the window highlighting the man's back as he rutted into Vickie. Ian stood there, watching the grunting flesh, the man's shaggy head lowered so he couldn't see his face.

He didn't time it, but each step he took coincided with a squeak from the bedsprings, adding to the rubbery feeling in his knees.

The man's head gave with a dry crack, like breaking Easter eggs.

He was thrusting into Vickie when the rounded side of the hammer sunk into his skull, causing him to collapse. At first everything was still, and then he moved, shoulders rising and falling, a marionette with tangled strings. Ian pulled the hammer loose and brought it down again, the crack a little wetter this time as if that egg hadn't been completely boiled.

The man stopped moving and a thin, pale arm snuck out from under him to grope up his back. "Bruce?" Vickie's hand continued up his neck to the back of his head. "Bruce, what's—" Ian watched as her finger sunk into the hole in his head like a thumb into a pie.

She shoved, her voice cracking like his dad's had. Squirming, she wriggled out from under him enough to meet his eyes and stilled, the mascara trailing down her face like clown makeup. Ian raised the hammer, ready to bring it down against her forehead, and Vickie closed her eyes, hunching in on herself.

He paused, watching as she waited for the hammer to fall. She was as evil as the man on top of her, but more than that, she was pathetic. He could see it in her eyes, the same nightmares in his. She would continue to see the smile in his dad's neck and taste the copper on the air. They'd never be rid of that.

She reached for him, nails ragged and spiked hair tangled against the top of her head. "Ian . . ." Whatever she was about to say died on her lips, eyes closing as more mascara ran down her cheeks. "Kill me." He didn't answer and she opened her eyes, shoving at the dead weight on top of her.

He dropped the hammer and walked away, abandoning that place.

DESERTED CITIES OF THE HEART

BY PAUL D. MARKS

Gateway Arch

Memory is a funny thing. It grabs hold and doesn't let go. Daniel Hayden wished he'd get one of those diseases where you couldn't remember, Alzheimer's, amnesia. Anything. He knew if he told that to certain people they'd think he was nuts. Didn't matter what they thought.

Daniel looked up, thought he saw a mourning dove flying through the Gateway Arch, heading out in the direction of Route 66. It was gone now. He wasn't sure if it was even there in the first place. Like Route 66, there but not there at the same time. What was left of that legendary highway passed right through St. Louis. Once America's Mother Road, much of it now decommissioned, it existed more like a ghost or a shadow on the land. Daniel had always looked on it as an escape route. But escape to where? Besides, escape was nothing more than an illusion. Wherever he went he'd take his baggage with him.

He wanted to forget the last three months had ever happened. Yeah, he wanted to shut those memories out. He didn't want to think about yesterday. Didn't want to think about today. And he definitely didn't want to think about tomorrow. He never thought it would turn out like this.

"I wish tomorrow would never come," he said out loud. But there was no one around to hear him.

Three months earlier

Daniel lay on the grass beneath the Gateway Arch, staring up at its clean, sweeping lines. It seemed to rise all the way to heaven, getting lost in the glare of the tawny late-afternoon sun. He liked coming here on his lunch hour or after work sometimes. It was only a five-minute walk from the office.

He liked to daydream about being somewhere else. But he knew he'd never leave St. Louis, never get on a jet bound for anywhere, never get in a convertible, top down, and head west on Route 66. Never. Probably never make it to LA or New York either. No, he was happy enough with his life in The Lou. You didn't hear much about St. Louis in the news. Not many movies or TV shows took place here. But there was that old midnight movie classic, *Meet Me in St. Louis.* His parents would watch it every Easter. He hated it. Just a musical fantasy, nothing about it was real. And nobody he knew spontaneously broke into song or dance, unless they were stoned. He sure as hell wasn't the type to spontaneously break into song, but he did have a dream of being in a band once. Played rhythm guitar in a quartet. Even wrote some songs. He wanted to play the blues like Albert King on his Gibson Flying V, but his friends wanted to play rock. So he bought a Fender Telecaster and they rocked out. His parents wanted him to have a secure job, something to fall back on. He loved hacking computers, so they convinced him that working with computers was the way to go. And though he had a passion for it, and even loved his job, it wasn't the same as playing music. Eventually, he sold the guitar—it felt like he was selling his soul.

Dreams fade. New ones take their place. He still wanted

to accomplish something, maybe move up at work. He was good at it—IT tech for CyberGen Management Systems, a high-powered information company that did a lot of government work. Not the most exciting job in the world, but any job's exciting if you put your all into it, he thought. He was just an average guy. Successful, if not rich. Decent looking, if not movie-star handsome. But not a freak either. He knew he'd never set the world on fire.

"Nice day," the young woman said. Not the most original opening line. And where had she come from? He'd had no idea she was there.

"Yeah, especially for this time of year."

"My name's Amber. Amber Loy."

He didn't think she looked like an Amber. Amber should be more exotic. She was on the plain side. Not unattractive, just not flashy. Looked about twenty-five—twenty-five going on thirty. Hair a mousy brown pageboy. Hardly any makeup except for bright red lipstick. He liked that. Black patterned nail polish. He wasn't sure about that. Green eyes, kind of dull. No sparkle. Definitely not an Amber.

"Daniel Hayden." He felt awkward. But what else do you say before you start talking about your favorite movies and groups, how many times you've read *Infinite Jest* and just what the hell it means. And why was she talking to him? What did she want? To sell him religion? Dope? Undercover cop, trying to bust him?

"Mind if I sit here?" She didn't wait for a response. That made him suspicious.

"Can I ask you something?" he said.

"Sure."

"What do you want?" He didn't know how else to say it. Social graces weren't his strong suit.

"Nothing. And you're certainly blunt."

"No point beating around the bush."

"You're alone. I'm alone. I'm new to St. Louis. Don't know anyone here and was just wondering what there is to do. I was also wondering if there's some Wi-Fi hotspots near here." She tapped her messenger bag, so he assumed it held a laptop. "Need to catch up with the world."

Daniel was wary. He wasn't the kind of guy women just started talking to out of the blue. He didn't really like her much. She seemed ordinary and forward and looked like a hipster wannabe, just trying a little too hard. And now she was intruding on his quiet time. Invading his space.

Awkward silence filled the air over ambient noises: boats, cars, planes, people, the wind tacking along the Mississippi. But he couldn't hear any of it, couldn't hear the young woman now seated next to him. Like outer space, his space under the Arch was void of sound. He didn't know what to say. Figured she didn't either since she wasn't saying anything. Had they run out of things to talk about already?

He glanced over at her, the thick hipster glasses and ironic George W. Bush T-shirt that said *What, Me Worry?* on it. He thought she might make a PBR appear magically out of her bag at any minute.

"So," he said, because anything was better than this titanic silence, "what do you like—"

"What? Now you're going to ask me what bands I like. And, of course, I have to say some dumb shit like some obscure band that nobody's heard of and as soon as anybody does hear of them, I have to move on 'cause they're not cool anymore." She looked over at him. "Go ahead, stop me from making a fool of myself at any time."

But he didn't want to stop her. He knew exactly what

she was saying. She leaned into him, invading his space even more. Extended her arm, phone in hand.

"Say, *I'd rather be dead than cool*," she said.

"Kurt Cobain."

"Right, now smile." She snapped a selfie of them.

"Do I get a copy?"

"Sure, what's your number?"

He told her.

"Well, I gotta go." She started pulling her stuff together. "Hey, maybe we can get together for coffee?"

"I don't think so, I'm kind of busy." He watched her cheeks flush. He'd hurt her feelings without meaning to.

"Oh, busy, I get it—I can take a hint."

"Hey, I didn't mean anything. I'm just kinda stressed from work, let's get coffee."

Coffee went better than he had expected, so they decided to do something over the weekend.

"I can't believe we're coming here," he said, as they approached Meramec Caverns, a little over an hour's drive from St. Louis. "It's so . . . middle class."

"Bourgeois," they said together.

"It's so lame it's cool." She laughed. "And we can make fun of all the tourists, they're so fucking midtown."

"While they make fun of us. We're tourists here too."

"Exactly. Hey, like them in their khakis and deck shoes."

She'd wanted to come here, do something touristy, since she was new to the area. She thought it would be funny, but he really did like Meramec Caverns, even if they were a little middle class. He used to come here with his family, when things were good. Had fond memories of it. His father always making silly jokes and his mom taking pictures. He began to wonder what he was doing here with Amber. It'd been almost a week since they'd met under the Arch. He was starting to like her, even though he didn't want to. Spent the whole week thinking about her. Wondering what it was about her that he liked. Why was he obsessing over her? She wasn't trying to impress him or put on an act for him. Maybe that's what he liked about her.

"They say that Jesse James hid out here," she said.

"Yeah, but despite the sign over there, nobody knows if it's really true."

"Must be true if the sign says so."

She squeezed his hand. Stuck her other hand in the air and took a pic of them with the sign in the background. In big neon letters, it said, *Meramec Caverns—Jesse James Hideout.*

"I always thought it would be cool to be an outlaw. You wanna be an outlaw with me?"

The drive back was long enough for them to find out all the things they had in common: the Avengers, computer games. Even the Rams. He told her about wanting to pick up the guitar again. Since she was driving, they somehow found themselves at Guitar Center.

"What do you like?"

"I don't know. They're all out of my price range, at least anything good."

"Well, like what?"

"Gibson Les Pauls, ES-335s, or SGs. Fenders. Those seem to be what a lot of people play, but what I'd really like is a Flying V, like Albert King played."

"So why don't you get one? Live a little."

"I've lived . . . a little," he protested.

They left without buying anything, hit Atomic Cowboy

for grub. She'd heard it was cool. He'd been there a few times, liked it well enough. Both ordered Atomic Fries and cheeseburgers. "Hold the chipotle mayo," they said together.

"We do have a lot in common." She smiled at him, pulled him closer. Grabbed another selfie. "We both like the Rams. Both work in IT, or at least I used to and probably will again once I find a job here."

"I'd help you find something, but we don't have any openings."

"Oh, I wasn't hinting or anything. I still need to get settled. Your work sounds pretty deck though."

"Nah, I'm just an IT guy," Daniel said.

"IT guy with a security clearance."

"I just show 'em how to do what they need or fix the systems when they break down." He didn't like talking about it. CyberGen Management Systems did some heavy lifting for the Defense Department, the FBI, and other government agencies, as well as about half the Fortune 500. Like Las Vegas, what went on in CMS stayed in CMS. "And we're both into computers and gaming. *World of Warcraft. Assassin's Creed.*"

"I'm into a new game, *Deserted Cities of the Heart,*" she said.

"That's a mouthful. Don't know it." But the title struck him. He imagined a world of bare trees and misty breezes. Disillusioned lovers walking on desolate beaches. His love life might as well have been described as a deserted city of the heart. He'd had a handful of girlfriends. And two relationships that had lasted over a year. But even when he was in them he'd felt alone and lonely, in a way that he didn't with Amber.

"I really like it. I go there to get away from the world."

"I go to the Arch for that. Even though there's people around, I can shut it all out."

"That's how I see *Deserted Cities*."

They walked out of Atomic, hand in hand. He was close enough to know that she didn't use perfume. He could smell her, a faintly sweet smell. Almost no makeup. Definite hipster vibe, while he was definitely no style. He didn't understand it, but he was falling for her.

Other guys might not look twice at her. She might not fill their dreams. But his dreams weren't the clichéd dreams of those other guys, superficial blondes with superficial intellect. She was understated in every way. And he was falling for her—hard.

She'd only been in The Lou a few weeks, but her Washington Avenue Historic District place was already decorated. Posters, including Andy Warhol with a Salvador Dalí mustache, dream catchers, and retro furniture. Spare, but it looked like someone actually lived there. His apartment of six years never looked or felt like home. She put out some PBR and bacon-wrapped doughnuts to munch on.

"Tell me more about what you did," he said.

"I was just a low-level IT grunt," she responded, lighting a joint, inhaling, and passing it to him—snagging a selfie of them, he with the joint in his mouth. "More like customer service, only it was in-house customer service. Anything complicated, they'd call my boss. But you're really in the thick of it."

"I know what I'm doing, but I still just have a low-level security clearance."

His head swirled pleasantly from the beer and pot. They made silly jokes that they probably wouldn't have laughed at if they'd been sober.

"You wanna play some games?"

They moved over to the Sony PlayStation.

"*Deserted Cities of the Heart?*"

"Sure, I'll play."

"It's better when two play." She grabbed the controller. "It's a role-playing game. You have to pick an avatar. The goal is to find love in a future society where love is outlawed. If you do find a lover, you have to keep it a secret from The Executive. If the Praetorians—storm troopers—catch you, they imprison you, you lose several turns and go back a level."

"Interesting, different from most of the games, first-person shooters and all."

He chose Orion as his avatar, a strong warrior and great hunter. She was Anwen, Welsh for beautiful, and her avatar was. In cyberspace we can be anybody or anything we want to be, he thought. Live out fantasies and you don't even have to leave St. Louis. It's like turning off the lights, you don't have to see people as they really are with all their flaws.

They swigged PBR, smoked more dope. Munched on those doughnuts, jammed on the game. He was walking down an isolated road in the middle of nowhere. Ghostly trees seeming to talk to him. The ruins of skyscrapers in the distance.

"Jeez," he said.

"Something wrong?"

"I don't know. All this dope and the game—I feel like I'm really in it. Living it, breathing it. Time stands still—like there is no time."

"That's what's so cool about it. You're in another world."

They went deep into the deserted cities, down one level after another. Hiding out from the Praetorians, ducking them as the game sucked them in deeper and deeper.

Daniel felt woozy. "I need a break," he said. "This is spooking me."

"Sure. It can get too real. Sometimes more real than real life."

They lay back on the couch for several minutes, neither saying a word. Sipping beer, munching doughnuts.

"You ever try hacking?" she said.

"No, not really."

"Not really?"

"Well, white hat I guess. Except—"

"Except?"

"Well, I guess everyone does a little," he said. "I broke into my nephew's school. Changed his grade."

"That would be more fun than just playing games. It's real life and it's dangerous. Makes you feel alive when there's a threat hanging over you."

"Threat?"

"Yeah, like of being discovered."

He was feeling no pain. He wasn't in the room anymore. She wasn't there. He was driving a vintage '65 Mustang convertible, tooling down 66. The road never seemed to end. He could drive and drive and drive and never arrive anywhere. That's what he liked about it.

"Let's do it," she said.

He snapped out of his reverie, the dream of the open road fading faster than the last chord on a blues riff. "Huh? Do what?"

"I thought you said you could get in and out of anywhere without leaving a trace."

"Yeah, but—"

"Live dangerously."

"Where do you want to go?" Daniel took a hit on the joint.

"Let's go into Dalloway's."

"What, you wanna steal some credit card numbers?"

"No, I just want to see if we can do it."

"Easy," he said.

She brought her MacBook to the couch. They bounced around inside the Dalloway's Department Store's *secure* computers, checking out people's spending habits. They went deeper into some of them, could find out almost anything about anyone.

"Scary. We're all open books. Better not have any deep, dark secrets," she said. "Show me how."

He showed her how to hack into Dalloway's. Stoned or not, she picked it up fast. He didn't stop to think, or maybe his mind was too foggy, that as an IT tech, she would have known how to do most of this already.

"Let's hack into where you work," she said. "I bet there's a lot of secrets there."

"I can't do that. I'll get fired."

"I thought you said you could go in and out of anywhere and not leave a trace."

"I can, but—"

"I dare you. I'll bet you a hundred dollars you can't." She said it jokingly, but it was one of those jokes that was serious underneath, at least that's how he took it.

Between the PBR and the pot his inhibitions were down for the count. He knew a back door into CMS's servers. He was inside in less than a minute.

They poked around, starting with the people who worked there.

"Jeez. They know everything about us, don't they?"

"I think we should get out," he said. "We've seen enough."

"Look, I'll bet that guy's a real loser. Phillip Tannen, what kind of name is that?"

"It's a normal name."

"Not when you're stoned."

"He's my boss."

"Definitely a loser. Oh my god, did you know he was into magic—a magician. How dorky is that?"

That cracked them up, though he'd never thought it was funny before.

They looked up several people, making fun of them for this or that. ROTFL at everything.

"Hey, let's look up people in the Witness Protection Program," she said.

"I can't do that."

"A thousand bucks says you can."

"No. Why should we?"

"Because we can."

"Because we can?" He hesitated, but was soon back at the keyboard. Via CMS's system, they probed around in the Federal Witness Protection Program.

"Wow," she said, "some of these guys are real creeps. Now that guy looks like a mobster. Anybody else here in St. Louis?"

He continued scrolling through the list of protected witnesses.

"What about her?" she said.

"Carole Cooper?"

"Yeah, let's see what she's up to." She stared at the screen.

He barely remembered the night before as Amber made him breakfast. He scarfed his food down, had to be at work in less than an hour—wearing the same wrinkled and dirty clothes from the night before; people would notice. They'd know he'd been with a woman, but they didn't need to know that he and his girlfriend—she was his girlfriend, wasn't she, or at least on the road to becoming his girlfriend?—hadn't slept together yet.

They made plans to meet at Atomic Cowboy for dinner after he got off work.

His head was still foggy, filled with cotton candy, as he made his way to the office.

. The day dragged on, his fat hangover making time slow to almost a complete stop, like in *Deserted Cities*.

He walked out to the CMS parking lot, half expecting to see Amber there, even though they'd agreed to meet at the restaurant. He got to Atomic about five minutes late. Traffic. Amber was late too. He took a table, ordered a PBR while he waited for her. Half an hour later she still hadn't shown. He texted her. No response. Should he be worried?

He decided not to wait any longer. Driving toward the river, he could see the Arch in the distance. The Arch. Where they'd met, just a few weeks ago.

He tried her cell again. Still no response. Drove to her place, rang the bell. No answer. She'd given him the code to her building's lobby door. Once inside, though, he couldn't get into her place. He waited outside, but she never came home. Sitting in his car, he called hospitals and the police. But there'd been no reports of an Amber Loy having been in an accident. Was she with another guy? Was he jealous? He'd never been jealous before. He finally went home.

His apartment seemed cold and lonely. For these past days with Amber it seemed like home, a place he wanted to come back to. He pulled a PBR from the fridge. He texted her. E-mailed her. Called her cell. No response. He flicked on the TV, hoping to get his racing mind off her. He never thought he'd fall in love. Aren't they the ones who fall the hardest? He passed out on the couch.

The moon trickled in through the half-open blinds, as Daniel woke around midnight. Groggy, he picked up his cell, called Amber—still no response. What the hell could have happened to her? He rolled off the couch. Tired, rubbing the sleep from his eyes, he flicked on the bedroom radio, went into the bathroom to brush his teeth. Something on the radio caught his attention. Daniel walked slowly from the bathroom to the bedroom.

"... *The body found in the Mississippi near the 'Captains' Return' statue has been identified as Christa Czerny. Ms. Czerny had been in the* Federal Witness Protection Program, *living under the alias of Carole Cooper in the Lafayette Square neighborhood of St. Louis. She had been relocated here from Chicago, where she was due to testify in the trial of Morgan St. Jacques, a well-known,* alleged *crime boss. When questioned, FBI spokesperson Leticia Adams said the Bureau had not yet discovered how Ms. Czerny's cover was blown and had no leads on the killer.*"

He stared at the radio. Wasn't sure what he was staring at, what he was hearing. His head was filled with bricks, still fuzzy from last night's party at Amber's.

He had to sit on the edge of the bed to keep from falling over. Something about this story, this Carole Cooper. Something about it was familiar. He'd heard the name before. Couldn't remember where.

Damn! It came to him. He ran for the bathroom and puked into the toilet, not knowing if it was the beer or guilt. Grabbed his cell. Dialed Amber. Still no fucking answer. He washed up quickly, flew out of his apartment. Drove the ten-minute drive to Amber's in six minutes, lucky not to have gotten a ticket.

He entered the building using her keypad entry code. Went to her unit. Banged on the door. A neighbor poked her head out. He didn't care. The neighbor went back inside. "I'm calling the police!" she yelled.

He thought he might have to kick the door in, but that would definitely bring the cops. Tried the handle and it opened. He was surprised at what he saw—or didn't see. The unit was empty. Cold, clean, and completely cleared out. As if no one had ever lived there. No clothes. No bacon-wrapped doughnuts. No artwork on the wall. Nothing. He thought he was hallucinating, still high from last night's beer and THC. This couldn't be. He sat on the bare hardwood floor. Leaned back against the wall, feeling very alone.

He didn't know what his next move should be. Call the cops? Try to find her? What would he do then? Beat a confession out of her? Tell her he loved her and they should leave the country? His mind spun in circles.

It didn't matter. He was in love with her, much as he'd never wanted to be. But he would find her. He would confront her. If he had to, he'd turn her in to the cops.

He came back the next day with a bag full of gear, searched every inch of Amber's apartment. Nothing there, not a hair in the drains, not a stray sock. Found a couple of partial fingerprints with the print kit he'd brought. He talked to the building super. Got her to show him Amber's application. She even made a copy of it for him on her all-in-one printer. She liked his eyes.

He figured he had three choices. One: go to the cops. But that wouldn't work. He didn't want to spend the rest of his life in jail as an accessory to murder, or whatever they would charge him with. He wouldn't last two days in prison. Or, he could go to Morgan St. Jacques and his mobster friends that Christa Czerny was due to testify against. Yeah, that was a good plan. The other choice was to start with Christa Czerny and work backward from there. But where would that lead? Back to the mob guys. But he didn't care about them. It was Amber who betrayed him. Yeah, Amber—like that was her real name. And it was Amber he wanted now. He wondered if she was the actual hit man, or just the decoy they'd used to get him to find the person they wanted to off.

He had to track her down. She had probably done research on him. Knew all about him. She'd insinuated herself into his life. That first meeting under the Arch was no accident. What a fool he was. What a loser.

He tried to recall everything she said. More lies probably, at least most of it. But maybe there was a shred of truth here or there, something he could latch onto that would lead him to her.

Amber Loy certainly wasn't her real name and everything on her rental application was a lie. So no point in trying to follow up on any of that. But people who changed their names often used parts of their real names. No, she was too smart for that.

He had a friend in the St. Louis PD who could run the prints he'd found through IAFIS, the FBI's Integrated Automated Fingerprint Identification System. But he didn't want to bring anyone else into his nightmare. He hacked into the system, ran the prints. Nothing came up—he knew it wouldn't.

His skin crawled, throat tight with desperation. He'd been played for a fool and didn't like it. He had no idea where to turn, how to find her. But he would. He had to. He loved her. Maybe he'd fallen in love too quickly or too stupidly. And now he was obsessed with her, even though she'd betrayed him. Obsessed in love and obsessed in hate. Either way, he had to find her. He'd start with the places they went.

He drove to Atomic Cowboy.

"Have you seen the woman I've come here with?"

"I don't even remember you," the manager said.

He described her to the manager, but it didn't ring a bell. He wanted to show him her picture, see if he'd seen her. Realized he had no pictures of her. They'd taken several selfies, but they were all on her phone. She'd promised to send them to him, but never did. She was smart.

She could be anywhere. Probably out of the city by now. He should give up, but he couldn't. He went home, crashed on the living room couch. Flicked on the TV from the remote, Turner Classic Movies. An old Bogart flick called *In a Lonely Place*. He heard one line of dialogue before going under: *"I was born when she kissed me. I died when she left me. I lived a few weeks while she loved me."*

Nerves firing, unable to sleep, he woke up an hour later. Saw his PlayStation in the corner and knew one way to find her, sort of. He fired it up. Went into *Deserted Cities of the Heart*, melded into his avatar. A hunter now—on the hunt for Anwen.

He walked through streets filled with rubble and toxic waste. Acid rain and hail pouring down. Dodging the Praetorians.

He found Anwen—Amber—in an abandoned train station.

Orion, I would have recognized ur signature anywhere.

That obvious? he said.

I'm sure u didn't come here 2 make small talk. U want something?

Yeah. You sold out to The Executive.

U want 2 kill me. Gotta catch me first. She ran off down the platform, jumping onto the tracks. He chased her until the tracks stopped dead at the edge of a bottomless ravine.

She climbed into an old rail car. A gun materialized in her hand. She fired at him, grazing his arm.

She threw the gun. He ducked. Charged her. She hit the wall, cornered.

Okay, she said, almost admitting defeat. But Anwen—Amber—would never admit defeat. *U can ask 3 three questions.*

What's your real name?

Well that one's out of bounds, ha ha.

Why Carole Cooper or Christa Czerny?

Because she was about to testify. It was just a gig for me, nothing personal.

And now there's nothing at all. Like she never even existed, he said.

She existed in the computer.

No, she existed in the real world and that's where you killed her.

I didn't kill anyone. Get 2 ur next question.

Why me? Daniel asked.

U had access.

Did you ever love me, even for a second?

That's number 4. Ur out of questions. She vaulted past him, jumping back onto the tracks, yelling as she went: *Have fun finding me. The chase is half the fun!* Her avatar smiled and she was gone. He couldn't catch her.

User Anwen has logged off, appeared on his screen in vivid red letters.

All he thought about was her, Amber or Anwen or whoever the hell she really was. Obsession became his life. She'd tricked him. Made him break the law—no, he did that on his own. Either way he loved her, couldn't stop thinking about her. He logged onto *Deserted Cities of the Heart* every day. Couldn't find her. Then every hour of the day. He saw her avatar once more. Asked if he could at least have a relationship with her in the virtual world.

It was so easy 2 get what I wanted from u. Men are so e-z. That said, I did like u. Still do. But I had a job 2 do. I'm a professional.

He had no response for that.

The phone rang. Phillip Tannen, his boss, asking where he was. He made excuses. Tannen bought them, for now. Ten a.m. and he still hadn't showered or shaved, or even eaten breakfast.

He turned back to *Deserted Cities*. It was the only place he might have her now. She was gone. The empty streets taunted him. He was alone.

He fell asleep at the PlayStation. The doorbell woke him early the next morning. He looked through the peephole: his boss, Phillip. He didn't answer the door, went back to the Play-Station, back to *Deserted Cities*. He couldn't find her. An hour later, the doorbell rang again. UPS. They left a large rectangular package. He carried it inside, opened it, and pulled out a vintage Gibson Flying V. A note printed on the mailing label read simply: *Forget the past. Live your dreams.* He kicked the cardboard package, tossed the guitar on the couch. Went into the bathroom, showered, shaved, and headed to work.

Waiting at the elevators, he saw a woman on the far side of the lobby. Mousy brown hair, thick Buddy Holly glasses, and a fedora with a feather. Amber? The elevator arrived, but he was sprinting across the lobby after the woman. She disappeared out the door. Or had she never been there? He charged out the door onto the street looking for her.

No matter where he looked, Amber was everywhere and everyone. And nowhere and no one. But he knew where to find her: *Deserted Cities of the Heart*. One day, she'd be there again.

He finally went home. Picked up the Flying V, plugged it into the little amp he'd bought, and slammed out a blues riff. Went into Albert King's "I'll Play the Blues for You."

Guilt ate at him like the cheap beer and spicy food ate at his insides, killing him from the inside out. He'd hang at Atomic as long as his money held out. And that wouldn't be too much longer. He'd lost his job. His apartment wasn't far behind. His hair was grown out and shaggy now. He wore the same clothes most days, because most nights he slept in them, right next to the PlayStation, so he could check in on *Deserted Cities* at any time.

He kept going back to Atomic Cowboy, hoping she'd pop in some night. False hope, he knew. She probably didn't live in St. Louis, and even if she did she was probably out on another *gig* now. Doing someone else. Another victim. Another dupe.

He got out of his chair, headed toward the front door, put his hand on a woman standing there. She turned abruptly.

"I'm sorry," he said. "I thought you were someone else." The scorn on her face said she didn't buy it. But damn, she sure looked like Amber, especially from behind. They all did. And none of them ever were.

It had been three months and he hadn't seen the flesh-and-blood Amber again.

But visions of her continued to haunt him. She was everywhere. Every hipster woman with big glasses. Every hipster woman with brown hair.

Every woman who barely fit her specs was Amber.

Every mote. Every speck of dust that glided across his field of vision.

He saw her everywhere. But all of them were mirages.

Amber was nowhere. Nowhere at all. Not even in the deserted cities of the heart.

And even if he'd found her, even if he could stifle his love, sick as it was, and sear her eyes out with hot pokers, he knew it wouldn't bring Christa Czerny back. The only thing that brought her back was a joint and a pint which, these days, he had to get with a five-finger discount. And in the swirling pot smoke he would conjure her face, not Amber's. Christa's. Her story. Make up things about her. Good things. Give her the life he'd stolen.

Eventually, Daniel found himself back at the Arch almost every day. He didn't even know how he got there. Every woman he saw was either Amber or Christa. He'd walk toward them. They'd all turn away. He looked like a bum.

He hoped to see Amber—Amber was easier to handle than Christa. Guilt ate at him for his part, inadvertent as it was, in Christa's death. But Amber—there was no guilt there. Only stupidity and vanity. Still, if he had the chance to get back with Amber—

He'd lost his job. His apartment. His self-respect.

There was no escape. Not down Route 66. Or in the bottle or a blunt. Because in the haze of smoke there were always the faces. Carole. Amber. Amber. Christa.

Good or bad, he couldn't forget Amber. Couldn't stop looking for her.

He followed the shadow of the Arch across the lawn, wishing—praying—there was no such thing as memory. Hoping every day for Alzheimer's or amnesia. There was nothing left of him. It was like he had never existed.

"Move along," a cop said. They didn't want transients

littering their park. He thought he was invisible, but you're never invisible to a cop.

The Arch's shadow drifted over him as the late-afternoon sun morphed from yellow to gold. He thought about going inside the Arch, up to the observation platform. Wondered if there was a way to get outside the observation area so he could jump. He stared up at the Arch, realizing that it went up on one side, but it came down swiftly and steeply on the other.

BLUES FOR THE RIVER CITY

BY COLLEEN J. McELROY

The Ville

The old men had stopped speaking to each other long ago—when their sons were young, full of themselves and what they could do in this world. The men had carried their anger for years, nursed it like bitter vetch, a bad batch of bathtub hooch, anything that could stand between them and common sense. It mattered little that the brew was not of their own making, that it was in the air, the topsoil, the very foundations of the city they called home. From the moment they could stand on their own and walk unaided, they had swallowed it drop by drop in the spit they produced until they became used to the sour taste. They pushed into this anger, learned to keep their heads down and their eyes open.

"Hard work," they told their sons. "Onliest thing you can count on."

"Pay attention," they said. "Don't let trouble catch you unawares."

"Mind where you're going before you get there."

There were times when the old men thought all of that talk fell on deaf ears. Their sons, Cohee, Wheeler, and Russell, hid behind a teenage façade of silence, an affliction of growing up every father in this world failed to understand. These men thought their sons were stubborn and pigheaded, more ready to turn to the streets than get out of the rut the white folks had fixed for colored folks. The old men still lived in the 1940s world of CCC camps and WPAs, the shadow of war, and the ever-present racism that was determined to keep them riveted forever in a state of uncertainty, a sense that they would never be regarded as men, that they would always be forced to answer to the summons of *boy*!

"Hey, boy, git over here."

"Let the boy clean it up."

"Stupid boy, what did I tell you?"

"Lazy good-for-nothing boy."

"Black boy . . . Colored boy . . . Nigra."

If truth be told, their sons were bristling to strike out, to be men and step out of the shadow that had kept their fathers patiently waiting for something good to happen. Except it never did. Not in the Ville, that section of the city that nailed them to boundaries, visible or not. Outside of the Ville, they had no names, recognized only by color or gender, or whether they walked with a swagger or looked white folks dead in the eyes.

Wheeler was the tallest of the three, lanky and agile with quicksilver hands and a lopsided grin. "A real gone guy," the neighborhood girls called him.

Cohee was slower, broad shouldered and muscular with little sign of the good humor Wheeler used to edge his way out of a fix. Cohee, like his father, tackled business head on, blustering and baiting, and seemingly begging for a fight. Wheeler was slick, smooth where Cohee was rough, and light where Russell was dark. Russell rarely let on to what he was thinking; he had deliberately flunked math his freshman year in order to stay in the same class as his buddies, and never told anyone how he could calculate the problems in his head. What good would it do to triangulate the exact distance between Natural Bridge Road and Kingshighway if the Jim Crow law was always waiting for you to cross the line?

The city was saddled below that place where the Missouri flowed into the Mississippi, midland country that had been a trading post for native people centuries before. That river was a beacon for those who did business directly on its shores, and for those who watched for what business the river might bring them. Sooner or later, everyone found themselves on it, or near it, or fighting the pull of it. City government was planned around the river; city traffic swarmed toward its banks, and most of all, since the time of the fur trappers, the business of the river was the business of the city. A statue marking the merger of the two rivers had been erected in front of Union Station, the hub of the railroad, Gateway to the West, a constant reminder that the first business of the city was the flow of traffic through it, either by rail or the mighty Mississippi. Those leaving by rail took note of the Wedding of the Rivers fountain as they entered the station. Those with business that served them well left in first-class style. Others left with catch-as-catch-can.

"You know what the porters say when they see hobos jumping the train?" Wheeler's father often joked. *"I'd like to stay here, but the blues keeps moving me on."*

In the Ville, folks knew they could no more change the tide of business in their favor than they could stop the Mississippi from flooding its banks by plugging that fountain. Their sons were not yet burdened by thoughts of what seemed impossible.

Some mornings when Wheeler watched his father take extra-special care with his uniform, making sure the seams were pressed straight, collar stiff, and shoes polished to a mirror shine, he wondered if that was all he had waiting for him, a place in the sleeping car porter's union, a job that would take him to the edge of tomorrow and back, always returning home to the same old grind, the same old same old.

"Bro, gots to be something better out there," he told his friends.

"Gots to be," they echoed.

Often they convened at Brick's Garage which Cohee's father managed, a dump of a place that looked like it had accidentally gathered old tires, a rusted hoist rack, and one lone gas pump, the old-fashioned type that had a glass container showing everyone how much fuel was available. The garage was a neighborhood institution in that part of the city where few licensed mechanics ventured. Once in a while, Harry let the boys pump gas, or change a gasket, nothing big but their hands got dirty and they walked beneath the car hoist marking the undercarriage parts with chalk. Best yet, Harry had promised his son a jalopy roadster for his sixteenth birthday, provided the engine was up and running as smooth as any 1949 model. But it was Russell's father, John, they favored. He had fought in Luzon and had come home with shrapnel in his knee, the only colored man they knew who had actually seen combat.

"A mistake," he told everyone. "I could work the radio better than the white cats, so they took me."

"That's where Russell got his smarts," folks said.

They called him Sarge, though he had not worn his uniform since the war ended four years earlier. Without thinking about it, they mimicked him, never mind that the only jobs he could find after the army were as a daytime bartender at Mrs. Scales's Tavern and moonlighting as a janitor for the city. Weekends, all three of them might go with him to speed up the cleaning of places like the Fox Theatre on Grand Boulevard, where they could walk up and down the aisles, stroking the red velvet seats, with no one there to tell them colored folks were not allowed. And those nights when Sarge had to drain and clean the swimming pool at the white high school on Natural Bridge Road, they went along to help. Sarge taught them to swim a few laps before they started the work, but made sure they cleaned up after themselves.

"Won't do to let them know we been here having fun by our lonesome," he said.

The year they made the varsity team changed everything. In truth, Wheeler and Cohee made varsity, while Russell was a drummer, the best the marching band had ever had by all accounts. That year, everything, for better or worse, centered around the football field. Russell lifted the harness of the big drum on his shoulders each afternoon, while Cohee and Wheeler tested their endurance on the playing field. Rumor had it that the following year, the city was going to set up the first intramural game between a white high school and a colored high school. Coach was determined their school should be the colored school in the competition.

"You can't be all brawn and no brains out there," he said. "This game takes brains."

Wheeler and Cohee dutifully lowered their heads and pounded the practice dummy. It's true that they wanted to impress Coach, but more to the point, they strained to impress Vera Mae Madison, a cheerleader who wanted, most of all, to wear somebody's team jacket emblazoned with the school logo and mascot. And she wasn't all that picky about who the lucky player would be. Vera Mae clouded their vision.

Just watching her walk by made them hurt worse than hours on the practice field on empty stomachs.

Once upon a time the goose drank the wine,
The monkey played the fiddle on the streetcar line . . .

The first time they saw Vera Mae, she was signifying and hand slapping, her hands moving so fast, left to right, criss-cross in and out, they could barely keep up with the rhythm. She was in the center of a ring of cheerleaders, her bobby socks hanging sloppy over her brown-and-white oxfords, pleated skirt flared like a sprung umbrella away from her hips, and sandy-colored hair tamed by two cornrows that ended in thick braids brushing her shoulders. Her legs were Vaseline smooth, long and muscular, and her laugh was a short burst of energy, like the referee's signal to start the game. Already, she was marching into the sassy woman she would become long after her encounter with them. But that day, the sun made her shield her eyes, and with the light just right, she spotted the boys and weighed her options. It didn't take much. They were already half the way there.

"Somebody's nose is wide open," Cohee grinned.

"You the one gots your nose open," Wheeler said.

Russell had nothing much to say right then, but on his way home he went to Kresge's five-and-dime and bought a bottle of Coty nail polish. "You two just flapping your lips," he told them. Then he winked and gave the bottle of Coty's Brilliant Red to Vera Mae. Wheeler and Cohee seemed to take Russell's move with a cheerful *Way to go,* for who would not want to wish his best friend luck with a girl who smiled just so.

* * *

Mornings began with the screech of the Hodiamont streetcar
as it veered toward the heart of the city. By the time it rumbled
around the curve and passed the blocks of brick tenements
latticed with fire escapes, the noise had pulled everyone out of
sleep. That sound was better than an alarm clock. It let them
know when they were late and when they had time to linger
over the bit of breakfast bread or oatmeal. When his route
did not allow him to be home, Thomas made sure his son,
Wheeler, had a hot breakfast rationed for him to heat and
serve, the napkin folded and flatware on the table the same
as he did mornings in the dining car. And he added a dash of
cinnamon to the sugar the way his wife had done before the
cancer took her.

You sit down and eat, he told his son in the note he left on
the table.

But Wheeler never did. Always on the run, he grabbed
a bite and latched the door, still chewing as he hit the front
stoop. "Hey, bro, let's get on the good foot!" he would yell
when he reached Russell's door.

Their next stop on their route was to swing by Brick's to
pick up Cohee. Twenty minutes tops before heading to school.
At least that was their route before they met Vera Mae. To
include her, they had to detour off Franklin Avenue and cross
the streetcar tracks away from the school, adding fifteen minutes to the trip. When Vera Mae started hanging out with
them, no one said it was all right—but none said it was wrong
either. They simply gathered her into the fold, maneuvering
to be the one who walked beside her, shoving and shadowbox-
ing on the sidewalk. Now and then, Cohee even broke into a
doo-wop falsetto, "*Ve-rah, be my girl, ooh-ohh-oo . . .*" but she
remained calm, walking at a parade pace as if none of that
foolishness had anything to do with her, the morning sun add-

ing a kind of glow to her pale skin. "Light bright and almost white," folks said. But never to Vera's face.

They filled the sidewalk, zigzagging back and forth around Vera Mae, forcing anyone passing to stop as they went by. Even the smaller kids on the way to Dunbar Elementary taunted them: *"Two's a company, three's a crowd / four on the sidewalk is not allowed."*

Older women planted themselves firmly in their path, sucking their teeth *tsk-tsk* at such bad behavior. And folks who lived in the basement, in the under-stairs daylight units, could only see their legs, and banged on the window panes as their loud talk filled the entryway, their shadows interrupting whatever meager light could wander into those rooms. Their antics kept the drunks stumbling away from daylight, and scattered stray dogs scavenging for bits of food in the alleys. The more attention they got from Vera Mae, the grander the day seemed to be. To avoid being late, they had to run the last two blocks, but they usually made their first class in the nick of time, easing into their seats just as the morning bell stopped ringing. The teachers cut them some slack for being late because, after all, the talk of integrating football games was growing hotter, and the team needed all they could muster. Coach was another matter. More than once Cohee and Wheeler broke ranks to get next to Vera Mae and her cheerleading squad. It wasn't hard to spot them. Among the dark-haired girls, Vera's hair stood out almost gold in the afternoon light. Russell felt pushed aside, and banged his drum louder at the other end of the field. Coach even took notice, and when he paid attention, everybody paid attention. And Lord knows, the boys were getting a lot of attention hanging around Vera Mae.

It took some getting used to, this way Vera Mae's crew had

of swarming around her all of the time. Everyone wanted to know why they had hooked up with her, or, more to the point, why she was interested in them. More than once, Cohee almost got into a dust-up when someone walked in front of him while he was talking to her. Wheeler looked like he was about to pop at any second, until Russell started trash talking and everyone backed down. But Russell saw he'd drawn a smile from Vera. He took to having his mother make something special to share with her at lunchtime.

"Don't get too stuck on that yella gal," his mother said. "You need to study to get into college."

"Don't worry, Moms," he told her. "Vera Mae's smart. She's gonna be right there with me."

His mother, unconvinced, returned to cleaning up the kitchen, humming, "Um-hum," as if she were singing a familiar tune.

Tired of running interference off the football field, the boys tried to take Vera Mae someplace that wasn't so familiar. The Fish Shack? She had been there and so had her crew. White Castle? Even the freshmen class hung out there, listening to R&B on the jukebox, munching ten-cent burgers.

Russell heard about the drummer with Count Basie's band at the Club Riviera—"Rocking and shouting," he said. The Riviera was the biggest supper club in the city where colored folks didn't have to use the back entrance. Because they were minors, the best they could do was look at the fancy wheels folks came riding in on, rhinestones and silks flashing in the seconds it took to walk from the car to the door. Vera lasted about five minutes.

"I could see this at the movies," she said, and turned sharply as if the drum major had signaled to her. She did not look back, knowing the boys would follow. And they did.

"There gots to be a way," Cohee said.

"Movies, man. She's talking movies."

"Not the Antioch," Wheeler said. "That place smells like rotten eggs."

Russell grunted. "I don't mean that funky old Antioch. I'm thinking the Fox, downtown, bro."

"They don't let us in the Fox, man. What you fixing to do? Walk up to the ticket box and say, *I want two tickets, please, Mr. Sir?* Kick your butt from here to Vandeventer."

"How many times we been in there and ain't nobody kicked us out yet—" Wheeler started to object, but Russell cut him off.

"I got it covered," he said. "I can figure the time it takes to get in and out with nobody knowing the diff, get it?"

He talked them through it and they slapped hands to seal the deal. But with all that glad-handing, they had forgotten one of the cautions their fathers offered: *Mind where you going before you get there.*

The movie, *Road House,* was playing at the Fox, and Vera loved movies with gangsters and gun molls. Wheeler set up the date, and made her promise she wouldn't tell anyone where they were going. She agreed only if she could wear his letter jacket for the rest of the month.

The evening they took her to the Fox, the streets were slick with rain. A downpour widened the distance between houses with eddies of water swirling toward the open maw of gutters. The gratings held scraps of newspapers, cigarette butts, the head of a broken doll, anything else that could not be immediately swept into the sewer. Even in the posh section of town, where the lights from the Fox Theatre beckoned, and each night the streets were swept by a legion of workers, trash swirled in the drains. While the rain fell, the city's waste flowed freely, and most folks stayed inside to avoid getting drenched. Russell was counting on that when he swiped his father's key to the service entrance. He figured that with luck, the rain would mask their comings and goings, everyone bent on getting out of the downpour, and the usual bunch of thuggish whites hanging near the entrance would head home as soon as the movie ended. Weekends, he'd watched them standing in front of the theater, talking like *Archie* comics, smoking Lucky Strikes, and watching the girls walk toward the corner bus stop or soda shop, more interested in keeping their hair slicked back than anything else.

"White trash," his mother called them. "House so dirty I can't hardly get it clean."

But that evening it was raining, and as the old folks said, "Nothing's so clean as a hard rain."

Russell had calculated the time they would need to get through the service entrance and up the stairs to the balcony in the dark before the exit alarm light would start to blink. In fact, he had counted the steps more than once: two right inside the door, ten to the first floor, twelve to the balcony, and two on the other side of the velvet curtain that kept light from filtering into the theater. Divide that speed by all four of them trying to make the landing, and he was sure all he needed was three minutes to get them seated at a safe distance from the evening crowd. Twice, Vera Mae had to be shushed. The first time, she stumbled on the staircase.

"Won't do to have white folks thinking we in here all by our lonesome," Russell whispered.

They inched their way into their seats. The light from the silver screen was as strong as the darkness in the aisles. Wheeler remembered the stories his father told of looking from the dining car as the train rumbled through the countryside at night, and how, in the distance, he saw the light of a window, the darkness around it swallowing all it belonged to—the house, the barn, even trees. "Didn't know a soul who lived there," his father said, "but that light caught my eye and I couldn't hardly shake it."

Wheeler turned away from the screen and let his fingers tell him when he'd found his seat. The others followed. Thanks to the sticks of Juicy Fruit Cohee shared with them, Vera was quiet during the movie until the end, when the neon lights announcing the Roadhouse were barely visible through the night fog, and Ida Lupino started singing about her lost lover as if the blues was the only sound she could hear: "*We'll have this moment forever / but never, never . . . again.*"

Wheeler claimed it was the sound of the rain that pulled them out of the spell of the movie, but Russell figured it was the sound of Vera weeping that startled him. No one expected that. To be sure, Vera was pretty, but in a rough kind of way. Crying was a whole new way of looking at her. Her sobs brought him straight up in his seat, muttering, "Damn!" He needed to get them out of there before the house lights came on and all the white folks spotted them. The credits were beginning to roll when he hustled them into an exit row and the pitch-black hallway. In that darkness, they could still hear Lupino crooning for her man, and they felt as lost as the characters in the movie.

Sarge spent nearly an hour searching for the key to the Fox before he called the garage. Cora was still out in Kirkwood cleaning that white woman's house, so he knew his wife hadn't taken the key, and he knew where he had left it this morning before he started his shift at Mrs. Scales's. When he heard the boys weren't at the garage, he reached a simple conclusion and shook his head. "Damn boy don't remember a thing I taught him." He said it again as he started his car, a rattle trap Harry had fixed and given to him. The rain had not let up all day, and KATZ predicted heavier rain later that night. At the intersection, the Chevy skidded on the first set of streetcar tracks he crossed. Sarge had to remind himself that the tires were bald and gaining little traction on the wet pavement. He worked to keep his mind on his driving, fighting the thought that the boys had put themselves in harm's way.

Rain glistened on the street like glass beads breaking in his path. The light played tricks with his eyes. "Shoulda never took them to work with me," he muttered. He could feel his neck tightening up, the headache returning. The cardboard pine tree air freshener Harry had hanging from the rearview mirror danced in and out of focus. Sarge stopped right in the middle of the street, and for that moment under that thin curtain covering the windshield, he was back in Luzon, shadows dancing in the trees, noise grinding in his head. He wasn't supposed to be there. It was a mistake. The only colored man in the squad and they wouldn't even give him a gun. "Boy, just work the radio," they said. "And when we say *run*, you run like hell, Rastus." Who could hear the mortar shell when everyone was laughing? He gripped the steering wheel. "Run!" he yelled. "Run!" His voice so loud it drowned out the Chevy's ragged motor.

Russell couldn't run, not just yet. He was trying to get Vera Mae onto the fire escape, but she was protesting, saying something about her head scarf and the rain. "All morning," she said. "Took me all morning to straighten my hair." Wheeler whipped off his jacket and threw it to her. As soon as she caught it, she refused to let Russell help her. She draped the jacket over her head and stepped onto the fire escape as if it were a taxi pulled up to spirit her home.

"Come on!" Russell yelled at her. "We gots to get outta here 'fore we trip the alarm!"

He heard the alarm switch click one second before he pushed the door shut. Cohee was on the lowest level, the hinge already loosened to swing the last section to the ground, a grinding noise that triggered the red alarm light. The whole alley was suddenly bathed in that light, an odd sort of carnival ride that took over and made it difficult for them to see. Looking up was easier, and the white boys who had been standing near the entrance door came around the corner just as Cohee reached the bottom rung and held it closer to the ground. It was quite a sight: Cohee anchoring the fire escape while Wheeler tugged Vera Mae by the arm, and Russell behind her, pushing as she slid from one step to the next.

"Ohh, lookee," a tall redheaded boy said, "monkeys escaped from the zoo."

"What you doing up there, boy?" another said.

"Looking for your mama!" Cohee yelled.

"What you say, nigger?"

Cohee let go of the ladder and started for them. On cue, a sheet of rain washed through the alley, stopping everyone, it seemed, in slow motion. Wheeler didn't have time to say he recognized the team logo on their jackets from the white high school on Natural Bridge Road, not with the fire alarm going off, everybody cursing, and Vera screaming about her hair. Without Cohee there to catch her, she stumbled on the last rung of the ladder and crashed to the ground, one leg bent awkwardly under her, her hair busting loose, all her earlier efforts with the hot iron shrinking in the rain.

Someone from the Natural Bridge school shouted, "What you coons doing with that white girl?"

They all turned to peer at Vera Mae, wet and hurting, looking more like a discarded rag doll some kid had thrown in the trash than a slick cheerleader. The onslaught of rain reduced her to one long scream, and Vera Mae had a fine set of lungs.

Wheeler laughed. "What white woman you talking about?"

Cohee raised his fist again. "Cracker, you want some of this?"

That's when Sarge's car rocketed into the alley, the Chevy backfiring as he popped the clutch. For a second, no one knew which way to run. They could hear police sirens racing down Grand Avenue, and Sarge's car coming at them from the other direction. In the rain, the beam from the headlights seemed to bend, first toward the wall, then down the middle of the alley, one blink in one direction, blink again and another direction. Russell could have told them that was called a parallax view, but having recognized his father's car, he knew he had some more important explaining to do.

When Sarge's car lurched to a stop beside the fire escape, the Natural Bridge boys were the first to move. "This is some shit going down," Wheeler said while the sirens grew louder. As if in agreement, a streak of lightning lit the alley, thunder rolling right behind it. The boys from Natural Bridge pulled their jackets on straight and signaled, *Catch you later*, as indeed they would when football season started. Cohee flipped them the bird, but he allowed Wheeler to steer him toward Vera Mae. Russell opened the car door.

"Pops?" he said. His father didn't seem to recognize him.

"Run!" Sarge cried out.

"Pops, you take your medicine?"

"Run!" he answered.

"Shit! I gots to get him to the hospital," Russell said.

"Vera too," Wheeler told him. "She's bleeding bad."

Russell wouldn't listen to the arguments against him driving with no license and no permission to drive his dad's car. The fuzz was closing in, sirens howling closer, and the alley was no place to be questioned. Russell fishtailed the car in reverse, and headed down a side street toward the Ville. The trick was to avoid the streetcar tracks where he could lose control. Sarge was slumped over, holding his head. Vera was in the backseat with Cohee and Wheeler, her body curled as if she had landed mid-somersault. Nothing could stop her moaning.

I just need to make it to Homer G., Russell thought as he turned onto Page Avenue. He wondered where his father kept the medicine that the docs had given him at the VA. Better yet, he wondered what he would tell Vera Mae's mother when he finally got her home.

Years later, the old men still wondered what they could have done that night, how they might have stopped Sarge from slipping into a place where he recognized no one but the demons in his head. "Shell shock," they told the doctors when they were itching to label Sarge as crazy. The men were ignored, for what colored man would have shell shock from a war that gave him so little in return? And what good was any of it if you couldn't rise up and help your friend? They embraced Cora, but in the end, she moved to be closer to the sanitarium where her husband was. And Russell had stopped going to school anyway. That year, when riots broke out after the colored team beat the white team in the first integrated game, Russell wasn't there to cheer for his buddies, and before long, the whole neighborhood had changed with the school zone redistricting, whites fleeing to the suburbs.

The talk in the barbershops took note of the changes in the city.

"When it's all said and done, we the ones best go with the flow," the men said.

"You got that right," they all agreed.

The long and short of it was nothing much changed for them, even years later when the army was integrated and their sons were serving in Korea; the men could barely stand to read their letters, full of stories about the white cats in their outfit. The streetcar tracks were gone, paved over for bus traffic, but occasionally the old men swore they could still hear the bell announcing the streetcar's arrival at the bend in the road. If they put their minds to it, they'd tell you their hearing was keen enough to separate the noise of street traffic from the *whoosh* of barges on the riverfront. To hear them tell it, street noise was gravelly and hoarse while the great river softened the sounds, smoothing out the rough patches the way a cobbler tanned leather. In warm weather, they sat on the porch after a rain storm, each on opposite sides of the street, switching stations from KQZQ to gospel, watching the gutters fill where the currents of the Mississippi loosened its banks and carried the rich soil and debris of St. Louis industry to the Delta.

FOOL'S LUCK

BY LAVELLE WILKINS-CHINN

Central West End

It was that crazy little thing called love. He loved her, and there was evidence. The first time I saw her, he was arduously pursuing her down my street, a flying gazelle, her dress up, legs hurdling wide open over cracked, buckled sidewalks, across parking lots, edges of lawns, showing all the neighbors she didn't wear panties and gleefully squealing like it was the most fun she'd ever had. The two were keeling and staggering drunk; him stumbling and falling, her weaving on wobbly high heels until he was on his feet, then they took off again. It was a queer dance.

I had just stepped off the bus from my new school. I hated my new school. My teachers hated me too. Me and all the alien, grandiose, Afro-nappy-head kids, bussed from the North Side: our first year performing on a new stage called integration. All roles maliciously acted out, definitely not a good day. Frustrated nerves electrically raw, I saw her. And then him chasing her. I was embarrassed, ashamed, dejected; like the Temptations song, I was a big ball of confusion. It wasn't a something-so-strange-I-hadn't-seen-it-before kind of thing. It was simply that he was my favorite uncle and vulnerable. Just one look and Ray Charles could see she didn't give a shit about him.

He was closing in on fifty—she was thirty-something. Magazines later confirmed she'd been a fashion model years before. So what? Her hair was silky and long down her back, with blond streaks. Stunning? Paaaleeeez, to *me*? HA! But there was this: her legs, always striding on stiletto high-heeled mules. Her torso was shapely in excessively skin-exposed, titillating dresses. Extended fake lashes winked, brushing chiseled cheekbones. Heavily drawn kohl mascara framed her iron-chipped eyes, seeping black streaks into crevice-cracked crow's-feet covered in eye shadow of wild plum or shocking pink. Possessive, reading eyes, interpreting and storing everyone's weaknesses. Mother's wisdom said eyes were windows to the soul. I believe it's true. Looking into her eyes was just like falling down into two bottomless black holes. A pro in every sense, life's unexpected hard bits concreted her face. Carla was a high-wire act off-balance.

My uncle was well known around parts of town, especially little hole-in-the-wall taverns and dive bars, so she'd probably heard about his fool's luck by word of mouth. Unk was coming into lots of moolah: a federal government settlement large enough for him to never have to work another day, and then some. This according to a letter dated September 1, 1968, from Washington, DC. It was delivered to our house when Unk was on one of his road trips. It took twenty years for the government to admit that action in World War II's Southwest Pacific Theater had damaged him severely and permanently. During his military service Unk's long-term assignments were collecting and burning human body parts in the Philippine jungles, leftovers from several massacres. After months of pickup jobs, decapitated heads began speaking to him—tormenting hallucinations. From 1946 through 1949 he was hospitalized in mental wards up and down America's West Coast.

Tall, loose-limbed, a perfect scarecrow build, Unk's voice

was strong, a melodious, rich baritone, announcing good times when he was gliding down the street: "*Look out, ole Macky's back!*" With his favorite song, "Mack the Knife," he joyously serenaded passersby in long-stride waltzes down the avenues of North St. Louis—especially when he was drunk. Which was most of the time. On good days he was usually well dressed: beautifully cut black suit, crisp white shirt against gleaming mahogany skin, impeccably groomed, shoes shined and sharp, newspaper folded under arm, handsome, movie-star smile. One night at the Keyhole, a little back-alley dive down by the riverfront, Carla tripped over the doorjamb, colliding with Unk sitting sprawled-legged on the jukebox, singing his tune.

Occasionally Unk brought her around and she stayed in the car, never coming inside our house. Thanksgiving when he escorted her inside, I wanted to cry. Thanksgivings were sacred to my mother, so bringing guests to her house for dinner? Well then, this was serious.

To compound this tragedy, I had big problems at school. I had been an honors student every year through eighth grade. My grades had now slipped to a B average. My mom came to the school to talk to my teachers and was told I was on the verge of suspension for *insolence.* Hey! Can I help it if dramatic sarcasm is my *nature*? I told Mama those teachers never called on black kids when we raised our hands for questions or to lead any special projects. So, defensively, my mother talked to the principal, Mr. Kelb. He told her although I was a good student, I caused disruptions in class and it (meaning I) wouldn't be tolerated by the faculty, or by him. If I expected to succeed, said he, I must cease opposing (back-talking) teachers in class. Mama assured him with her honey-dripping Southern charm that I would no longer cause any disturbances because (and this is when she dropped the bomb) she would sit in on my classes for a week or longer if needed, along with the parents of other bussed students. Mama and her advocacy group were planning to monitor classes, an action suspiciously objected to at first by administrators, but as a block unit captain, my mother had connections with district aldermen and other black civic leaders. They couldn't stop her. Afterward, neither could I—from daily grilling about homework to being a proper Christian.

Mama invited my classmate and rebellious comrade Leslie and her widowed mother, Ava Bell, to our Thanksgiving dinner. Mrs. Bell formerly taught elementary school and she, too, monitored our classes. With the two extra leaves, my mother's dining table seated ten people comfortably. There were twelve total gathered and squeezed in: close family friend Sharon and her boyfriend Willie, Mama's cousin Justine, her husband Clarence, their son Conrad whom everyone called Connie Chub, Mrs. Bell and Leslie, Uncle Ransom, Carla, and of course me, Mama, and my dad.

Mama blessed our table saying thank you, Lord, for all blessings we've received. I'm so grateful to have my family in good health, etc., in the name of Jesus. Shooting bullets out my eyes through Carla's buoyant cleavage, I tried killing her before I choked on the heavy meal laid before us. Mama glanced at my wickedly focused face and sent me to the kitchen to help bring out more dishes. In the kitchen, my face firmly held with her right hand, pointing to my mouth with her left, she said, "*Don't* you be nasty on this of *all* days. *This* is a blessing-filled, *godly* day and *you* will *not* be rude and *un*-Christian. When you go back to that table *you will* smile even if it *kills* you and be nice and courteous to your uncle's friend." Oh Lord! She didn't know . . . it truly almost killed me.

Oh, the shark, babe, has such teeth, dear
And it shows them pearly white

Sitting down again my antennae beeped to Unk's comment: he was glad he was finally making wedding plans. Meeting friends later, he and Carla were going to the riverfront—they were planning a little reception after a civil ceremony at the city courthouse really soon. When Clarence pushed his chair back, stood stiffly, then awkwardly bowed after Unk's announcement, Cousin Justine looked up at her husband as though he'd lost his mind. Willie belted out a hardy laugh then gasped on something. I think Sharon kicked him under the table. Connie Chub offered muffled congratulations, ham stuffed into his mouth. Mrs. Bell smiled and looked confused, checking other faces. At that point, personally, I was in shock. This was apparent to Leslie, judging from the concern on her face. No one opposed, but none seemed pleased either. Including my mother. My dad just grunted at the news, gulping down his beer.

Unk was Daddy's younger brother. The only thing they had in common besides the same mother and father was a love of reading newspapers, but if trouble was around, they'd looked out for each other. Mama said she hoped Unk was going to settle down in one place and quit hopping around from town to town. Then everyone quietly ate. Sharon's silverware clinked loudly and I glanced over. Looking as evil as I looked stunned, she chewed that bird like it was still alive and trying to get away. Holding up a glass of wine, Carla stood to give a phony toast. All mouths gaped, except Unk's; he beamed up radiantly at his future bride. I needed to vomit and, uttering excuses, left the table. Leslie, being a bright sensitive girl, followed me to my room. She knew I couldn't handle this bullshit. We listened to music in my room and talked about teachers, students at school, and what little progress there was since monitoring began. When her mother knocked and then opened my bedroom door, I didn't want her to leave. I asked if they would stay for dessert, but Mrs. Bell said my mom had wrapped plenty of food with dessert for them to take home. Walking them out I peeked into the dining room, where Connie Chub was still eating dessert with his loony dad Clarence, then into the living room where everyone else sat. Thankfully, Carla and Unk had left already for the Keyhole.

When Carla found out Unk's settlement was stalled for months in government red tape, she started fucking all the men in our family.

All the wives except one put up with it. I'm sure Mama's constitution was sufficient warning, so Daddy wasn't on the radar. Sharon told Carla she was going to fuck her up and for good. Carla laughed and told Sharon, "God's already fucked you up." This was a reference to Sharon's abnormal physique; I'd discussed this with Sharon when I was eight. She told me that when her mother was pregnant, her father didn't want another mouth to feed and pushed her off a roof. That was in Chicago in the hot summer of 1921. A month later, Sharon was born premature with a curved spine. Despite some early years of hard knocks, Sharon's face was pretty: a high forehead, button nose, and large, wide-spaced brown eyes. Her arms, hands, legs, and feet were all long, slender, and elegant, but from the rear, her back humped like a camel's. She was the color of a camel too, a satin, sandy camel. Her subtle makeup was perfectly applied, enhancing her prettiness. Her hair was always coifed in smooth, swept-up French twists or chignons with sexy tendrils covering her delicate ears. She was a professional seamstress, dressing in such a refined way that the protrusion on her back was barely noticed. Standing four feet eleven inches, she was a wildcat underneath her pinkish-pearl manicure. The sure way to rile her was to mention the hump. She liked to fight dirty too, pulling knives out from her frilly bosom with the force of a man weighing 250 pounds or more. She weighed less than a hundred pounds soaking wet.

One evening, Sharon went into the Keyhole after work. (Cooking was not her thing.) She loved their fried tripe sandwiches, famous as the best in St. Louis. She noticed Carla at a back table flirting and sitting on a man's lap. Looking closer, Sharon saw that the man was Willie, her boyfriend. She squinted as Willie grinned down Carla's bosom. When he looked up, Sharon was slipping around the crowded tables and he deftly shoved Carla to the floor before flinging his arms wide open. He laughed, gurgled, "Here comes my baaaaaabbbby! Hey, baby, come sit down and join me!"

Sharon flipped the table over and glasses, beer bottles, and innocent bystanders went flying everywhere. Two backhanded slaps and Willie was off the chair. Swiftly turning, she repeatedly kicked Carla in the ass as she scurried along the floor. Bending over, Sharon was ripping at the fabric down to her bosom when Unk staggered out of the bathroom. He rushed over, pinning Sharon's arms down to her sides, picked her up like a doll, and carried her out of the joint kicking and cussing. Willie held the side of his stinging face, skulking close behind.

The last duel between Sharon and Carla was legendary. The really funny thing, Sharon wasn't married to anyone in the family, but Unk called her "Wifey" because she was the only one who'd let him sleep on her floor when other women put him out. Willie and Unk were tight drinking buddies. When he was in town, three days out of seven Unk would be lying on their bedroom floor talking and drinking "Rosie O'Grady" wine with Willie all night while Sharon bitched and complained.

Unk made it clear to everyone he'd take care of Sharon for as long as he lived. Carla fucked with Sharon every opportunity she got, as well as anyone else she thought posed a threat. Tired as she was of grift, drift, and hustling without a permanent home, Unk's settlement could change her circumstances.

Before their meeting, according to Unk's various river rat sources, her circumstances were this: rich family heritage, old Main Line money that settled in Boston following the Civil War. After college she moved to San Francisco, entrenched in bohemian life choices that didn't square with her Brahmin upbringing.

In 1964, she returned home, swinging her malnourished three-year-old boy on her bony hips, father's identity still unknown. What was known was her police record citing a string of heroin and cocaine convictions among miscellaneous other illegal activities. Her parents stripped her of her child, her trust-fund status, and formally stated certain boundaries. Feeling forced to leave, her pride demanded she never look back. *Ever*. When she surfaced in St. Louis circa 1969, needle tracks marked her inner arms, the creases the back of her legs, between her toes, and surely other, undisclosed body parts. She subsisted on a variety of drugs along with wine, beer, gin, vodka, and, on very good days, Johnnie Walker Black Label. Good days came around more often after she hooked up with Unk.

Unk was a better entertainer than almost anyone. After

his military service he tried working in Vegas show biz. He worked mostly as a porter, waiter, and whatever else he could do, until stress broke him down and he was admitted to a psychiatric ward—working long hours waiting tables, serving crown rib roasts that soon transformed themselves into talking severed heads. Between admittance in psychiatric hospitals he'd bum around the country. He could tell jokes, sing better than anybody in our family, play harmonica, and do impersonations of anyone, famous or not. He'd leave on job-hunting trips across country just to be in a different city—Minneapolis, Seattle, Tijuana—then he'd come back with two or three vagrant buddies tagging along. They'd stay in St. Louis awhile, then wander off again. Whenever he'd come home, he'd always have fascinating stories to tell us. After Carla came along he stopped wandering off alone. He couldn't trust her to be loyal when he was *in* town. It wasn't her nature.

After Christmas, Unk took Carla down south to meet more family. Big mistake. One town they visited was so small everyone there was kin to everyone else on either their mother's line or their father's line. Those countrified women welcomed them, at first. Carla flirting overtly with their men didn't raise a hair. Until the men came home with their pockets picked clean. That did it. All of their money, earned hard in cotton fields, box-production factories, and various backbreaking, mind-sapping labor, gone. Insufficient wages that already couldn't support huge families, gone. Some had as many as nineteen children. Gone. One woman tried to blow Carla's head off with a double-barreled shotgun. Unk got her out of that town quick.

In Memphis, Carla's playing field was larger, so they lasted a bit before being kicked out. And when I say kicked, I mean kicked *hard.* Redneck-Confederate-Southern-Comfort hard. A cousin of Dad's called scared to death, letting him know he was driving Unk nonstop three hundred straight miles to a St. Louis hospital. When my parents reached the emergency room, the attending doctor warned them before they went in to see Unk. Broken leg, he had stab wounds in all his vital organs and his upper thighs, broken ribs, and possibly other as-yet-unidentified bones, and kick bruises all over, including his head and face. Mama said Dad looked terrified. He leaned down to Unk's ear and in a quivering hiss said, "Get rid of Carla as soon as you're out the hospital. She's either going to get you killed, or kill you herself. Ransom, you're too *old* to play the fool. She's making death come to you quicker than needs be. It's time for you to *enjoy* your life brother, *not* step back in misery."

Mama says Unk's swollen, blackened eyes filled with water, his lips trembled, when he rasped, "I can't, I *can't.* She's in my blood."

Leaving, Dad turned to Mama sadly and said, "She's going to kill him soon and all these years he waited for nothing 'cause that settlement is going up in smoke. He's never going to have peace, even in the grave."

Dad's prediction was truth. As he spoke I believe Carla had already plotted how to bury Unk. A year or so later she was so bold that Unk actually admitted he could taste poisonous chemicals in the food she cooked. One day he furiously jumped up from their kitchen table, knocking it over, and roared: "Carla! You are *not* going to kill me!"

She answered, "You're already dead."

Then he said, "I'm taking you with me!" And Unk clenched her throat, forcing the life out of her. As they struggled she coaxed him toward the open back door that led out to a cobbled patio. The witness, a neighbor across the alley, stood in his backyard listening to the cursing and scuffling, and shouted at Unk through the open door, "Mack! Let her go! Don't—" just as Carla twisted, turned him, and kicked him as hard as she could.

He fell back, busting through the screen door, falling head first down the concrete steps, banging his skull on the patio. She let him lie there. The neighbor ran into his house to call Dad and an ambulance. Unk spent three days in a coma before he died. Everybody told my father he should file charges against Carla. He refused. He said she'd regret everything she did. "My brother was good to her," he said, "and she abused him, so I know she's going to pay for it somehow. Just wait and see."

I was totally enraged, eager to fight. I was tired of being called nigger by grotesque retards at school, tired of stupid-ass teachers with correspondence-course degrees telling me I wasn't smart enough, tired of trying to be a good Christian. Two months after Unk's funeral, I came home from school and Carla was sitting on our front porch like a welcomed guest. I ran up the steps and jumped on her, clawing her face and throat, screaming, calling her every whore-bitch-slut name I could think of. I told her *she* should be dead! *Dead!* Mama heard me, ran out of the house and grabbed my arms, preventing me from throwing Carla off the side of the porch. Carla choked on laughter. Mom turned and slapped the shit out of her. She laughed and laughed and laughed.

The next spring it rained cats and dogs for nine straight days. When it stopped, the leftover, winter-scuffed potholes were filled deep with water. The sun came out big and beautiful on a Saturday morning and everyone on our block was so happy to see it, every excuse was given to be out in the sunshine. People cleaned yards, grilled barbeque ribs and chicken, and gaggles of kids ran up and down the streets or played in puddles. Mama made salmon croquettes, a favorite of Sharon's, and asked me to walk a plate of food around to her house. Willie had been drinking nonstop, still grieving Unk, constantly whining that he had no one to go fishing with anymore, worrying Sharon to exhaustion.

On the way there I thought about changes at school. As a graduating senior every assignment now required careful decisions, carrying much more responsibility. When I approached Sharon's house I saw a man sitting on the edge of a gigantic pothole at least six feet across and more than likely four feet deep. He had a fishing pole line down in the hole. Getting closer I could see it was Willie. His eyes were closed and he had the pole braced between the slats of his lawn chair. I doubled over, almost collapsed on the sidewalk. Sharon came outside onto her porch and saw me.

Between giggles I said, "Sharon, why don't you get him out of the street?"

"Any fool thinks he can catch fish in the middle of Kingshighway needs to be left alone," she said, then sympathetically shook her head. I could see the corners of her mouth sneak-creeping into a smile. She loved that old fool Willie.

I heard a car racing at police-chase speed. I turned to see Carla's brand-new red convertible Mustang burning rubber as she braked, skidding to a squealing stop, the car's bumper less than a foot from Willie's lawn chair. Sharon slyly slipped off her shoes, ducked, and eased down to street level as Carla jumped out of the car leaving the door open. On an extreme carnival speed-high, absolutely wild, Carla screamed at Willie, "Getthefuckouttathestreet!"

Willie opened his eyes, red as stop signs, but otherwise didn't budge.

"Getthefuckouttathestreet!" Carla grabbed the lawn chair, shaking and yanking it—"Getthefuckouttathestreet!"—trying to pitch Willie into the pothole. "Getthefuckouttathestreet!" She must have sensed a shadow-presence then because she jumped, and spun around.

"Oh, ho ho, here comes the little humpback troll." Her insults were cut as Sharon pushed her into the pothole. Carla splashed, kicked, cussed. Sharon squatted down, pushing Carla's head under filthy water as Carla blindly reached for something to grab ahold of. Nearly drowned, her head bobbed as Sharon pulled, knocked, and banged it around the edges of the hole; Carla gulped, sputtered, and regurgitated sewage. Before she could grip anything, Sharon wrapped that wench's wet hair around her wrist until the scalp was tight to her fist. She popped the switchblade from her bosom like a jack-knifing pro, precisely cutting off all of Carla's hair that she held in her fist.

Sharon stood, untangling the hair, stretching out all four feet eleven inches, holding her arms up so everyone outside could see. Carla screamed through bloodied lips. Her legs hiked along the side of the hole before slipping, sliding, and falling back into it. Sharon threw the loose hair back at Carla's face with victorious witch cackles. As she moved to her porch, I saw her slip strands of hair into her dress pocket.

Wearily, Willie reached over in the pothole and tugged at Carla's blouse. Her drug high was so completely blown she didn't know if it was Sharon and jerked around, twisting and cussing, until her blouse came up, covering her face. Wearing no brassiere, her breasts hung heavy and bare for all to see. Instantly wide-eyed awake, Willie pepped up and shouted over his shoulder, "Haaaaaaaaaayyyyyyy, haaaaa, haaaaa, haaaa! Somebody come help me get this weird fish I caught with big milk-jug titties!"

Less than a year later, Carla called my dad almost every night, saying Unk was haunting her and she couldn't sleep. She was scared, didn't want to stay in her house alone. Given no Christian sympathy, nada, she awoke one night really strung out, running and screaming out in the streets until she found Sharon's house. Sharon said she was babbling crazy, begging, "Please, *please*, help me, I'll give you anything, an-y thing you *want!*" Sharon told her she didn't want anything from her. The episodes went on for weeks. Then Carla had a stroke—a crippling, mind-debilitating stroke. Results? Invalid.

Dad tracked down Carla's family to let them know. The family's attorney instructed him to put her into a nursing home and send the address. Someone would be getting in touch. But they never did.

You know when that shark bites with his teeth, babe
Scarlet billows start to spread

Nursing home name registration: *Carol Anne Adams*. She's thirty-nine years old. The only person who visits her is Sharon. And—probably—Unk.

ATTRITION

BY CALVIN WILSON

Downtown Newsroom

I f procrastination hadn't existed, Jarvis Trent would have been the guy to invent it. He liked to think that the more time he spent not doing something, the better the results would be when he actually got around to doing it.

That went a long way toward explaining why Trent turned up early one November morning in a downtown St. Louis newsroom, with no one else around except an intern who was unlucky enough to be working the cop beat. Trent moved past rows of bare desks—unadorned by photos or flowers due to a series of layoffs—before finally settling into one that was as far away as he could get from the chatter of the police radio.

He unzipped his fake-leather folder, pulled out a tape recorder, and flipped it on. The third-billed star of a clichéd indie movie about corruption in a small town began to ramble on about her commitment to doing one for the industry, one for the art.

Trent started to yawn when he felt the presence of someone behind him. Before he had time to turn around, he heard a voice: "Are you a professional?"

"What?"

"I said, are you a professional?"

It was his new boss, Tatiana Briggs. Brought in to replace Sid Murdoch, whose midlife crisis had dictated that he relinquish his post as A&E editor to become a writer/editor-at-large, concocting think pieces that no one was particularly interested in reading, but would give him something to do until he retired and eventually died.

"That story should have been filed yesterday afternoon, at the latest," Briggs brayed. "You're way past deadline. We're running a wire story instead."

"But I just have a few more quotes to—"

"You should have gotten it in on time." Briggs was clutching her handbag as if she was afraid he might grab it. "We're not having any more of this," she said, adding just as she turned to leave, "That's not the way I run things."

Management had brought in Briggs, who had been a business writer at a San Antonio weekly, to impose law and order on the arts and entertainment writers who had gotten into the habit of turning in copy too close to deadline. In her grayish pantsuits and sensible shoes, she looked like every self-centered prig you'd ever had to put up with your whole life.

Trent was a general assignment arts writer, and up until now he had liked his job. Mostly he wrote about things that the other writers on staff were unaware of, uninterested in, or too busy to handle—things like jazz (which the pop music guy said hurt his ears) and modern dance (which was situated in a black hole that neither the theater critic nor the classical music critic cared to explore).

But with Briggs on board, the Monday planning meeting had become his own special ring of hell. Where Murdoch had conducted it with a lighthearted pragmatism, Briggs was nothing but business. And for someone who had been appointed A&E editor, she didn't know much about art, film, books, theater, or music—neither classical nor pop. When Claire Shannon, the book review editor, mentioned that she was considering a freelancer's review of a Samuel Beckett biography, Briggs thought she was referring to the character on the nineties TV show *Quantum Leap*.

Later, Trent asked Claire what she thought of that exchange.

"Oh, you can't expect her to know everything," Claire said.

"She's an arts editor and she doesn't know who Beckett is?"

Claire just shrugged and busied herself at her desk, her nose back in her books. It figured. She was just like the other writers, too frightened of losing her job to do anything but acquiesce to an idiot.

Trent wouldn't have described himself as easygoing, and some people might have described him as prickly. But considering the vast array of personalities he'd encountered in his years in the newspaper business, he could honestly say that he had never experienced anything more uncomfortable than strong dislike. That is, until Briggs showed up.

As the weeks went by, Trent could feel himself getting more and more resentful of her presence. The way she'd assign stories as if she actually knew what needed to be covered. And the high-handedness with which she shot down good ideas and promoted bad ones. It also galled him that everyone else seemed to be kissing up to her.

Trent could remember visiting his uncle in Memphis years ago and playing with two other boys. It was a boring afternoon, and his aunt's cat was hanging around. When the cat ducked under a chair, Trent got an idea: he persuaded the other boys to help him corner the cat. The chair was up against a wall, and the boys were positioned so the cat couldn't escape.

Before long, it began to hiss, but Trent—who was stooping at the front of the chair and looking straight at the cat—had an instinct about these things. At what he imagined was the exact moment before the tabby was about to scratch his face, he backed off. The cat bolted from under the chair to God knows where. No harm done.

But with Briggs around, Trent finally understood how that cat must have felt.

Eventually, it was all just too much.

Trent zipped his jacket all the way up to his collar as he stood waiting for Briggs to arrive at her house—a cheap-looking affair that he supposed was the best she could get on short notice. Or maybe she was just cheap. He knew her car, a beat-up 1996 Saturn that she didn't bother to wash. All she had to do now was drive up.

She usually left the paper around six p.m., and it was already five forty-five, so it wouldn't be much longer. No one was out on the street, maybe because it was starting to get cold. He was about to zip up his jacket again when he remembered that he already had.

And there she was, the Saturn rattling along as if it needed a tune-up and oil change. Briggs parked the car, scurried to her front door, and unlocked it. That was when she felt a push, then something hard on the back of her head. Then nothing.

Trent had taken a risk: someone peeking behind a curtain could have seen him ambush Briggs. That was one of the things he hated about himself—his impetuousness. But he was glad he'd read that news report a couple of years back about quicksand along the Mississippi River.

Things went pretty much as Trent had expected they would. Briggs wasn't important enough for the police to put much effort into looking for her. Anyway, Trent knew that life was nothing like TV. Most crimes didn't get solved.

Briggs's sister Esther flew in from San Francisco, stayed in

St. Louis just long enough to make it look good, then headed back. Claire was appointed arts editor with no raise in pay. She wasn't much of a disciplinarian, but the staff had gotten the message about punctuality, and management felt no need to bring in another Genghis Khan—especially considering the money being saved by not having to pay Briggs.

With Briggs gone, Trent felt better than he had in years. Whatever gene stopped people from committing heinous acts wasn't part of his DNA, but he'd known that for a long time. It wasn't a matter of whether he could kill someone, but whether he thought such action would be appropriate given the circumstances. If he ever met someone like Briggs again, he might take similar steps. Perhaps make further use of a hammer and a big plastic bag.

Although he seriously doubted such a thing would ever happen again, it was nice to have the option.

TRACKS

BY Jason Makansi

The Hill

Damn! Trisha thought, squeezing her hand brakes in front of the flashing reds, clanging bells, the line of coal cars approaching from the west. She thought about dashing across the rails. Then the barricades descended. Suddenly, feeling the burn in her thighs, she welcomed the forced rest. She dismounted precisely, swiveling like an indicator on a scale in a doctor's office. Then she unleashed her medium-length, loosely curled blond hair from her helmet.

The ground rumbled. Her aching buttocks reminded her to spend that hundred dollars for a better seat.

"Damn all this coal and global warming," she muttered.

She propped her bike against the high chain-link fence topped with barbed wire surrounding the RC Pharmaceutical plant. To her left, the huge storm-water drainage canal passed underneath the roadway. Her half-gloved hands mopped the sweat burning her eyes. She positioned her helmet on the sidewalk behind her head and lay down. Above her was a cloudless cobalt sky.

It's good to be forced to slow down, she thought, not really believing it.

She was startled by a shrill warning whistle, another freight train passing on a separate set of tracks fifty yards or so behind her.

What if both trains get stuck? she wondered. *Well, if I had to, I could always follow that storm-water drain, or whatever it is, out of here.* She glanced at the sloping concrete embankment and the roadway bridge ahead of the tracks. She'd never seen but a trickle of water in it. The small office building across the street was lifeless on a Sunday morning.

She closed her eyes, which were often complimented for being as blue as the sky above her. The moistness in her thighs absorbed the heat. Her head cooled. She had an urge to fondle herself, lifted her head to look around as if she just might.

What seemed distant at other times—the factory, the canal, the office building—now seemed to close in. The urge passed.

An Italian-flag banner flapped from a nearby streetlight.

This definitely is not the Hill, she thought, chuckling about the quaint Italian neighborhood to the south. Not far in the other direction was lush Forest Park where she had met her friends for their regular Sunday-morning workout.

Her breathing returned to normal. Both sets of trains were moving slowly. Soon, she felt uncomfortably exposed, not to mention baking, so she crossed the street and sat under an awning on the steps of the little office building.

A discarded plastic fast-food tray rolled down the opposite side of the street, collided with a sturdy weed, got knocked off course, bringing Trisha's gaze to a small area of desolate landscaping: a few large rocks, faded mulch, nothing green. Across the way, beyond a large parking area with only a few rusted shipping containers, she watched a short, dark, thin man framed against the stark white backdrop of the factory siding exhale smoke against the stagnant air. He tossed his butt, and wandered toward the fenced perimeter.

This is straight out of a Hopper painting, she thought.

* * *

Earlier that morning, Slinky Watkins drove into Miller's back lot and parked her truck.

"You don't have to work weekends," her boss had said repeatedly. "Miller's Capezio is plenty satisfied with your performance."

She preferred it though. She liked to pull and stretch and fondle the fabrics, silk sleeves, ruffled skirts, and supple shoes that the dancers bought from Mr. Miller. She'd slide a garment under her armpits, across her back, and under her crotch, places where her skin was more sensitive, her body more responsive. Sometimes the garments returned by the dancer's parents still smelled sweetly of a young girl.

Once she didn't hear Mr. Miller's car. Her ears were flat against her head from the super-tight legging she'd fit over her head. Slinky yanked it off just in time, when she heard the door open and the piercing automatic bell. Her boss was startled to find her shirtless. Thankfully, the day wasn't so warm to have the air conditioners turned on, yet warm enough that someone working alone just might want to cool off by taking their shirt off. Slinky barely had breasts. In fact, she had the smallest breasts of any woman she had ever seen. What she never understood was why her cherry-red nipples, the size of small cranberries, never seemed to relax. Against her pale skin, they looked like swollen sores. She wore a bra only to hide them.

Mr. Miller had reversed course immediately. Slinky acted like nothing unusual had happened.

"Hey, I'm only trying to save on air-conditioning," she said moments later, walking past him.

Mr. Miller was a kind employer. If he was able to overlook her five years of hard time at the Missouri Eastern Correctional Center, he could overlook catching her shirtless on a Sunday morning. He never mentioned the incident.

Adapting to the train schedules was part of working at Miller's, from the first tremble of a coffee mug to the deafening noise and nauseating smell of brakes grinding against metal. Occasionally, two sets of trains passed simultaneously on Sunday morning at around 10:48 a.m. Once, Slinky watched a lone jogger, stuck between the tracks, wait a long time. He stomped his feet, cursed, and waved his arms—no match for the futility of his situation.

She liked to see the bikers in their bright, tight body suits, colorful, reflective, the clothing like separate skin. Fluorescence of epidermis! She liked the phrase so much she wrote it down. She remembered how she learned the science word for skin. "Your epidermis is showing! Your epidermis is showing!" the kids in elementary school yelled on the playground. She loved that word, but she hated remembering her childhood.

Such thoughts always led to that really mean girl at the swimming pool that one summer, who yelled, "Ugh! Her blood is showing! She *is* a girl!" when her period had started and she had no idea about it. The girl encouraged her friends to tiptoe toward her as a group, like she was diseased. They pointed "down there" and joked and laughed, surrounding her near the fence. Two of them poked her with their fingers. Hysterical, Slinky searched frantically for something to keep them away, reached for the skimming net with a short metal handle hanging off hooks on the fence, and beat back her tormentors, but not before she'd gashed one of them along her cheek, deep enough for a dozen stitches and a permanent scar. That girl's father, a lawyer who worked for a prominent downtown firm, saw to it that Slinky was barred from going to that pool again.

She never forgot who caused her all that grief.

In high school, Slinky did math with the boys in the science club and insisted on taking up wrestling. She loved the feel of the tight outfits. The contact with others aroused her, even though it was fighting. Her brothers and her father taught her how to fight but not about what would happen to her body. They wrestled and horsed around all the time. Those were the only times she *didn't* feel awkward about her body. The coach lauded her prowess on the mat, but the boys' parents eventually had her removed from the team. No more epidermis contact.

Now, she heard the high-pitched squeals of metal on metal. She looked at the old industrial clock behind its thick wire cage: 10:42. Right on time.

She pushed her solid, curveless frame from the desk and turned to look out the office window. A woman with her bicycle. Beyond the fence across the street were the inactive loading docks. The all-white exterior and fluorescent purple company sign with its flowery cursive lettering accentuated the sun's glare. She could see the humidity separate from the air, the kind of day perfect for being in a swimming pool. The more Slinky stared at the cyclist, the more she became the girl who made fun of her first menstrual bleeding.

Were any cars waiting? None! Her face brightened. The bicyclist had two minutes to reverse course. She checked the parking lot around back. She looked toward the open concrete storm canal. Once, during a flash flood, there was so much water flowing by, she worried that the canal might spill over. Someone could throw a body in there and not see it until the drain met the River des Peres. Mr. Miller told of a time when they did find a body down there and had to call the police to remove it.

At 10:48 a.m. the train approached on the tracks behind her building. Slinky smiled. Her skin, her epidermis, prickled pleasantly. Her throat constricted. She swallowed hard.

She returned to the office. The bicyclist was gone but her bike remained. Slinky's smile evaporated. The only escape was through the storm drain. Not a good idea. Some kids found that out the hard way once. Mr. Miller and his warehouse crew had to rope tow them out.

She hurried to the front entrance, peeked out the long vertical side window. Her smile returned.

Slinky found a tight, stretchy maroon leotard in the stock room. She thought how the word rhymed with *retard*, a name she was called often as a kid. She returned to the front entrance and pulled on the door with steady hands, but trembling so much inside she could barely hear herself think. The onslaught of the trains' clanging assaulted her ears before the laden heat of the morning whacked her face. In one motion, she threw the fabric over the girl's head and tied it behind her. Then she grabbed one arm in a half nelson, put her other arm around her neck, pressuring the Adam's apple, and dragged her into the foyer. She knew how to put to good use the arms her coach said resembled dinosaur bones. The cyclist did not struggle. Being fit for one sport didn't make you fit for another, Slinky thought.

"Look at it! Ugh!" The voices reverberated in her skull. She felt the pointing fingers indent her skin.

VJ, the guard, noticed the bicycle, but the rider was missing. It looked expensive, but what did he know? The last time he rode a bike was in India. Bikes there sure didn't look like this one. That was back when his name was Vijay. When he used that name, people thought he was a dumb immigrant. When he changed it to VJ, people thought he was a savvy foreign-born American.

He pulled his half-pint out of his back pocket, drained the last swallow, and popped a fresh stick of Doublemint into his mouth. He rubbed his belly. Ten seconds and he'd have the fence unlocked, the bike hidden in a shipping container, empty for years except for the time he discovered those teenagers drunk on an overcarbonated mix of Coke and beer, jeans around their ankles, awkwardly fucking like they'd never done it before. He relieved them of all of their cash, threatening to turn them in to the authorities, before he sent them packing toward the hole in the fence they'd entered from. For good measure, he copped a feel from one of the girls.

What the hell, he thought, *not like there are many perks to this job*.

He made a dash for the bike.

Slinky mashed her pelvis against the tight black Lycra lining of the cyclist's buttocks, then against the back of her thigh. She relaxed her other hand from restraining duty and forced it down into her own pubic hairs, finding her spot. With her forefinger, she massaged vigorously, rubbing against the biker. Only a few seconds later, her body spasmed, shuddered, then stilled. She paused long enough to smell sex on her fingers.

Sensing her attacker momentarily distracted, Trisha reached into the front pouch of her cycling shirt and pulled her emergency air pump out so sharply, it expanded like a big switchblade. The hard plastic snapping valve lock had hurt her many times when it accidently came down on her thumb. Her aim was true when she swung around. She caught the aluminum tube against the person's right cheek, the plastic valve tearing at a nostril. That stunned her attacker enough for Trisha to break loose while her attacker's hands gripped her face to contain the bleeding.

Outside, Trisha stumbled and grabbed the stair railing. She felt as if she were going to barf. Her grip was like glue. The railing shook, as though it would come out of the bolts in the cement. In her distress, she forgot how she even got there, then remembered, and saw that her bike was gone. She ran into the street, thinking her attacker might chase her, and nearly collided with the first car that had passed through the first railroad crossing, only to slam on the brakes before the next crossing. She approached the driver's side, motioning hysterically for the man to roll down his window. He gave her an angry look, tried to ignore her, then motioned her in the direction of an SUV with an official-looking insignia on the side and an emergency light on top.

As Trisha hurried toward it, she had the presence of mind to ask herself what she would say. She had not been raped. That old line, *You should see what the other guy looks like*, came to her. Recalling the moment she swung at her attacker, she realized something not quite right about his face, a softness, a frailty. He looked more feminine than male.

He could easily have abducted her, or worse. No clothes taken off. No blood, no scratches, no bruises. No evidence. Still, she felt violated, humiliated. What about her bike? She could at least report it stolen. But she had no evidence she had a bike. Wait! Her helmet! She ran back and found it on the steps. But who could have taken the bike? Had someone come from the woods behind the factory?

A pickup truck scratched out of the lot adjacent to the building. It approached the railroad crossing to the left just as the gate lifted. Thinking this might be her attacker, she considered running after the vehicle, hoping to catch the license number. The last train car, an engine colored dirty yellow and coated with grease, got more distant with each second. The truck was well gone before Trisha had taken a first step toward it.

She then walked to the other railroad tracks toward the SUV, realizing after a dozen or so steps that it had left. She stopped on the sidewalk, bent over, and began bawling. Driver after driver held up by the trains passed her in a huff in both directions.

Tears exhausted, she looked up and saw the guard at the far end of the industrial lot. She ran in his direction between the fence and the storm-water canal, which she now realized was much deeper than she'd thought.

"Hey! Hey! Please, can you help me?!"

VJ started toward the fence, beyond where the windows and doors had been boarded up as long as he'd been working here. He'd been expecting his "drop" at 11:05 a.m. at the one part of the property overlooked by the security cameras.

His older brother, the "genius" financial consultant, bragged that making money was all about vacuuming up nickels and dimes in transaction fees. Well, VJ could play that game too. Whatever this powder was they refined in here, people out there were willing to pay a boatload of money for scrapings off the rolling lines.

Startled upon hearing a plea for help, VJ turned in Trisha's direction, ignored her for a second, then stopped.

"Someone attacked me in that building over there. My bike was stolen! Could I make a phone call?" Her arms hung limp on the stiff wire fencing.

"That's against policy," he said, taking in her breasts, framed by the wired openings.

"Could you at least call 911?" She sighed heavily.

Still loopy from the heat and the last of his whiskey, VJ thought about the teenagers in the storage container. How appealing this woman was, even mussed up, darling white-girl freckles dotting her cheeks, pinkish splashes on her arms, thighs that looked like they could grip and hold an industrial-sized vat.

"Wait, was your bike over there?"

"Yes."

VJ looked at her, then down the railroad tracks, at some distant point. Who was he kidding? He wasn't going to fondle this woman. He was one incident away from losing his job and being shipped back to India. His brother would never help him again.

"Okay, lady, I saw the bike and took it in for safekeeping. I'll level with you, I *thought* about selling it if no one claimed it. But I didn't steal, okay? We make deal? I bring your bike back over to that fence. You don't mention a word."

Trisha looked at him, disgusted, then relieved. He was being halfway honest. Well, maybe a quarter-way.

"Do you know who the hell works in that place?" She pointed to the building.

"No idea. I see cars parked in front, people enter and leave, but I couldn't ID one person."

Miller's was right across the street but from this spot it seemed to Trisha a mile away.

VJ went to retrieve the bicycle.

In his absence, Trisha, tears brimming all over again, became aware of the quiet. A bird chirped here and there. The rails pointed silently toward the vanishing point, utility poles overhead and hushed. A rusted valve that probably hadn't seen flow in years jutted out of the bone-dry concrete canal. Except for the guard walking toward her bike, all was at rest. Whatever just happened had moved on.

PART II

A POETIC INTERLUDE

FOUR ST. LOUIS POEMS
BY MICHAEL CASTRO
Gaslight Square

IN ST. LOUIS HEAT

the heat
  the men
    in blue

jeans
  on the black
    corner
by the Chester
    Pipe
      Shop

lean
  //#
    all
afternoon

    against
  the caged
storefront

GASLIGHT SQUARE

gutted storefronts
crumbling movie theater
empty picture
frame wall trick-
ling brick rubble
into street
eerie
& dimly fluorescent
uninhabited
save for one
solitary
stocking-capped black man
bent over
in loose drab overcoat
staggering between parked cars
in the driving rain

ST. LOUIS BLUES REVISITED

Blue is the blues of this town
Blue as the cold cop
Who killed Michael Brown
Blue is the blues of this town

Blue is the blues of this town
Blue heat street sign blue core flame
Gas blue blaze haze glazes a name
Blue is the blues of this town

Blue is the rain song, like tears it comes
From blue whale clouds that rumble like drums
Blue is the blues of this town
Blue is the blues of this town

Blue is the whiskey that gnaws in the gut
Blue is the uniform makes a man strut
Blue is the lead in the gun chamber rut
Blue is the blues of this town

Blue is the ghetto, blue the stone rubble
Blue the dope powder, blue the hope bubble
Blue are the trains, the veins, the migraines
Blue is the blues of this town

Blue is the ballpark, blue all the museums
Blue the caged monkey who swings between screams

Blue is the Arch & the gateway of dreams
Blue is the blues of this town

Blue is the hit man, blue in a bottle
Blue is the street girl, blue her eye shadow
Blue is the beat of the street & the news
Blue is the blues of this town

Blue is the song, blue the bird songster
Language as long & as strong as a dinosaur
The trees' teeth are chattering—airplane chainsaw
Blue is the blues of this town

Blue is the smoke over rims of the stacks
Blue is the waterfront, blue both sides of tracks
Blue is the love that is eaten by cracks
Blue is the blues of this town

HALLOWEEN

Today all the hungry ghosts
wail
all the world's sorry chains
creak
all its light leaks
into the dark
where hidden horror lurks

It's Halloween!
Gargoyley guys
& shrewy witches—
the underside
is the scratch we itches

A parade, in masquerade
of tiny boys & girls, wide open
bags & palms, stream through seedy suburbs'
leaf-mealed lawns

innocents
trickling trick-less

stifling yawns

gathering more & more
door to door
treats
from shadowed neighbors' smiles

sweets & coins
dispensed straight up or
with weird & twisted, hidden wiles—

cold cash &
bidden fruit they there-
fore dare not grasp or eat
without exploratory
pause

preferably
laboratory
analysis

Once home
they sift through eager fingers
offerings that they sought, & brought

mull possibilities—
laced treats & hot pennies
strained food for thought—

& later bodiless, near
nauseous, overwrought
they wrestle in the bed

wispy demons of the mind

reflections of this bitter world of humankind
whose cool coins', glad hands' & twisted smiles'
impact instead
may burn, or sicken, or, finally

kill you dead

PART III

THE COUNTY

A PALER SHADE OF DEATH

BY LAURA BENEDICT

Glendale

"Hey, can I help you do that?"

When the boy approached me the first time, I was trying to wrestle a marble-topped plant stand from where it had caught on the corner of an antique mirror. The cargo area of the Suburban was crowded with the *objets d'art* and detritus I'd thoughtlessly grabbed in my rush to leave the Glendale house. My house. The house I'd been driven from with a restraining order displayed by the fat off-duty cop whom my husband, Gavin, had hired. The August afternoon was stupidly hot, and I was irritated. The last thing I wanted was help.

"My dad said your kid died."

The whole load shifted when I let go of the plant stand and turned to look at the boy standing a couple of feet away in the street.

He looked about ten, maybe three years older than my Jeremy would've been in November, and his face and limbs were brown the way a kid's skin gets from spending a lot of time outside in the summer. The khaki shorts hanging below his motocross T-shirt were worn, but looked too formal for play. My guess was that they were part of someone's hand-me-down Catholic school uniform. He wasn't a bad-looking boy: too skinny, but with widely spaced brown eyes with full lashes, and an awkward, lopsided grin that was almost charming.

I peered over his shoulder at the brick bungalow across the street where I'd noticed him sitting on the porch the day I'd come to sign the lease on the duplex. All of the curtains and shades were shut tight. A square of plywood filled the tiny attic window in the inverted V of the eaves. It didn't look like anyone lived there, let alone a boy and his dad. I wondered if there was a mother involved.

"He drowned." He said the words matter-of-factly as though he didn't think I knew.

Was I going insane? Who would say something like that to a complete stranger? I wondered if something was wrong with him. As far as I knew, my face hadn't been on the news in the year since the trial had ended. The guy who rented me the duplex must have recognized my name or face and told the neighbors. *Shit.* Why hadn't I caught that little flare of recognition and subsequent steeling of the jaw I'd come to expect whenever I told someone my name? But I was out of options. There was nowhere else for me to go, except out of St. Louis. And I wasn't ready for that.

"I don't need any help. Thanks." I quickly redid my loosened ponytail and turned back to dislodging the gilt-framed mirror we'd gotten from one of my great-aunts as a wedding present. Screw the kid's idiot, nosy father, and the rest of the jerks who were probably this minute peeking out of their JCPenney curtains.

One by one, I pried things out of the Suburban and carried them into the apartment: the mirror, a piecrust table that now had a massive scratch on its face, a delicate set of antique curio shelves that had held my mother's teacup collection (the collection was a casualty of one of our disagreements, and I had thrown the first three cups at Gavin's head, then the remaining ones at the wall because I had—obviously, strangely—felt I needed to finish the job after he crawled out of the room).

The boy had stepped back into the middle of the street. The way he stood watching, but not saying anything else, creeped me out.

I'd just deposited a bamboo-patterned umbrella stand that I knew Gavin was particularly fond of on the porch when I saw a red Camaro turn the corner half a block away and accelerate. I glanced from the car to the boy, who was staring blankly at the back of the Suburban, to the car, and back again. The car would hit him straight on, perhaps knocking him up, over its hood, and into the air. And I would be the only witness. I hurried off the porch, shouting and waving at the boy. "Car! Get out of the road!"

The car's horn blared, and the boy looked toward the sound. Finally he turned and ran for the curb in front of his house. As he bounded up the porch stairs, I found myself noticing how the bottoms of his feet were gray—almost black—with dust.

The owner of the duplex and his wife lived in the apartment above me, but there'd been a note on my door when I arrived that said they were going out of town to a couple's retreat for the week, and would I mind watering the flowers in the front yard. The handwriting was loopy and girlish and there was a bloated happy face with big oval eyes at the bottom of the note. The wife, certainly. She'd stood at her husband's side, her manicured fingers wrapped possessively around his rather flaccid upper arm, while we discussed the rent and their insistence that, no, I couldn't have a cat. "Allergies," she'd said, rolling her eyes. "I don't want to get all puffy!" Her sweater and skirt were carefully matched—surely bought as a set—

and her peach lipstick was coordinated with her nails. Though we were both barely thirty, we would never be friends.

My apartment was long and narrow, not quite a shotgun, but not more than two rooms wide. The ceilings were high and the carpet was new, even if the wallpaper was atrociously floral. Every single wall was covered with flowers or stripes or stripes with flowers sprinkled over them. Again, I suspected the wife. How she had managed to find wallpaper from the 1980s, I couldn't imagine. But the trim was freshly painted, and despite the noise from the air conditioner laboring in a living room window and the loose bolt on the back door that only worked if you set it just right (I made a mental note to ask Mr. Universe to fix it), the place had a homey feel to it that I didn't mind. I would be living here alone.

That morning I had woken up for the last time in the bed that Gavin and I had shared for ten years. The softly worn Frette sheets I'd splurged on for our seventh anniversary had felt delicious against my skin. Tonight I would be sleeping on the cheap futon and frame I'd bought online and had delivered to the new apartment. I hadn't even thought about sheets for it. Somewhere in the bags of things I'd brought from the house there were two blankets. As long as the air conditioner kept working, I would be all right with one of those.

I had until three thirty to get what I wanted from the house. I looked at my watch: two. I could just make it there by two thirty.

Over the phone, Gavin had mocked my plans to carry everything to the apartment using the Suburban. "When are you going to give up this bullshit martyr act, Becca? You should hire a mover. I gave you plenty of money."

I hated the sneering tone in his voice—so bizarre and un-familiar, so different from the calm compassion he'd shown me

for so long after Jeremy's death. This wasn't the gentle man
I'd married, the new law school grad who, five days after we
returned from our honeymoon, gave me a photo in a heart-
shaped silver frame of the two of us on the beach in Cabo
San Lucas. Sometimes it freaked people out how closely we
resembled one another: the same brown eyes, thick dark hair,
slight, athletic builds. In the photo—it was still on the dresser
in the guest bedroom, dusted every week by the conscien-
tious Libby—our heads tilted toward one another, we smiled,
a little drunk, a little sunburned, and deeply in love. But it
was as if I couldn't even remember that smiling girl anymore.
When I looked in the mirror now I saw lines on my forehead
and around my mouth. I was heavier. I'm sure it's one of the
reasons Gavin gave up on me. He'd never be able to accept a
size-twelve wife. And when he'd stopped grieving, he'd turned
impatient. In my heart I had forgiven him for calling the police on me when I'd lost my temper. I had even told him he
could keep his half of the house, even though I had a right to
it. It was ridiculous that he was afraid of me.

I went to the empty Suburban, grabbed my thermal cup,
and took it to the kitchen. After filling it with ice and lemonade from the rattling, not-perfectly-clean fridge, I opened the
cabinet I'd stocked the afternoon before and stared up at the
two bottles of Beefeaters. I felt the inside of my cheeks pucker
with desire and the spit gather in my mouth. No. I wouldn't.
Not this afternoon. I could make myself wait.

The off-duty cop had relocated from our front porch to his
massive king cab pickup truck. It idled, windows up and surely
frigid with A/C, in front of the house, undoubtedly driving our
next door neighbor, Mrs. Grable, crazy. She disliked strangers.
And noise. And dogs and children.

When I got out of the Suburban and started up the ivy-guarded walk, he stepped out of the truck. I tried to wave him back, and even made a joke.

"Hey, I'm allowed to take the silver if I want."

He didn't crack a smile, just locked the truck and hustled up to the door. I'd forgotten that I didn't have a key anymore.

Inside the house, where I already felt like a stranger, I gathered . . . things. I had no sentimental list, just a cold feeling in the pit of my stomach. I'd moved all the shoes and clothes that I wanted early that morning. But so many of them didn't fit me anymore—those I'd left in our custom bedroom closet, clotting the drawers and hanging in disorganized clumps. The disorganization, the sense of disarray, would irritate Gavin. Maybe that's why I was leaving them. Since there was no way I could ever be the woman I'd been before that horrible afternoon, I was leaving her behind. He could have her.

The door to Jeremy's room was closed. I'd said goodbye to it that morning, taking only his second-favorite lovey—a one-eyed lamb—from where it rested on his pillow. If I went inside that room again, my resolve might break. I might beg Gavin to let me stay just because I would be close to Jeremy's things. But no. I wouldn't even try. Gavin had humiliated me enough. I had to get the hell out.

In the kitchen I put the coffee grinder, all the spoons from the flatware drawer, and the set of expensive chef's knives Gavin's sister had given us as a wedding gift into a box. Then I took the dishtowels and tucked them around the things in the box. I removed all the tea and spices from the cabinet and spread them over the counter, but I only put the tea in the box.

Three fifteen.

I hurried upstairs. Pressed for time as I was, it gave me a

small, anxious thrill to stop and unmake the bed I'd reflexively made after getting out of it that morning. Would Gavin sleep tonight on the same sheets I'd slept on without him? I didn't know. He'd slept at the athletic club downtown all week. We were separated. Officially strangers. What would he do if he came home and found me still at the house? The cops might drag me off in front of the neighbors. *Again.*

At the last minute I took Gavin's pillow, clutching it to me as though it were a small, misshapen child.

I barely remember driving back to the apartment. The street was empty, but I missed the turn into the narrow drive-way, and so kept driving and turned right at the end of the block to go around. But I didn't make the next turn. The neighborhood dwindled after five or six blocks and became a commercial area I hadn't been to before. I passed a Catholic church, a gas station, a hobby shop, and an enormous bill-board advertisement for a pain management clinic. But not far from the billboard was a small stone building topped with a worn sign of its own that read, *Bridget's Bide-a-Wee.* From the name it sounded like a creepy children's day care, and for a sliver of a second I was thrown back to Jeremy's first time at the Methodist church's Mom's Morning Out, and the way he had hurried over to the big plastic playhouse, stopping at the door to wave goodbye to me. Then the sun chanced to glint off the unlit neon martini glass balanced on the end of the sign, drawing my attention. I pulled into the lot and parked between a battered Mercedes and a generic blue Chevrolet sedan and rested my head on the steering wheel until the air in the car turned hot and thick. When I couldn't bear it anymore, I went inside. The first martini hit the spot.

I crouched on a limb of a tree growing beside a dark lake. I listened. Tapping came from beneath the water and I bent forward to hear it better, to try to see what it was. All was blackness except for a few cold shafts of sunlight beating past me through the trees, but they didn't reach the water's surface.

Taptaptap.

Taptaptap.

I leaned forward to get a better look until I was forced to stop, my hair nearly yanked from my head. Putting my hands up, I found the branches of the trees had twined themselves into my hair, which had grown far longer than I remembered. I pulled, gently at first, then began to tug. But the tree held fast.

Taptaptap.

Taptaptap.

Now I was awake, my eyes open to the sun streaming in the uncovered window a few feet away from where I lay. Which was . . . where? There was an empty bird feeder in the shape of an apple attached to the window with a suction cup, and a blank wall of siding beyond it. I didn't remember the window or the bird feeder and worried that I might still be dreaming. Then a shadow passed across the blank wall. A large bird? No. Something stealthy, moving quickly. A glimpse of brown hair and tan skin.

My eyes moved to the wall around the window. Wallpaper. Tiny flowers and pastel stripes, like a little girl's room. I remembered the boy and his dirty feet. Jeremy's empty room behind the closed door. I was aware of someone near me. Light, sleeping breaths.

I tried to turn my head but my hair was caught by a man's arm. Alarmed, I jerked away, not caring that it hurt.

The man threw his arm up over his face, but not before I saw it: roughly handsome with a pale mustache and a light coat of fine whiskers over his chin and jaw as though he hadn't shaved in two or three days. His eyelashes were pale too. His own hair was on the long side, reminding me of a boy I'd dated in high school.

"Your blond period," my best friend Stacy had called it, when I'd dated three blond guys in six months. Stacy. Really my *former* best friend. She'd first sworn her faith in me, answering, "Never!" if anyone asked her if I was capable of killing my own four-year-old child. Then she'd moved away just before the trial, unwilling to appear as a character witness, saying her deposition was enough. But I'd heard her voice on the phone. There was something in it—some half-truth. Hesitation. I begged, but she hung up.

The man made a moaning noise, and muttered, "Shit." With his other arm he pushed away the blanket that lay over his legs and scratched his crotch, which, like his arm, was covered in pale, curled hairs. He didn't have a morning erection like Gavin so often did. When was the last time I'd seen Gavin naked? Three months? Five? The last time we'd tried to have sex, I'd stopped him because I'd forgotten to refill my pills. And he'd been angry, saying it didn't matter, we were married and Jeremy had been gone over a year. That was the night of the teacups, and my first half-bottle of gin.

Suddenly realizing that I was naked as well, I pulled the other half of the blanket over me, knowing it was too late, trying to remember (and yet not remember) the day, the night before.

Done scratching, he rose up on one elbow and glanced around. "Hey, where's your bathroom? I've got to piss like a racehorse."

"Through there." I pointed to the doorway leading to the central hall of the apartment.

He sat up and leaned over the edge of the futon to retrieve

a pair of black cotton briefs from the floor and carried them with him to the bathroom. When he was through the door-way, I saw Jeremy's lamb where it had been mashed beneath him. A scream caught in my throat. I snatched the lamb to me, brushing it off furiously with my hand to remove any trace of the blond man. When I was through, I laid it carefully be-neath the futon out of his sight. Out of his reach. Whatever I had felt for him the night before—and it must have been *something*, yes? even if I couldn't remember it?—had been replaced by contempt.

I pulled on the shorts I'd been wearing the day before, do-ing my best to ignore the unpleasant residue of our coupling between my legs, and took a T-shirt from one of the open bags on the floor.

When I picked up his jeans from the edge of the futon, a wallet slipped out. His driver's license read, *Michael Francis James*, and he lived on a street that wasn't far away from where we were on Landsdowne. It made sense, given that we'd met at a bar in the area. At least I thought we'd met at the bar. I remembered sitting at a table alone and ordering food with my martini because it seemed too strange, too decadent to go into a bar in the middle of the day and *only* order a drink. And I remembered a man and a woman coming over to the table. Had there really been a woman? Blond, like him, I thought, wearing a loose pink shirt, telling me I looked awfully down. And that was all. Nothing until the morning and the tapping at the window.

I replaced the wallet, my hand shaking. I bent to pick up his boots and shirt as well.

What is happening to me?

His voice came from the kitchen. I hadn't heard him leave the bathroom. "Hey, Becky. You don't have any beer?"

Beer? I didn't even drink beer.

He stood in front of the open refrigerator, black underwear in place, a slack but not large beer belly peeking over their tops.

"You need to leave." I held out his clothes hoping he wouldn't see my hands shaking. My head hurt like hell, but I spoke as forcefully as I could.

"What?" He seemed genuinely puzzled.

"This was a mistake." I fumbled for his name. "Michael. Mike."

"What the fuck?"

"No, really. Go."

"Huh. I didn't take you for a love-'em-and-leave-'em type." He let the refrigerator door close. "Not after all your crying to get that toy out of your car. You wanted to bring some pillow too, but it wouldn't work on the bike. Real tears and all."

I gestured with the clothes again. "Here. Please."

He shook his head. "Let me get a fucking drink of water, at least."

I waited while he took a glass from the counter, filled it from the tap, and drank. When he was done, he dabbed rather delicately at his mouth with a paper towel. But then he let the paper towel fall into the sink.

Taking the clothes from me, he tried to look me in the eye, but I turned away and he gave an unpleasant little laugh. He dressed in the bedroom. When he came out I was standing at the front door.

"For a decent fuck you're a cold bitch, you know that?"

There was a shadow of hurt in his blue eyes that almost moved me. But I just opened the door.

Before he crossed the threshold he bent to pick up something from the welcome mat. It was a yellow rose with pink curled edges and a long green wire stem. He examined it before he handed it to me.

"Fake. It figures."

I shut the door behind him and went back to the bedroom. My hands were still shaking. Outside, a motorcycle started up. The sound of the engine surged, then faded off down the street.

Whatever I'd done, I was desperate to undo it. I took off my shorts and found the underwear and shirt I'd been wearing. Balling them together with the blanket from the bed, I went, naked, through the door in the hallway and down the basement stairs. I stuffed everything into the washer and coated it with a capful of detergent before setting it on *Hot/Heavy Duty*. In the bathroom I showered, scrubbing myself as hard as I could—particularly between my legs—with a bar of soap and the chunk of loofah I'd brought from the house. Almost ten years with the same man, and I couldn't even remember having sex with this Michael person. What if I were pregnant? Or he'd given me chlamydia or some other disease? *Oh God!* I rinsed my mouth again and again with the shower water until my throat was choked with hot water and tears.

After showering, I opened a window in the kitchen and set the air conditioner to high to get the stench—perhaps imagined—of sex with a stranger out of the apartment. My head hurt like crazy, so I took four ibuprofen with a yogurt smoothie from the fridge. It wasn't filling, but I figured it was vaguely healthy. The drinking of it kept me away from the lemonade and gin. Not that it would have mattered because the gin bottle sat empty on the counter, and I wasn't going to open the second bottle. Ever.

The thing to do was to get out of the apartment. I had no

job to go to. Not yet. But I was going to have to think about it eventually. I'd had to give the landlord and his wife rent in advance for six months because I didn't have one. Apparently this was how the rest of the world lived. How sheltered I'd been with Gavin and his steady paycheck.

I found my purse and checked my wallet. The cash and credit cards were still there, so at least the guy hadn't robbed me. I went out onto the porch, locked the door behind me, and headed for the driveway. And, nothing.

No Suburban. *Shit.* I closed my eyes. The keys were in my hand, and the extra set was—*damn*—probably still on Gavin's key ring. It made sense that the Suburban was still at the bar. I was going to have to walk there and get it.

The ibuprofen wasn't doing anything for my headache, and I was thirsty before I even turned the corner. I was hoping the place wasn't as far away as I thought it was, and was cheered to discover that the first couple of blocks were very short, bisected with alleys lined with tiny garages built at the same time as the early-twentieth-century houses. Neighborhoods didn't come much more established than this one. It was the kind of area where residents got to be like family, raising generations of kids who went to the same schools, married each other, and moved into houses down the street from their parents. But there were also enough people that I might be left alone. There was no law saying I had to talk to anyone. I knew of even cheaper places in St. Louis to live, but the area seemed relatively safe. I was only a little afraid to be living on my own—something I'd never done before.

Of course, the word had gotten out, hadn't it? There might be people who objected to my living there. People who believed I'd killed Jeremy even though I was found not guilty. People had opinions.

The houses thinned out as I approached the more commercial area where I thought the bar was, and they were older, more run down. I was amazed to see that one house—set back from the road on the tiniest of rises—had rough synthetic grass for a front lawn. Up at the top of the slope, there was a row of vibrant yellow and purple tulips as well. But tulips didn't bloom in August. Like the flower on my doorstep, they were all fake.

I bent to run my hand over the plastic grass where it met the cement to know what it felt like. It tickled, and I thought how strange and bold someone had to be to put fake grass in front of their house. Then I caught a movement out of the corner of my eye.

"Hi."

"Shit, you scared me." Realizing I'd said the word *shit* to a little boy, I automatically followed with, "I mean *shoot*."

"Where are you going? Can I come?"

I looked beyond the boy. There was no sign of any adult with him. At least today he was wearing black flip-flops and brown shorts that were baggy but looked like actual play clothes. His cheek wore a smear of white like he'd been into paint or something. I had to stop myself from reflexively wiping it off.

"Where's your dad? You shouldn't be this far from home by yourself."

He shrugged. That was all the answer I got.

"I have to get my car." I turned away and started walking. "You should go home," I called over my shoulder. And I hoped that he really would. But, of course, he didn't. I knew he'd follow me all the way to the bar. Then he'd probably tell his father. The father would tell the other neighbors, and someone would tell my landlord. God, where was all this going?

It might not be safe for you, Becca. Come to Florida. Come and live with us. My mother had believed me. She worried for me. But her life was complicated. I couldn't handle my stepfather. No, I had to stay.

The boy followed a few feet behind me, his shoes making a slapping sound on the sidewalk. It bugged me, but as headachy and thirsty as I was, everything was bugging me. I wondered what we looked like to the cars driving by. I wasn't used to walking places. I felt conspicuous, and it was made worse by the boy's presence. What would people think? That I had asked him to come with me?

By the next block, the houses were gone completely.

"Listen, you need to go home, okay? You can't come with me."

"Did you know that wherever you are there's a spider within three feet of you? I learned that at school. Hey, isn't that your big truck?" He pointed.

Bridget's Bide-a-Wee was still half a block away, but the Suburban was hard to miss, alone as it was in the parking lot. The pub was closed. It was too early to have a drink, anyway. I thought of the lemonade at home. So cold from the fridge. I willed myself not to think of the Beefeaters. I would pretend it wasn't there.

"Yeah, it is."

The Suburban was stifling with heat. The boy stood at my shoulder looking in.

"Hey, it's got leather in it. My dad says leather in cars is for suckers."

"Does he?"

"Can I ride in it?"

I glanced around the empty parking lot, still feeling conspicuous. Could I possibly tell him he had to walk home, given that I lived across the street? Someone might snatch him from the sidewalk. The irony of the thought wasn't lost on me.

"Go around the other side and get in."

He gave no reaction except to run around the back of the truck to the other side like he was afraid I'd change my mind.

I climbed in and started the engine and turned the A/C on full blast. The boy got into the passenger seat and started touching everything as though he'd never seen the inside of a car before. But he didn't speak. Only touched. Finally, he settled back and peered at me expectantly.

"You have to put on your seat belt."

He nodded. "Okay."

On the way out of the parking lot, he said, "That's the snow cone place everyone goes to. They have tiger juice. Have you ever had tiger juice?"

"No," I told him. But I could take a hint.

I pulled into a space near the metal trailer with the giant snow cone on its roof. When he started to get out, I told him he had to wait in the truck. To my surprise, he didn't show any sign of disappointment. He really was a strange kid, and I thought once again that there was something not quite right about him.

I parked in the driveway.

"Can I come inside your house?" He'd finished the snow cone in about two minutes flat as we sat in the truck and then he folded the paper cone into a tiny triangle. When he was finished he handed the triangle to me as though it were a gift. "You can have it," he said. His hands were small, like a much younger child's. I thought of Jeremy's hands. How tiny they'd been when he was born. Gavin had worried that they might break if he touched them.

Suddenly I wanted the boy away from me.

"You have to go. Go home or something."

"Why?"

"Because I said. Don't . . ." I was about to tell him not to tell anyone he'd been with me, but I realized that it didn't sound quite right. Just the thought made me feel guilty. Worried.

"Go!" My voice was too loud for the inner space of the truck, but I couldn't help myself.

The boy showed no surprise. He opened the door with slow deliberation and got out. I didn't look to see where he went.

A few minutes later I headed inside the apartment and drank several glasses of water. Then I turned the air conditioner to its lowest setting and wrapped myself in the remaining blanket. I fell asleep clutching Jeremy's lamb to my chest.

I woke feeling like a new person. And I was starving. After a dinner of macaroni and cheese and a tall glass of lemonade with gin—really, only a little gin, not more than a couple ounces—I went out to the porch swing with a book, finally feeling a bit more relaxed. There was just enough sunlight left to read by. I'd brought only a small box of books from the house: Agatha Christie paperbacks I'd read in high school, *Jane Eyre*, *The Hitchhiker's Guide to the Galaxy*. Nerdy stuff that Gavin had thought was charming.

The street was quiet except for a staccato flow of people coming in and out of a house near the end of the block. It looked like a party.

Across the street, the boy's house was dark. I told myself that I was stupid to worry. I hadn't done anything wrong. I'd given him a ride home and bought him a snow cone. That was all. No one could fault me for that.

The people coming and going from the party were young, much younger than I was. Maybe college-aged. Some guys were tossing what looked like beanbags into a brightly painted box in the front yard, and every now and then a voice would erupt in laughter. They held big red Solo cups that they re-filled at a keg on the porch. I wondered idly what would happen if I wandered down there.

I wasn't so bad to look at, was I? I put the book aside and gathered my hair into a soft pile over my shoulder. I hadn't put makeup on in weeks, but it wouldn't take me long to run inside. The Michael guy, now that I thought about him, maybe hadn't been so bad. He'd liked me. Told me I was a good fuck. No. A *decent fuck*. Now there's a gentleman for you! I laughed out loud to think of it. It felt good to laugh.

Out in the trees, the cicadas started up, and the noise from the party got louder. Had I imagined it, or had a light come on behind one of the window shades in the house across the street?

Where was the boy? I hoped he was safe inside his house now that it was getting dark. I wondered what he had looked like as a baby. Jeremy had started out fat-cheeked and round, with dimples on his elbows, face, and knees. But he'd quickly turned slender. So slender, in fact, that the doctor had been concerned. Worried that he wasn't getting enough to eat. Later, she'd sat on the witness stand, answering questions in her squeaky, butter-wouldn't-melt-in-her-mouth voice, talking about percentiles and motor responses. She'd been recommended highly too. But she never liked me, the bitch.

The boy liked me, though. I bet his parents would like me too. I could feel my resolve to keep to myself drifting away.

I went inside to refill my glass and drank it down quickly. Seeing a container of grocery-store chicken salad in the refrigerator, I tried to remember if I'd eaten dinner. I wasn't hungry, so maybe I had. It wouldn't hurt me to lose a pound or two, anyway.

I made another drink and started back out to the porch. The apartment was cool, but there was nowhere to sit except the bed. And I wasn't tired. I needed a television too. Gavin didn't like to watch television, so we'd only had the one. I opened the front door.

"Gavin."

He'd come to me.

I set my drink on the edge of the empty umbrella stand and threw my arms around his neck and buried my face against the slightly stiff collar of his maroon sports shirt. It was an expensive-looking shirt. One I'd never seen before. I had to touch him. To feel his skin against mine.

But instead of holding me, he put his hands on my shoulders and pushed me away so that I upset the drink. It splashed on my bare legs, but I didn't care.

"Becca, stop it."

"You came. Why are you here?" I said it even though I knew he was here to take me home. The crappy apartment melted away from us. Yes! I'd been an idiot. So had he. He knew we'd come to the wrong decision about my leaving.

He looked over my shoulder into the darkening, empty living room, then back down at me.

"You called me."

"No, I didn't." Had I called him? I couldn't remember. Why couldn't I remember?

"You asked me to bring you the extra keys to the Suburban. But you're drunk. You shouldn't be driving anywhere."

Even in the dim light I could see contempt in his eyes. It wasn't any different from the last time I'd seen him. And why didn't he smell like himself? He had a faint scent of flowers about him, like expensive perfume.

"But you know what, Becca? I don't give a shit if you kill yourself."

Then he did the most violent thing I'd ever seen him do. He threw the keys as hard as he could against the wall. Maybe I imagined it, but I thought I saw tiny chunks of plaster fly into the air.

I laughed. "That was fucking mature."

He stared at me. He looked sick, his face twisted like I'd never seen it before. His breath came fast and short, and the cords of his neck stood out in relief. He was thin, and looked older than his thirty-five years. He hated me. I could see it now. I had been the one who was confused.

"Don't call me. Don't come by the house again because I'll have you arrested. I'm having the locks changed. Stay the fuck out of my life, Becca. You're fucking poisonous. You killed . . ." He stopped.

"What? What were you going to say?"

"You killed . . ." But again the words wouldn't come.

I thought of the lemonade and gin soaking into the carpet and didn't care. I thought of the neighbors who might be looking in the windows and didn't care.

"I have to get out of here. I can't be here with you." His hands had balled into fists at his sides, a fighter at the ready. He would kill me if I said another word. I could feel it.

But I didn't care. I started to move away. Out of his range.

"Wait," I said over my shoulder. "Wait a second."

Somehow I knew he would wait. He was frozen. Mesmerized just as surely as he'd been on our first date, and on our first walk on the beach together in Cabo, when the wind off the water had blown my hair back and misted us with spray, and Gavin had held my hand so tightly.

"Wait," I called again from the kitchen. I found his things in there. He should have them.

The living room had darkened further. I held out the coffee grinder, lifting it up so he could see.

"I took this. It wasn't fair. I don't even drink coffee." I laughed. Did I sound nervous? Yes, I'm sure I did, because I was.

He wouldn't even look at the grinder, but stared at my face. God, he was so handsome. Yet he'd spoiled it all.

Finally he turned away from me. Rejecting me, and everything I had to offer. He had come to see me just to show he could be without me again. Had he ever loved me at all? Loved Jeremy? Seeing him now, I understood we'd been in his way. I couldn't let him leave.

I dropped the coffee grinder where I stood, hardly noticing when it hit my foot. But he kept moving toward the door.

I stabbed him just above his belt on his left side first, in the soft part of him I knew so well. I'd caressed him there as he guided himself into me so, so many times. I almost fell against him, surprised at the easy way the knife seemed to guide its way into him. He'd always insisted that we keep our knives sharp. "They're actually much less dangerous that way," he liked to say. "A regular table knife can do much more damage."

He cried out and stumbled, but kept moving. He reached for the doorknob.

I wanted to see his face. "Stop, damn you!"

Removing the knife was a little harder, but I got it, and without looking at the blade, I aimed for his neck. It didn't go in solidly but sliced the side of his neck just as he got the door open. Even in the near darkness I could see the spray of blood coat the doorframe. I felt it too, tepid and wet on my face like water from a sun-warmed ocean.

Gavin arched forward, but didn't fall to the ground. Then he was coming back up, as though he would stand. He teetered a moment, his head collapsed onto his chest, then began falling, falling back toward me, so that I had to jump out of the way.

He hit the rug.

The boy stood before me in the doorway, his shirt and face, the entire right side of his body, covered in blood. He had caught Gavin as he'd fallen forward, and now he pushed him back inside.

Had I fainted?

I opened my eyes to see eyes, white in the darkness, white in his blood-splashed face. I squeezed my own eyes shut, trying to remember. I scrambled up, still dizzy, but the boy held onto my arm so I wouldn't fall.

"Look at you," I said.

He didn't respond for a moment. He looked down at Gavin and I followed his gaze. Gavin's face was turned to the wall. It was dark enough that his hair, his ruined neck, his shirt appeared to all be the same color: an infinitely deep gray. Not quite black.

"Did that man hurt you?" The boy used the sleeve of his bloody shirt to wipe one eye clear.

"He hurt me." Was it a statement of fact? I wasn't sure. I couldn't think. My brain was cloudy and words felt thick in my mouth.

He tugged on the hem of his shirt. God, his shirt! The poor thing.

I led him to the window to get a better look at him. He looked so helpless. I touched his cheek with my finger.

He stood in the bathroom doorway, watching, as I ran the tub water. I had plenty of thick towels and a couple wash-cloths. We had so many. Two full bathrooms for the three of us, and it was shameful the way I was always buying new shower curtains and towels. When the tub was about halfway full, I knelt and bent my hand back and pressed my wrist to the water's surface. It was a little cool. I made the water mix a bit hotter.

Then I stood up. "Look at you. What a mess!" I extended my hand and he came slowly to me. "Hold up your arms."

I lifted his T-shirt over his head, tucking my hand into the neck of it so it would stretch over his face without bothering him. There were stains on his torso where the stuff on his shirt had come through, and the sun had left lines on his up-per arms so that he looked as though he were wearing a shirt of pale ivory. I felt vaguely guilty about that. Children should always wear sunscreen. Only bad parents let their children go outside without it in the summer.

He coughed and I looked closely at him. Was he ill? Maybe a summer cold. He was shivering.

"Hurry. Get in the water."

He turned around and slipped his shorts off and got into the tub.

I looked around for toys. Something for him to play with. But there was nothing.

"Let's get you clean." I took the bar of soap and washcloth and wet them in the water—which had quickly clouded to a deep shade of pink—beside him. I rubbed the washcloth with soap until it was foamy and took his chin in my hand. He closed his eyes as I wiped his face, rinsing the washcloth in slow running water from the spigot. When I started on his neck, he put his hand up to take the cloth from me.

"I can do it."

I laughed and let the cloth go, sitting back on my heels. Children! They were always so anxious to be independent. "Get behind your ears. You don't want potatoes growing back there."

The bathroom light was bright yellow and cozy but the dark of the hallway was leaking inside. It was as though we were on an island. Safe.

Idly, I looked at his clothes on the floor, wondering how I would get them clean. First, I thought, they needed a good soaking. I got up and stoppered the sink before filling it with cold water. I put the clothes in and watched the water color like the bath. I tried to remember how he'd gotten so soiled. I liked washing clothes in the sink, liked the way the cold water felt on my skin.

"I'm done."

"That was fast." I tried to keep the skepticism from my voice. He hadn't washed very long. "What about your hair? You have to wash your hair."

He grinned and held his nose and slid beneath the pink water, which made him look bigger than he was. It was like a trick. An optical illusion.

I waited for him to come right back up again. He had let go of his nose and was lying in the water, perfectly still. Now his eyes were open. Staring. My breath caught and there was a cold spot in my chest.

"Stop it!"

No response. His hair floated around his face.

"Jeremy!"

I leaned over the pink water and pulled him up by the

shoulders, which were narrow and slick. He coughed, spewing water, and shook his head wildly, making more droplets of water fly.

"Don't do that! You scared me!"

Lying at the bottom of the tub. His eyes open. A single perfect bubble escaping his mouth and rising to the surface, breaking into the air.

He coughed again. "Let go."

"You have to wash your hair." I let go of him, but my hands were still shaking.

"I want to go home now."

I took the bottle of shampoo from the end of the tub and squeezed a quarter-sized puddle into my hand. The water dribbled from the spigot, but I set the shampoo bottle down and turned the water up with my free hand.

He put his hands on the edge of the tub and tried to stand, but I pressed my shampoo-soaked hand against his chest. He wasn't clean! He needed to be clean! His skin made a loud stuttering noise as it slid over the surface of the porcelain, and he landed on his bottom.

He began to scream, opening his mouth wide so that I could see his teeth. Several were brown. Half-rotted. How was that possible? All those trips to the dentist. The way I'd helped him brush his teeth every night—what I was seeing couldn't be true.

"Stop it, please! Sit. Down." I tried not to yell at him. I really tried. Grabbing his arms, I forced him further into the water, tried to get his head under the spigot.

Scattered bruising. A clear mark on his throat. Aspirated water in the lungs.

"I'm just going to wash your hair, Jeremy. Stop it. I'm not going to hurt you. Be still!"

No defensive wounds. Water contamination of the evidence.

But he wouldn't stop. Now he was twisting, his mouth open. Water spraying everywhere. If he didn't stop, he would hurt himself. He needed to calm. To be clean again.

He gave another wrenching twist, and my slickened hand slipped so that he was able to reach me with his mouth, with those brown, broken teeth. They scraped my forearm then got purchase, and I felt the skin pop, and at the center of the pain I had an image of Jeremy poking his finger into a package of ground beef I'd left on the counter. *Pop-pop-pop.* Laughing, watching me with those bright shining eyes. *Pop-pop-pop.* Running away to the living room, laughing at me from behind the couch.

I drew my arm to me, putting my own mouth against the emerging blood as he shot from the tub, knocking me back. On the way out of the bathroom he slipped, but grabbed the doorframe to right himself. One of his feet pushed against my thigh, and I reached to grab it. Then he was gone.

Again.

I ran after him down the dark hallway to the living room. Through the rectangle of the open doorway I could see the glow of the streetlight reflecting off the window of the house across the street. He was already down the steps of the porch, his painfully thin form outlined in a halo of yellow. As I got closer I saw there were other people too, standing in the street, heedless of any cars that might want to get through. I quickly stepped over the still form in the doorway and onto the porch in time to see him dodge past them. Not one reached out to stop him.

When I called after him he didn't look back, but kept running. I watched him run up the porch steps, so clean. But I feared his feet weren't clean enough. He hadn't had time to scrub them. He was just a boy. A little boy. And little boys don't really care about things like that, do they?

Finally, a light came on in the window beside the door where he stood banging so loudly that I thought the wood might splinter and break. I wondered who was on the other side, and felt sad that it wasn't me.

I watched until the door opened and the boy hurried inside, but I never saw who let him in. Out in the street the people standing beneath the streetlight shifted into two groups: the larger one moved toward the boy's house; the second approached the curb in front of my apartment. Were they coming to welcome me? I glanced around my empty living room. Everyone would have to sit on the floor, and I had very little in the way of food for a crowd. There was nothing I could do. They would have to understand.

I looked at the man lying on the floor. His arms were flung outward as in a ready embrace. He looked awkward, and someone might trip. I knelt beside him and arranged his arms so they lay neatly against his sides. Just so.

HAVE YOU SEEN ME?

BY JEDIDIAH AYRES

Frontenac

The body is found in the walk-in closet. Not yet a body, still a person. The person is, among other things, a woman, a mother, and a model. In her system are trace amounts of alcohol, cocaine, oxycodone, semen, and a half-digested seafood dinner.

No note. No signs of struggle. No 911 call. The body is found by the maid. Who calls her boss rather than the EMTs.

An hour later Betts looks down at the body, pops an antacid, and thinks again of the black-and-white photo in his wallet. The one printed on cheap paper stock with the words, *Have you seen me?* beneath the girl's face.

Maybe.

Betts feels the itch to call the number again.

The first time Betts called the number he'd just listened.

A quiet and nervous woman answered. "Hello . . . Hello? . . ." Then, with more urgency, "Have you seen my daughter? . . ." A hairline crack in the voice, "Teresa? Is that you?"

He'd hung up. The feeling was too much. Too raw. It upset his stomach, but he held onto the flyer. He kept it folded in his wallet, sensing that he would call again. Another time.

It was the day after he'd seen her at the vacant property where she and her gutter-punk crew had been squatting. Betts was harvesting bricks from the site, taking out the entire west wall of the duplex just east of the park off North Florissant near the ice-cream place. He worked for a man named Kinds who worked for the man—Citizen Number One—who owned half the condemned and abandoned properties in the city and in counties to the west and south through various incorporated ventures. When Betts had loaded his truck he'd haul it to a warehouse on the west side of Jefferson. Foreman would pay him cash. Broad daylight job. Cops didn't bother them. Nobody cared about what they were doing, and other than the odd hand-wringing op-ed by some liberal white do-gooder with a fetish for all things poor and black and "authentic," his work drew little attention. The city was eating itself and he was part of the digestion process. The wild reclaiming the urban landscape. Now when he drove the streets he didn't see homes, businesses, communities—only money. Redbrick gold. Unused and unrefined building blocks to be reclaimed and repurposed. The neighborhood was littered with two- and three-walled structures being broken down in stages.

On his lunch break, Betts had gone into the house to take a piss. There was no plumbing anymore. No toilet, sink, or bathtub, nor an ounce of copper wiring left in the walls. But it seemed more proper than watering the weeds outside. Next to the closet that used to be the bathroom was a wall covered in flyers for missing children. Runaways and abductees. Many of them were vandalized. Eyes X-ed out with pen, cartoon cocks pointing at their faces, apocryphal legends claiming somebody's homo-faggot or dumb-nigger status. But a few of them were more carefully displayed, hung like family portraits on the wall. Betts had seen this kind of thing in other abandoned properties. Sometimes the long-term squatters made it homey by putting up pictures of their friends living and otherwise. He read them all. Every single one. Every time. He'd learned to swallow the catch in his throat before he choked.

When he came through the front door, he'd surprised the girl who was working on removing one of the flyers. It had been stapled into the rotting drywall and she was trying to be gentle with it, the stained, folded-up piece of paper impaled inside a building abandoned by the owner and being harvested for raw materials. She stood five foot nothing, fifteen going on fifty, black hair stuck up in bunches. Conspicuous hygiene disguised as style. Slight gap between her front teeth that she had the self-possession to make work for her. She was using a knife to pry the staples out of the corners when Betts entered the room. The girl was wary, but not skittish. She let him see her knife, but was casual about it.

He put his hands up, palms out. "Whoa, it's okay, girl, nobody gonna bother you."

She paused a moment to test the claim before returning to her work. Her hands were gentle, but the paper tore easily. Betts squinted at the poster she was removing. From the fading blue page the face of a boy, maybe ten years old, smiled at him. "He a friend of yours? Lamar? You know him?"

Without turning to look at him she said, "Lamar dead."

Betts felt something slip inside, but rallied. "You been living here?"

"I just wanted a picture." Her patience for him running low.

"Go ahead, I ain't stopping you." A staple fell to the floor and she moved on to the final corner. Betts gestured with his chin at the bottom of the poster. "Anybody called that number?"

"What you think?"

"I'd like to. Somebody should get word to Lamar's family somehow, let them know."

When she turned around, Betts caught an icy charge from her look and her whole life played out like a movie before his eyes. He saw the tired old woman in her teenaged eyes, the fierce young survivor she'd already become and the scared little girl she'd been last year. Born, forgotten, dead. Roll credits. "Don't do that."

"Why not?"

Her tone said that it should be obvious. "There's a reason he left."

The last corner tore free and the girl grabbed the picture and ran out the back way without another word.

Betts went over to the wall and examined the posters again. He searched until he found a photo with the same eyes and gapped teeth he'd just been talking to. Number at the bottom. "I'm sure your momma'd want to know too."

The body is no longer a person and fits neatly into the La-due Pipes & Paints van between the pipe snakes, generator, wrench sets, ladders, odd bits of PVC tubing, drop cloths, and plastic tarps. It's cold outside, good as a refrigerator. Betts gets in, pops the cap on a small bottle of Pepto, and points the clandestine hearse north on Lindbergh.

The Pepto isn't cutting it tonight.

He gets onto 40 and heads east as he fumbles through his pocket for his crumbling talisman. The photo is fading. The flimsiness of the product testament to the sense of futility in the printing. A half-full gesture. An atheist's prayer. In the picture she's maybe fourteen, awkward, not quite grown into those teeth and posed with her head tilted at the unnatural angle of a glossy old movie-star headshot that only highlights her vulnerability preserved in amber for maximum impact. Betts worries the torn edges as if he could smooth away the holes and watermarks, maybe restore a little dignity to the kid who'd had her freshman-year photo posted in a couple hundred supermarkets, bars, and convenience stores usually ten feet from the public toilet.

The number is not programmed into his phone. He never uses his personal phone when he calls. Always a disposable. But tonight caught him off guard and he needs to talk. Damn the consequences. He'll get a new phone tomorrow. He dials from memory.

It rings and rings, and for the first time is not answered.

The second time he'd called the number was two years later, after he'd removed a junkie's remains from the basement of the apartment building in Soulard. Kinds had pulled him off the main site and sent him to the location where the body'd been found by a city cop who'd chased some rip-and-run artists to their nest. He knew the smell as soon as he was inside, and when he found the vagrant's remains, he'd kicked it up to somebody who knew what to do. An hour later, Betts had been taken through the protocol. Clean the place out. Make sure the body is found. Somewhere else.

Inside he used a flashlight though it was barely past noon and sunny outside. The windows were boarded up and there was no illumination other than the odd patch of daylight visible through weather-worn spots in the plywood-covered windows. The place smelled like a pack of transients had lived the entire brutal summer there. He spent the rest of the day clearing out trash and loading up the old fourteen-foot U-Haul he'd bought off his wife's cousin when his second FedEx route had dried up in '09.

The cousin had bought the thing, an old U-Haul truck with no personality, off the Internet when he'd expanded his business and taken on the extra route. First he'd hired Betts on as an assistant for the holiday season in '06. When his bid for the second route had been accepted, he'd bought the truck and turned the old route over to Betts. Three years later the route dried up, but Betts kept the truck and paid it off working odd haul jobs. He strung together a mostly legit livelihood hauling junk or carrying bricks torn off abandoned North City buildings to West County construction sites. He filed as a private contractor and dealt mostly in cash and favors. That day he filled it with broken glass, waterlogged chunks of ceiling, chipped kitchen tiles, the odd Venetian blinds hiding behind a door, half a possum, and a couple of mildewed twin mattresses surrounded by needles, condoms, and skin magazines. It was near dark when he carried the body—a kid judging by the weight, dead from drugs or pneumonia or whatever the fuck, wrapped up in a single plastic sheet—out the door, easy-peasy into the truck, and it was only ten o'clock when he dropped him across the river. Betts placed an anonymous 911 call from a burner from the parking lot of PT's in Sauget.

After the vagrant, Kinds started giving him more sensitive jobs. Mostly cleaning up properties Citizen Number One wanted to sell or the odd midnight transport of office equipment from one anonymous white-collar location to another strip mall in the green, sunny suburbs, usually between real estate brokers and financial services offices. Betts never asked questions and he kept getting work.

After he saw the news the next day about the junkie being found, when a name had been applied to him and a family had been alerted, and with the image of his body lying in a heap on the dirty floor unclaimed and anonymous burning into his retinas, Betts reached for his cell.

The girl's words come back to him. *There's a reason he left.*

"Hello?"

"Yeah, I'm calling about the girl in the poster?"

"I'm sorry, what? Are you calling about Teresa?"

"Is that . . . is she your daughter?"

"Yes."

"I thought you might want to know . . . I saw her. She was . . . I think she's all right."

"When did you see her?"

"I think she's living with a group of kids. They're all runaways, but they seem okay."

"Where is she?"

"I think they take care of each other. I . . . um, I just thought you'd like to know."

"Please tell me. There's a reward if she's found."

Betts hung up.

The next time Betts called the number was after Citizen Number One killed a waitress he'd picked up at a sports bar. Crushed his car like an aluminum can on a lonely lamppost on the way to one of his South County fuck-pads. He had a concussion and a driver's-side airbag. She'd gone through the windshield and sheared off half her face. First responders found her in a roadside ditch twenty feet from the vehicle, the snow already erasing her.

Asshole had known enough not to use his own cell phone and grabbed the clean one he kept in his pocket. There was no hiding the car or the body, but Betts got a call to pick him up and spirit his drunk ass all the way home where, the news-print story would read, he'd stumbled in a daze and crawled into his bed until the police showed up the next morning to question him. He'd claimed amnesia. No memory of the girl or the event. He'd given blood and urine samples which were quickly misplaced in a simple bureaucratic chain-of-custody cock-up and that was that. Not enough evidence for charges.

The waitress's family tried to sue for wrongful death, but nothing doing. Three semesters at Meramec, two abortions, and a service job don't beat five generations of local industry and philanthropy. Not in any game. Her divorced parents split a quiet payout that no doubt covered a few years' rent and a couple of sporty vehicles, but was missed by Citizen Number One about as much as last season's wardrobe. A signature, a bonus collected by his attorney, and all was forgotten. As if the amnesia had been real and catching.

Betts's stomach was in ribbons. He saw the waitress in his dreams, head turned all the way around, the left side of her skull scraped clean, and her right arm planed from shoulder to elbow. Twenty-six years of not trying too hard adding up to a stain in the snow. And the prick in the papers expressing his condolences to her family, saying he didn't know their daughter before the night in question, and though he claimed no responsibility, he would be donating to D.A.R.E. and M.A.D.D. and setting up a scholarship for girls from her hometown of Rolla.

As Betts watched the guy on TV, he remembered driving away from the dead waitress in the ditch. Citizen Number One had sat beside him in the front seat of the truck talking to his lawyer on the disposable phone. He'd talked to his counsel all the way home, alternately berating and imploring the man on the other end, occasionally threatening to fire him or bury him in a deep dark hole. He'd cried a little bit, nearly puked once, but mostly Betts had felt anger radiating from him. The anger had made him seem buffoonish and pathetic. Betts had felt contempt for the man screaming into the phone. But on TV, cleaned up, sincere and sober and magnanimous—he scared the hell out of Betts.

Six weeks later, baseball had started again, another celebrity scandal was taking all the headlines, and nobody remembered poor old whatsername.

Except Betts. And his ulcer.

"Hello?"

"Can you tell me about Teresa?"

A pause to collect herself, then, "Do you have information about her?"

"I saw her once. She seemed . . ."

"You've called before."

He coughed into his sleeve, sending Alka-Seltzer through his nose. "Have you heard from her?"

"No."

There's a rustling sound of the phone being roughly transferred from one person to another and a gruff, male voice speaks to Betts: "Hey, you see that little bitch, you tell her she can stay gone. Ain't no money here for her. Alls our money is for our own house. She don't wanna live with us, fine, but she ain't getting no more handouts. Keep sellin' ass if she need money, and leave us alone. Don't call here no more."

Twelve-year-old Betts had seen them coming when he rounded the corner. Four eighth graders, among them Lil' Trey who, rumor had it, was the one who'd killed the math teacher Mrs. Tompkins's dog. They said he'd snatched the mutt from her backyard, taken it to the empty gas station, used to be a Sinclair on Olive, and beat it to death with a bicycle chain, then dropped it over the fence into her yard again. Betts didn't know what was going on, but by the way they'd got him surrounded, it was clear it was not going to go well.

"Yo, faggot, suck my dick."

Shoved from the front. Betts backpedaled into another kid who propelled him forward to Trey again.

"C'mon, faggot, I know you like to. Do it."

Betts tried to run, but was tripped up and kicked in the guts before he could get back up.

"Get him on his knees."

Rough hands hoisted him up and he tried to kick at them, but only exposed himself to worse. Melvin, the smallest and quickest of this crew, kicked him in the balls and all the fight left him. Betts squeezed both hands between his thighs and let the boys hold him upright on his knees. Trey yanked the hair on the back of his head. "You a little bitch like your brother, ain't you? C'mon, now, you like to suck my dick. I let you."

He didn't cry on the way home, but he let go into a pillow as soon as he'd closed the door to his bedroom. Blood and snot and tears ruining the sheets. It was anger, yeah, but mostly it was shame that he was screaming out. He couldn't say how long they taunted him or how many times he was hit and kicked, but his clothes were torn, his nose broken, and his left eye was swollen shut. When he didn't come down to dinner, nobody got too upset, but the next morning, when he didn't come out of his room, his mom raised hell.

Pretty soon his dad was threatening to break down the door and Betts knew better than to let that happen. "Goddamn, boy. Happened to you?"

By then Betts's soft core had hardened and he mumbled, "Nothin'."

The family was crowded into the hallway around him, including his older brother Tommy Jr. Mom fussing, Dad fuming, and TJ just knowing.

"Don't give me that. You tell me who did this to you and why so I know whose ass to go beat."

Betts shook his head. "I don't know them," he lied.

"Why they do it?"

Betts shrugged and got slapped on top of the head for it. "Speak up, now. Why they hit you?"

"I wouldn't suck a dick."

Mom gasped, Dad said, "Uh-huh," and Betts betrayed his only brother with a cold look. In TJ's eyes he saw fear and shame and sorrow, and his father continued, "That's right, no, you won't. I hope you gave something back, boy, did you? I din't raise no faggot, did I?" He was bluffing a hardy smile, but his dad caught the end of the look Betts and TJ were sharing, throwing a dissonant note into their chord, and Betts knew immediately that it was a moment of significance. He didn't understand it completely. Not right away. But that was the moment that things changed in the house.

A month later, Dad burst into TJ's room and whupped him good. Said TJ wasn't any son of his, and that he was going to take his name back. "Thomas Betts" wasn't a faggot name and TJ didn't get to keep it. Mom shrieked and cried for help, and things got wilder. TJ hit back, but he was only fourteen and it just made Dad angrier. Mom's crying eventually brought Mr. Jenkins and his boy from next door, and between the two of them they finally pulled Dad off TJ, who was already packing his life into a bag.

When he passed his brother in the hallway on his way out the door for the last time, TJ was sobbing and Betts didn't have anything to say.

* * *

The phone rings and rings. He's been calling all night, but not leaving a message. He's parked across the street from the dumpsite going through a whole roll of Rolaids waiting for the right opportunity. Plan is to place her in the alley behind the club where she's been seen buying drugs before. He's about to press *Redial* for the tenth time when he receives a call from Kinds.

"Yeah."

"How we look?"

"We're good. You might want to go over the room."

"Redecorating Monday morning. Got a crew coming to repaint, new carpet, everything. So we should be all good."

"Hey?"

"Yeah?"

"What about her kid?"

"That's not your problem. Concentrate on your end."

"I know, it's just, I know she's got a kid."

"Kid's with his dad this week."

"Oh."

"Get your head straight."

"It is. Just . . ."

"What."

"Gonna be a shitty week for the kid."

"Gonna be a shitty week for all of us. So do your part to keep it from being a real shitty year, huh?"

Twenty minutes later, he senses his moment's arrival, starts the van, and gets to the end of the block. He's about to turn right onto Washington when his phone rings again. He looks at the number, but it's not anybody he's expecting.

"Hello."

No answer.

"Hello?" He stops the engine and turns off the lights.

"Have you heard from Teresa?" He can hear the change in the atmosphere, but nothing is said. "Listen . . . she seemed like a good kid. Smart. She seemed tough, I think she's okay."

When the other end speaks to him, it's barely louder than a whisper. "Fuck you."

Betts switches the phone to the other side of his head. "Excuse me?"

"Teresa's dead."

It's Betts's turn to be silent.

"She's been dead for a year now and you need to stop calling here."

Something hot slides between his ribs, and lets all the air out of his lungs. Betts barely manages to be audible. "How did she die?"

This time it's a well-considered and dispassionate, "Fuck you."

"I'm sorry, I—"

"No." There's authority in the voice and Betts listens. "You don't get to say anything else. You had your chance . . . now . . ."

"Listen, I—"

"No, you listen. Don't call here anymore."

Dad died three years ago. TJ's name hadn't been spoken since he'd left that night and they'd never heard from him again. Not even after Thomas Sr. died. Betts saw his mom after the funeral. He'd helped her clean the gutters, paint the house, finally cut down the tree always threatening to fall on her bedroom, before they put it on the market and moved her into her sister's home. He'd meant to talk with her about TJ then, but the look in her eyes had brought him up short. What good could come from it now?

* * *

The guard buzzed him through the gate when he'd explained the situation—he needed to treat the carpet with a special solvent before the painting crew arrived in the morning. The guard called to get him clearance.

Betts got a call from Kinds while he worked.

"Everything okay?"

"Yeah, figured I'd go over the spot extra good, since there'll be more eyes on it tomorrow."

"Fine. Just run it by me first next time."

"No problem."

Monday morning Betts places a 911 call to the Frontenac Police Department, and he watches the confusion at the gates through binoculars from the top of the hill on the eastern side. He waits for the call from Kinds, which comes five minutes later.

He doesn't give Kinds time to speak, but answers the phone with, "I quit," before smashing it on the street. He crushes what's left with the heel of his boot and looks at the wreck of plastic on the concrete. "Good luck buying your way out of this one."

Tuesday Betts answers his door to two plainclothes detectives.

"I'm prepared to cooperate, but I want a lawyer."

Cop Number One says, "He's already in the car."

Wednesday afternoon the story of a mysterious tragedy at the home of Citizen Number One breaks. Police had responded to an anonymous call about the body of a young woman that was found inside the master bedroom. Citizen Number One had been out of town for a stockholders' meeting in Florida at the estimated time of death.

158 // St. Louis Noir

In a statement to the press, the family attorney expressed deep sadness on behalf of Citizen Number One and said he was perplexed over the situation. He stated that the woman was a friend who was visiting the home at the time, but added that while the cause of death was unclear, there was absolutely nothing suspicious about her death.

Autopsy results were expected in four to six weeks.

Four weeks later the autopsy results came back "inconclusive."

On the same day the body of Philip Betts was found, by police, in his Afton home after neighbors reported a suspicious smell. Foul play was ruled out though cause of death was not determined. Betts, forty-one, lived alone and was unemployed.

A ST. LOUIS CHRISTMAS
BY UMAR LEE
North County

I

December 2013

Bubba Gates thought of it as an out-of-town Christmas, like those an out-of-town businessman might have to celebrate on the road. Or what football and basketball players would do if they had games on Christmas. As Bubba drove the streets of St. Louis he thought about those Christmases as a kid in the Bootheel of Missouri. The Bootheel, Southern with only a slight trace of Midwesterness. Where young boys learn their work ethic in the fields chopping cotton and look forward to yearly trips to St. Louis to see the Cardinals play.

Christmas had always been Bubba's favorite holiday. On Christmas Eve his family would go to both sets of grandparents' homes and eat cookies, open presents, and stuff themselves on good Southern cooking. On Christmas morning the family would wake and open the presents under the tree after the reading of Luke, chapter 2, from the Holy Bible. Never all that much under the tree. Family farmers in the Bootheel never had all that much extra money for things such as gifts. Didn't matter to Bubba. To him it was about family and about love.

Driving the gray GMC conversion van, flipping through the radio channels during a KSHE 95 commercial break, heading along West Florissant past Bellefontaine Cemetery, Bubba couldn't find anything he liked. Black stations, pop stations, and sports talk radio was all he found. He didn't care for any of those. One religious channel was running a commercial, "*Remember, He is the reason for the season. Keep Christ in Christmas.*"

"Amen, brother. Amen, brother," Bubba said aloud to himself. A car pulled beside him at the intersection of Goodfellow with a pretty young girl in it. At forty, bald, overweight, and married with three kids, Bubba didn't even pay much attention to pretty young things like that anymore.

West Florissant started in the slums. Isolated black ghettos full of vacant lots, abandoned buildings, dope sellers and dealers roaming the streets, historic homes in a state of decay, Chinese carryouts, Arab corner stores, and American muscle cars with temporary tags racing up and down the street. It then turned into a mixture of ghetto and the black middle class in the North St. Louis County suburbs of Jennings and Ferguson. Ghetto had the middle class on the ropes like George Foreman had Muhammad Ali on the ropes in Africa. This time there didn't appear to be a rope-a-dope strategy, as strip malls were half-empty and boarded-up suburban homes dotted the landscape. Bubba liked what he saw.

It was past Ferguson in the city of Florissant where Bubba had set up shop. It had the right racial mix for one. There were enough whites so a group of country white boys didn't stick out. There were enough blacks so black guys coming to meet them also didn't stick out. Florissant was a northern St. Louis suburb in transition. Where older white people sat around and talked about the good old days. The days when the Catholic parish schools and sports teams were full. When the local North County high schools were bursting at the seams with white students. The winters when as soon as it snowed kids flocked to the Florissant Civic Center to ice skate and Killer Hill across the street to go sledding. When Mayor James Eagan ran the city with an iron fist and his pit-bull chief of police enforced his edicts. Those days were long gone in Florissant. Outside of the historic Old Town district the city now mostly consisted of five categories: old white people who wanted out but couldn't get anything for their homes, new middle-class black families seeing promise in suburbia, Section 8 housing and apartments, those homes now being rented out after subprime mortgage defaults, and lastly, those who were too tied to Florissant to leave. Either those who were tied to the city in a political or business sense and needed it to make money or maintain stature, or those in a life of crime who needed to stay because this was their hood and the local bars were their lairs. Again, just as Bubba saw Florissant to have ideal racial demographics for his purposes, it also had ideal economic conditions as a growth market for his product, meth.

After making a left on Dunn Road and a right on Waterford and a left on St. Anthony, Bubba was at his place. He saw the curtains drawn closed. The guys were waiting on him. They had probably cooked something special for Christmas. God love 'em. Before stepping out of the car Bubba heard a commercial that made him pause and think. It was for a local children's hospital and it gave him an idea.

II

Back in the city, Faheem and Danny stepped out of the Chase Park Plaza Cinemas. Neither Faheem, an African American Muslim, nor Danny, an Orthodox Jew, were celebrating Christmas, and both were generally bored on the holiday. The two couldn't look more different. Faheem was a tall and muscular, dark-skinned black man with a long well-trimmed sunna-style beard. He wore a black knit kufi cap, a black hoodie, and jeans that cut off above his ankle on top of his Tims. Danny was a short and pale white guy with a close-cropped reddish beard. Under his red St. Louis Cardinals baseball cap was a small black yarmulke. Although he was physically fit, Danny didn't possess any type of a menacing presence and looked like your run-of-the-mill white guy.

"That was a pretty good movie, I have to agree. Didn't think I would like it," Danny said, walking down the steps of the theater toward Lindell where their car was parked.

"Why not?" Faheem asked.

"Black people going on and on about all that slavery stuff. It was bad. Time to get over it though," Danny replied.

"Man, are you serious? Jews won't shut up about the Holocaust. Every year there are new movies and documentaries coming out about it. I could say the same thing. Yeah, it was bad, now it's time to get over it," Faheem said, laughing.

"That's different," a now irritated Danny shot back.

"How is it different?" Faheem asked as they got into their all-black tinted 2008 Ford Crown Victoria police interceptor model.

"The Holocaust wasn't that long ago. There are survivors still alive. The memory is fresh. And let's be honest, it was one of the greatest tragedies in the history of humanity. Slavery ended like a hundred and fifty years ago. Nobody's alive from that time. Also, always evoking its memory is tied to the grievance industry and a political agenda," Danny said from the passenger seat as he slipped on his shades.

"You gotta be kiddin' me. You're not serious, right? Like the Holocaust movies and remembrances aren't tied to a political agenda of supporting Israel. Like the two aren't even connected. If white people feel so bad about the Holocaust they should have given the Jews Germany or Austria. Palestinians didn't have anything to do with the Holocaust," Faheem said as he drove toward Vandeventer and made a left heading toward the Northside.

"Historic homeland. We were there first. That's what Muslims don't understand. You're always talking about—"

And just like that Danny was cut off. "Call from the Big Man, be quiet," Faheem announced. He answered the phone, said hello, gave a few *yes sirs*, and then hung up.

"What did he want?" Danny asked.

"Said he wants to see us. Said it's urgent. Wants to meet us in the Jamestown Mall parking lot by the movie theater," Faheem answered.

They argued a lot about religion and politics though they were good friends. Danny had attended Muslim Eid holiday celebrations, and Faheem had been to Yom Kippur and Passover meals. When they argued it was more about trying to figure out where the other was coming from than winning. Between two aggressive alpha males, discussions can take on an aggressive tone.

Faheem was born in Brooklyn, New York, into a large family. Both of his parents had converted to Islam in the early 1970s and were members of the black Sunni Muslim organization Dar al Islam, based at Masjid Yaseen in East New York. After the movement split in 1980, with some following the Pakistani Sufi cleric Syed Mubarik Shah El-Gillani, who sent his followers to establish rural "Muslim villages," and others following Imam Jamil al-Amin (formerly H. Rap Brown), who was based in the West End of Atlanta, Faheem's family went their own way.

As a boy Faheem moved with his father, his stepmom, and

all the other kids across America. Cleveland, Chicago, North Carolina, Oklahoma, Los Angeles, and places Faheem had forgotten, only to be reminded of later. Now his parents were old and settled down in Atlanta, the Black Mecca, along with thousands of other black Muslims from the East Coast who moved south to grow old and die. Faheem ended up in St. Louis after marrying a Muslim sister he had met while living in Northern Virginia, who wanted to come back to "da Lou" to be near her family. Without any real hometown, Faheem didn't object even if he found St. Louis slow, Southern, and country, and the Muslim community lackluster at best.

The River City Robinhoodz had recruited Faheem because they suspected he had experience in vigilantism. East Coast black Muslims, especially those out of Brooklyn, Newark, and Philly, had a reputation for robbing drug dealers, and for the security teams at mosques performing neighborhood street patrols. One day while he was setting up shop as a street vendor across from the veterans hospital on Grand and Enright, a representative of the RCR approached him. What they didn't know was that Faheem had never participated in such vigilante actions before. He had been just a teenager when the security team of Masjid at-Taqwa in Brooklyn did its thing. However, two of Faheem's sisters, who had been raised strictly on the *deen*, had become addicted to drugs and were out in the streets, making his hatred of drug dealers personal, and he jumped at the opportunity.

Danny had been recruited strictly for his military expertise. A St. Louis native, Danny had not been raised in a religious home. His parents were "high-holiday Jews" who only went to the synagogue twice a year. They weren't even really political Jews; they donated to a few pro-Israel groups and the Anti-Defamation League and had a few Chaim Potok books on their shelves, and that was about it. Growing up in the wealthy western suburb of Ladue, with its heavy Jewish population, Danny knew some serious Jews. He just didn't happen to be one of them.

Senior year at Ladue Horton Watkins High School changed all of that. Danny began dating a girl named Sarah, a Jewish girl who'd grown up in a home like his. The only difference was that Sarah had become fascinated with Jewish history and culture and began reading about the topics nonstop. In an effort to win her over and to get laid, Danny began reading the same books she was reading. Eventually that led the two of them to begin taking classes with Chabad, a Jewish outreach organization, and after high school they said to hell with college and moved to Israel. The two became observant Jews, Danny joined the Israeli Defense Forces, and Sarah stayed behind in an apartment in the Ramot neighborhood of Jerusalem. Arriving to Israel in 1999, Danny completed his Hebrew-language courses and entered the IDF just in time for the Second Intifada. He saw plenty of action on the streets of Hebron, Nablus, and Jenin, and the deeper he got into the conflict the more passionately Danny and Sarah embraced religious Zionism. They left the more pluralistic Ramot for an ultra-Orthodox settlement near Hebron known as Kiryat Arba. In the "hills of Judea and Samaria," Danny and Sarah, with their small children, felt they were a part of history and the redemption of the Jewish people. Then reality came calling.

Back in St. Louis there were problems. Danny's younger brother Scott had gotten hooked on heroin. St. Louis from the eighties to the midnineties had been crack city. Entire neighborhoods like Walnut Park, the JVL, Wellston, and Kinloch were decimated by the drug. Since the late nineties heroin had been coming back with a vengeance. Starting in the black neighborhoods of North City, North County, and the near South Side, it had spread all over the region. Heroin fatalities had become common. Scott was one of them. His body was found in a ghetto apartment building in the 5300 block of Cabanne near Soldan High School in a neighborhood known for drugs and crime. Ironically, the neighborhood had once been Jewish, before Jews migrated west.

Danny's parents were still grieving when he had to return home with his family. They settled into an Orthodox Jewish enclave in University City just off Delmar, and Danny found a job helping his uncle run a chain of dry cleaners. It was at one of the locations in Central West End one day that he met the Big Man. When he told the Big Man of his IDF experience and why he had returned to St. Louis, the rest was history.

The Big Man lived in a beautifully restored nineteenth-century home on St. Louis Avenue in the St. Louis Place neighborhood just north of downtown. That was where the RCR usually met. Today he wanted to meet at Jamestown Mall. Faheem headed up Vandeventer, cut through Fairgrounds Park, took North Broadway until it turned into Bellefontaine near the county line, and then cut across Chambers to 367 which took him to the Jamestown Mall/North Highway 67 exit.

The mall had once been a booming suburban hub for commerce. Large department stores, trendy shops, all the regulars at the food court, and a movie theater. These days the department stores had pulled out, the food court was almost empty, few stores remained, and grass grew on the parking lot. There had been a recent attempt to turn the mall into a flea market and the county had come in and shut the whole thing down one day because the indoor temperature was below fifty degrees. The movie theater had also recently closed.

Hard times for sure. The mall had risen and declined along with the blue-collar industrial economy of North St. Louis County. These things also made the mall a great place to meet and not be seen.

The Big Man was parked in an all-white Cadillac Escalade. He sat in the passenger seat listening to an old-school Isley Brothers CD while smoking an Arturo Fuente Hemingway Signature Cameroon Perfecto cigar he'd selected at Brennan's. The Big Man had read all of Hemingway's books while in prison. The driver was his nephew, Rodney. Unlike the Big Man, Rodney had never come up hard on the streets of North St. Louis, nor had he sold drugs. Rodney grew up in Berkeley in North County and excelled as an athlete, boxing for North County, playing football and wrestling at McCluer North, and going to Mizzou on a wrestling scholarship before his knee blew out. Back in St. Louis he began working for his uncle.

Faheem and Danny pulled up in their Crown Vic, parked, and hopped in the backseat. The Big Man was wearing an all-white suit with cream-colored gaiters, an off-white fur coat, and a hat to match. His wrists and fingers were full of gold jewelry that matched the chains and cross around his neck and the four gold teeth in his mouth. A dark-skinned, chubby, middle-aged black man, the Big Man founded the RCR for two reasons: to give back to the community as a way of atoning for his sins, and to stop the flow of meth into St. Louis. Crack had been bad for St. Louis, heroin was arguably worse: but to the Big Man, meth would be the worst. He could already see the effects. The dealers themselves were coming up from the Bootheel, the Ozarks, and other places in rural Missouri in search of larger and more lucrative urban markets.

What the Big Man hated most was the fact that these white gangs, racist to the core, had been using local black gangs to spread their product. The RCR had been shutting down meth houses, robbing dealers, and killing dealers for a while now. There were bounties on all of their heads. Unlike another local vigilante group, the RCR used guns and they took the money for themselves. They had no rich benefactor. No shame in being rewarded for good behavior.

"Merry Christmas," the Big Man said to Faheem and Danny.

"Yeah, have a good one," Faheem replied. He didn't want to wish him a Merry Christmas because he didn't believe in the holiday. He also didn't want to be rude. Danny remained silent.

"That's right, you two non-ham-sandwich-eating brothers don't celebrate the birth of Jesus. We gonna have to have a serious debate about that one day. Another time. Right now we got business," the Big Man said.

"What's up?" Danny asked.

"We got word from one of our sources this crew out of the Bootheel ran by Nehemiah Calhoun is gonna try to get a big shipment of cash out of town to him soon. His house is in Advance, Missouri, but it's too dangerous to get him down there. We need to get the money before it leaves St. Louis."

"How are we gon' do that?" Faheem asked.

"The guy running things for him up here is some country-ass cracker named Bubba. Bubba is renting a house in Florissant where some of his buddies are staying. It's a five-minute drive from here. Given the fact he's trusted by Nehemiah Calhoun, Bubba will probably be the one taking the money to him. Or at least someone close to him will be. We need you to go over to his house and keep an eye on his movements. See if he's leaving town."

"Why us?" Faheem asked.

"The rest of the crew are all celebrating Christmas. Matter of fact, I'm headed to see my grandbabies now," the Big Man said as he handed Faheem a piece of paper with the address written on it.

III

Bubba sat at the table exchanging Christmas gifts with his crew. Cartons of cigarettes, cases of bullets from Bass Pro, *Duck Dynasty* T-shirts, scratch-off lottery tickets, porno mags, and other items. Frank, the best cook in the crew, had prepared a ham with mashed potatoes and corn on the side. Apple pie and vanilla ice cream for dessert.

Taking out a brand-new bottle of Jack Daniel's, Bubba offered a red-cup toast for his friends: "Frank, Kevin, and Billy, this has been a great year. We've made a lot of money. Put food on the table. Our families are living good. Kids are wearing nice clothes. Back home they're playing with nice new toys. All of that is from the sweat of our brows. From this work we are doing here in St. Louis. That's what brings money back to the Bootheel. Thank God, thank Nehemiah, and on this blessed day thank our Lord and Savior Jesus Christ. To Family First!"

All the men raised their cups and echoed, "Family First."

Family First was not the official name of their group. Nehemiah had never sanctioned that. It was just a popular saying among them and some people had begun calling them by that name. They just saw themselves as a group of good ol' boys from southeastern Missouri. Good ol' boys doing what they had to do to survive and support their families. The factories were closed, family farming made almost impossible, and for them the way to go was meth.

Nehemiah had learned about meth from a cousin who lived in Independence, Missouri. It was there that Nehemiah got the meth recipe and found a few reliable cooks. Having sewn up business in southeastern Missouri and paid off the Bootheel cops he needed to, he knew that to increase the profits you had to move into the cities. Heroin and crack ruled St. Louis; Nehemiah knew this. What he also knew was that once people learned about meth, it would become their drug of choice with its lasting and cheaper highs.

Distribution was a problem. In white neighborhoods in St. Charles County, deep South City, Madison County, and the white neighborhoods left in North County where drug usage was high, it was okay for rednecks to set up shop. White people from the affluent western suburbs and the more middle-class southern suburbs tended to drive in to buy drugs. In the black neighborhoods in North City, North County, South City, East St. Louis, and parts of Madison County, it was not realistic to have a group of white boys selling drugs. They would stick out like sore thumbs. Plus, they didn't know anybody and drug dealing is a "relationship business," as Nehemiah had been taught.

That's where Nehemiah's childhood friend Bubba came into play. Bubba had spent eight years in Missouri prisons for a string of armed robberies. First at the "Gladiator School" in Booneville and then at Bonne Terre. There Bubba met quite a few black drug dealers and gang members from St. Louis. He put them in contact with Nehemiah, and they were now cutting into the heroin and crack markets with their new product in the black neighborhoods of St. Louis in a major way.

Bubba and the boys drank and told stories of their families and growing up as Lynyrd Skynyrd played in the background. Billy rolled a fat joint of Missouri-grown weed and they passed it around. Headlights flickered through the front window and Bubba got up to look to see who it was. All four men were armed at all times. Walking to the door Bubba waived off his friends.

"Merry Christmas," he said, smiling to the young black man named Rello walking toward his front door, his maroon '77 Cutlass Supreme parked in the driveway. Rello ran a few meth houses in the College Hill neighborhood of North St. Louis. He also acted as a middleman between Bubba and some dealers in the O'Fallon Park, Hyde Park, and Penrose Park neighborhoods.

"Merry Christmas, my dude," answered the short, thin Rello, wearing a black leather coat, True Religion jeans, new Jordans, and a black-and-white STL cap. His smile exposed two gold incisors. He handed Bubba five shoe boxes, which Bubba knew were stuffed with money.

"Looks like you're having a real lovely Christmas. How are the kids?" Bubba asked.

"Blessed man can't complain. We had our Christmas thing at my house, then we went to my mama's house, and now I'm going to stop by my other BM's house and see my other kids," Rello replied.

"What's a BM?" Bubba asked, prompting laughter from Rello.

"Baby mama, dawg."

"I see. Well, if you don't have anything planned for your kids to do, I have something in mind," Bubba said.

"Oh yeah, like what?"

"Come inside. Have a seat," replied Bubba.

Twenty minutes later, as Rello was leaving, Bubba walked to the next-door neighbor's house. The old white lady had given him a fruitcake for Christmas, and to return the favor he was bringing a plate of homemade cookies his wife had sent up. The lady lived alone. Her husband, a union pipe fit-ter, had died of a heart attack a few years back and her kids and grandkids, in typical white North County fashion, had all moved out to St. Charles County. Today the driveway was full as her relatives were visiting. Bubba knocked on the door and saw an unfamiliar face.

"Hello," said a fortysomething man with a comb-over, a seventies-era Christmas sweater, and a potbelly. Bubba thought he might be a son-in-law as he didn't have the family look.

"Hi, I'm the neighbor. I'm here to bring some Christmas cookies to Mrs. Shields," Bubba said.

"Oh, of course. Come right in."

Bubba walked into a house full of kids playing, torn Christmas paper scattered around, and laughter. Mrs. Shields came walking up to him smiling.

"Merry Christmas, Bubba. You didn't drive down to see your family?" Mrs. Shields asked.

"Leaving in a few minutes. Here are some cookies my wife made. Was wondering if you could do me a favor."

"Hope I can. What is it?" Mrs. Shields said.

"I don't have any wrapping paper and all of the stores are closed. Do you have any I can use?"

"Why, Lord, yes, of course I do. I got all kinds of paper you can wrap up presents for them little darlings with. Just let me go get some. Of course you're going to need scissors and tape too," Mrs. Shields said, before getting Bubba the needed items.

IV

"Do you think we should have followed the Cutlass?" Danny asked, looking from the car parked a few houses down.

"I thought about it. I don't know, man, Big Man told us to

watch the people in the house. Some redneck named Bubba," Faheem answered.

"Right, but you don't think that was money or drugs in those shoe boxes?"

"For sure it was. They weren't doing Christmas delivery for Foot Locker."

"So, drugs or money?" Danny asked.

"Definitely money. The drugs are coming from the white boys. That's whose bringing meth into St. Louis. The black guys, those cats are out on these corners selling the product. Definitely he was bringing back money."

"So, that's the money going to this Nehemiah, right?" Danny said.

"Yeah. Allah knows best: that's how I see it. Regardless, we gotta get those boxes."

Faheem kept an eye on the house and Danny read an article in an old *New Yorker* magazine as KWMU, the local NPR station, played inside the vehicle. A bombing in Iraq, more killing in Syria, civil war breaking out in the newly created state of South Sudan. That was overseas. On the *St. Louis Post-Dispatch* app on his phone, Faheem read about an Amber Alert for a kidnapped six-year-old boy and a number of local killings. "Ya Allah, *ya ar-Rahman*," Faheem said aloud.

"Look. They're leaving," Danny said.

"And they got a bunch of Christmas presents with them. In the Christmas spirit I guess."

"A bunch of presents. You think they left them boxes at the house?"

"Not at all. Those boxes are wrapped up as Christmas presents. Looks like we gonna be robbin' Santa."

"Yeah, but not here. The sun is still up and there are a lot of people around," Danny said.

"Right. We'll follow them and catch them at an isolated spot. Jack their asses of the money and whatever they got. I say a bumper-jack."

"You bump them with the car. I get out like I'm looking for damage, and when they get out I draw on them."

"Exactly. And if they start trippin', you light they ass up, inshallah." Faheem followed the man through the St. Anthony section of Florissant before they turned right onto Washington, passing Pirrone's Pizza on their left. Washington turned into Elizabeth after crossing over 270. The quiet street was lined with beautiful midcentury homes with large front porches and big front- and backyards. Had the homes not been in North County you could have got at least $500,000 for them; being where they were, you would be lucky to sell one for $200,000.

Faheem and Danny followed Bubba and his boys as they turned right on Chambers in the city of Ferguson and took that until it turned into Airport Road and the city of Berkeley. Passing a stretch of small frame houses and ghetto businesses, they turned left on Jefferson next to a liquor store. A couple of blocks up, near the intersection of Jefferson and 5th, near a stretch of new houses built after a tornado and before the Kinloch city limit, Bubba parked his car.

Faheem thought it an odd place for white boys to be hanging out. Then he noticed the old-school Cutlass they had seen earlier parked in front of the house. Bubba and his three friends got out with presents. The same black guy from earlier came out of the house with two kids. The kids took two boxes each and got into the Cutlass. Bubba and the black guy exchanged a few words and then both got in their cars. Bubba took the lead.

V

Bubba was being extra cautious. There had been too many robberies lately and the large amount of money, a hundred grand in each box, made him kind of nervous. One box the boys took for themselves and split four ways, the other four boxes went to Nehemiah. That was too much money to lose in a street robbery. Even though he hadn't been robbed, Bubba knew all about the different vigilante crews operating in St. Louis. If the day ever arrived when they came for him, Bubba would be ready. His aim was straight and he shot to kill, done it before and would do it again if he had to. Christmas presented an ideal opportunity to move the money and the kids were a great addition.

They jumped on I-70 and drove it east into the city and then took the 55/44 exit toward downtown and got off at Grand. A local children's hospital was holding an event for sick kids where the public was encouraged to donate presents. Bubba had some gifts to bring, the biggest being for himself.

"Man, what are these fools doing?" Faheem asked.

"I don't know, but whatever it is, we can't roll up on them with the kids inside," Danny answered.

"I know. That would be straight-up scandalous. We'd end up on the front page of the *Evening Whirl* for sure," Faheem said, referring to the local black-owned crime and entertainment newspaper.

"Somehow they got the kids involved." Danny shook his head, thinking of his own children. He sent his wife a text asking her how they were doing and thumbed through Facebook and Twitter as Faheem drove.

176 // St. Louis Noir

"A hospital? Why are they going to a hospital?" Faheem asked.

"I don't know. Maybe it isn't money in there. Why would they bring money to a hospital?"

Faheem parked the Crown Vic on Park, about a block east from where Bubba and Rello had stopped. From there they followed them on foot, leaving their guns in the car.

"If they're going into the hospital, there's no way we can get the guns inside," Faheem said.

"Well, there's probably a way. We would just need some time to figure it out," Danny replied.

"Look, we just gotta pretend like we're there to visit patients and try to get as close to them as possible, inshallah," Faheem said.

As the two of them followed Bubba and his boys along with Rello and his kids, they noticed a large crowd outside with a lot of children. Christmas carols were being sung and there was a guy onstage dressed as Santa, handing out gifts. The crowd was mostly mothers with kids, with the occasional dad mixed in, along with a few grandparents. Some of the kids appeared to be alone while others were accompanied by hospital staff. Bubba, Rello, and the rest settled into the crowd holding their nicely wrapped gifts as the kids went to play with the other children who were now being thrown treats by elves.

Looking to the sky, Faheem realized it was time for the *maghrib* prayer. He excused himself to go to the bathroom and make ablution and then pray.

Walking up to the security desk smiling, Faheem asked where the restroom was and was guided to one in the lobby. Once in the bathroom Faheem made *wudu*, washing his face, arms, hands, and feet, and then outside he found a barren piece of concrete behind the crowd and pulled out his portable black prayer rug. In front of the rug he placed his car keys and gloves to both weigh it down and act as a *sutra* (a separation from his area of prayer and other people).

Bubba, Rello, and the boys were observing the kids, making jokes, and lamenting the fact you could no longer smoke at such gatherings. Out of the corner of his eye, Bubba noticed a black man with a big beard and a Muslim-style cap praying in prostration. This was not something Bubba had ever been exposed to growing up in the Bootheel, but he'd seen plenty of it in prison.

"Rello, you know that guy over there?" Bubba asked.

"The Muslim?"

"Yeah." Bubba kept a close eye on the man.

"Naw, I don't know him . . . Hold up now. He do look kinda familiar. You know what? That look like that Muslim who robbed one of our meth houses on North 20th and Obear," Rello said, trying to get a better look.

"The one on the north side over by the water tower?" Bubba asked.

"Yeah, that's the one. Someone with that same description hit up a house on East John right around the corner from the other house. The question is, what's he doing here?"

"That's a good question. I think I'd like to know the answer to that," Bubba said.

The five men began walking toward Faheem, who by that time had finished praying and was rolling up his rug and fitting it into his back pocket. A hand touched his shoulder and Faheem turned around.

"Brother, I wish I would have seen you praying; we could have prayed together," a smiling, clean-shaven man of South Asian descent said in accented English.

"*Alhamdulilah akh*, I wish so too. Next time, inshallah. My name is Faheem *akh*," he said, reaching out his hand.

"Here they call me Dr. Khan. You can just call me Brother Abdul-Basit," the doctor said.

"Inshallah I will see you again. Maybe at the *masjid. As-salamu alaikum*," Faheem said, smiling as the doctor returned his greetings. When he turned around he was no longer smiling. Bubba, his three friends, and Rello were all staring at him.

"You know, fella, you look just like someone I been hearing about," Bubba said with a mean look on his face.

"Yeah, you look like the Muslim they say robbed a couple of our houses up by the water tower," Rello said.

"So what. Y'all come to bring me presents or something?" Faheem responded, staring them down.

"Kevin, Billy, show him the presents we have for him," Bubba instructed. The two men opened their leather coats and flashed their guns. Faheem had gone into the hospital unarmed; that mistake could cost him his life.

"Frank, take the keys. Take him to the van and tie him up. You ever been down to the Bootheel, boy? Don't think folks down there ever seen a Muslim. You should be a real treat for the locals. Maybe we'll cage you up like an animal and make you do your little prayer like a circus trick," Bubba chuckled.

"You coming with us?" Frank asked.

"No, you guys drive him back home. Take him to that abandoned farmhouse outside of Malden. We're not cooking there anymore. It'll be a good place to hold him until Nehemiah gets the chance to meet him. Tell me, boy, what crew are you with?" Bubba said.

"RCR," Faheem answered, looking him dead in his eye as a smile lit up his face.

VI

Danny had been waiting for Faheem to complete his prayers so he could say his *Maariv*, a customary Jewish prayer after sunset. When he saw the five men walking toward Faheem, he knew that somehow they must have recognized him. Danny texted the Big Man their location and a *911 code. The numbers weren't in their favor. Definitely not when they were unarmed.

Then Danny saw the group split. Three men, no doubt armed, leading Faheem away, and Bubba and the black man staying behind with the gift packages. For Danny the decision was easy. Money can be replaced—you can't miss what you never had—but Faheem was his friend. A good guy, a married man with kids, and a brother in the RCR. Danny would do anything to save his friend just as he'd fought to save his buddies in the IDF.

Growing up in a wealthy home in West County, Danny had never been in a street fight as a kid, and he hadn't been raised by tough men. He arrived to Israel a complete stranger to violence. Then came the weapons and combat training, and then came the real action. Hill to hill, street to street, house to house, room to room, gun battles. That, Danny was trained for and good at. While he had been trained in hand-to-hand combat as well, he had only had two real fights in his life. Once getting his ass kicked by a Palestinian cabbie in Jerusalem and another time managing to beat up a guy during an RCR takedown. Still, he'd studied the Israeli fighting art of *Krav Maga* and did pretty well in training. All three of the guys leading Faheem away looked to be out-of-shape rednecks. Danny would pray for the blessing of God and proceed.

* * *

Meanwhile, Bubba and Rello had other plans.

"Rello, get the kids and take me to your car," Bubba said as he began walking back toward the street.

"Come on, y'all. Come on, hear? Think I'm playin' if you want to!" Rello shouted out at the kids who began reluctantly running toward them.

"Had a feeling this was going to happen. Could just feel it in my blood. The hospital would draw them out. They probably thought we were going inside and left their guns in the car," Bubba said.

"So what now? Want me to drive you back to Florissant? It's no problem, I gotta take the kids back up to North County anyway," Rello said.

"No, take me to Union Station. The 20th Street side where all the cabs are always sitting."

"Why you wanna take a cab to Florissant? That's crazy. I'm offering you a free ride," Rello shot back.

"I ain't gonna go to Florissant. Going home. Down to the Bootheel."

"In a cab?" Rello asked with a puzzled look on his face.

"Yep. In a cab," Bubba flatly answered.

Danny followed the group and made a sober assessment. Even though the three white guys escorting Faheem didn't look like the most fierce of men, they had him outnumbered and they would get to the car before he could reach the Crown Vic and retrieve his weapon. Besides, he didn't even have the keys to the car so he would have to break in, taking up more time. Then Danny saw an opportunity. A hospital-issued wheelchair sat empty on the sidewalk—not an uncommon sight near a hospital. Patients roll away from the entrance to smoke a cigarette waiting on their rides and then just leave them there.

Danny sat in the wheelchair as the Grand bus was heading south toward its stop. The driver would have to step out of the bus and help Danny onto the wheelchair lift if requested. A couple of riders got off the bus who looked to be hospital employees going to work, and a couple got on ahead of Danny who appeared to be getting off work from the hospital.

"Excuse me, driver. I need help with the wheelchair lift, I can barely move," Danny said.

"I got ya," said the driver, a middle-aged African American woman with fake nails and an enormous amount of weave, makeup, and perfume.

When the driver stepped out and got behind Danny, he jumped up, pushed the chair away, and did a judo-style ankle sweep, knocking her to the ground.

"Sorry, I really am," Danny said as several passengers gasped. Dashing onto the bus with the wheelchair lift still down, Danny jumped into the driver's seat and made a sharp U-turn on Grand, almost hitting the median.

"What the fuck is this crazy-ass white boy doing? This some Columbine shit?" a black guy in his twenties yelled out as he ran toward Danny and punched him twice on the side of his skull.

A flash went through Danny's head, and while he realized he was going to be bruised, he knew what he had to do. He began honking the horn repeatedly, simultaneously speeding toward Faheem and his captors as the passenger tried to gain control of the wheel.

All four people turned around and looked at the bus. A flash of recognition entered Farheem's eyes and he began sprinting away as the bus hit all three of his captors and plowed into their van.

A disheveled Danny hurried off the bus. The passenger who had punched him chased him onto the sidewalk and tackled him. Two more men joined in and they began punching and kicking Danny while he was on the ground. Danny could taste his own blood in his mouth and pain shot through his back and ribs. As it was occurring to him that there was a real possibility he might die, two gunshots rang out.

The men cleared away and Faheem reached out a hand and pulled him up.

"Come on, we gotta get out of here with the quickness," Faheem said, running to the car. Danny hobbled after him.

"What was that all about?" Danny asked as he painfully got into the car.

"The white boy named Bubba and the black cat he called Rello recognized me or something."

"Where were they taking you?"

"Something about an abandoned farmhouse by Malden in the Bootheel," Faheem said as he sped off.

Danny's phone rang. It was the backup Big Man had sent. "We had some trouble. Out of it now. Driving away."

"Tell them to meet us on Ohio and Hickory in those ghetto-ass apartments where all the Somalis live!" Faheem yelled out.

A few minutes later they were at the apartments. The plates were taken off the Crown Vic, and after all of their personal belongings were removed, it was set ablaze. They got into an all-black Denali driven by two of their brothers from the RCR and sped off.

"Where y'all need me to take you?" asked the driver, a

young black guy and former amateur boxing star named Clyde. In the passenger seat sat Rodney.

"Stop by my crib in Pine Lawn and Danny's place in U. City. Then we headed out of town," Faheem said.

"Where we goin'?" Clyde asked.

"Straight south on 55. Down to the Bootheel. I don't like leaving money on the table. They won the battle tonight. That was the decree of Allah. We'll see who wins the next round," Faheem said, still seething at having been briefly taken prisoner.

"They didn't exactly win, Faheem. Those three guys are seriously injured. Maybe dead," Danny countered.

"Maybe so, but we came for their money and we didn't get it. Bubba left with the money, so it's Bubba we gotta find. And Clyde, stop by the Walgreens on Olive near Danny's crib. We need to do some nursing to my man right here," Faheem said, putting his arm around his Jewish brother.

VII

Bubba got into the first cab in line at the taxi stand, a red one. He was initially caught off guard by the driver being a woman. Sure, he'd seen female cabbies before, but this was a strikingly beautiful woman. Not a white woman but not black either. Piercing green eyes, high cheekbones, smooth olive-brownish skin; this was a real beauty, and Bubba wondered what the hell she was doing driving a cab.

"Say, honey, let's stop at the fillin' station on Arsenal and 55. I need a few beers for the road if you don't mind," Bubba said.

"I don't mind at all," the driver replied.

"So what's a pretty thing like you doing driving a cab anyway? Too dangerous a business for ya with all these creeps out here."

"I can handle myself."

"What's your name, dear?"

"Ezdehar."

"Huh, never heard that name before. Spanish or some-thing?" Bubba asked, trying to figure if he had a shot at getting laid.

"It's an Arabic name. I'm Palestinian," Ezdehar said, hop-ing this wasn't the beginning of a long, drawn-out political conversation. The guy seemed like a dumb redneck to her and the last thing she wanted was a political or religious exchange with his ignorant ass. She also knew once he had those beers in his system he'd become overly flirtatious so she wanted to keep talk to a bare minimum.

Ezdehar pulled into the gas station and decided to fill up the tank while Bubba was getting beer. As she got ready to check her oil, she received a text message. She glanced around and saw only one other car in the lot; sitting inside it was a thuggish-looking dude. The cashier inside, who she had seen before, looked like he was having a hard time staying awake.

Inside, Bubba grabbed a six-pack of Stag beer and some Gus' Pretzels. On the way back to the cab he noticed how petite the driver was while she was still checking the oil.

"Need help with that, honey? That's a man's job," Bubba stated, putting his hand on her shoulder.

"I'd really appreciate it. All I know how to do is put gas in this thing and drive it," Ezdehar said, smiling and batting her eyelashes.

After putting the beer and pretzels in the cab, Bubba came around to help her out.

Ezdehar was small but had a very athletic and fit body. Her husband was a wrestler and had taught her a lot of moves. In her circles, those moves came in handy sometimes.

As Bubba began to read the oil, Ezdehar made her move. An ankle sweep from behind followed by a rear choke hold. Bubba, much larger and stronger, resisted and clawed, but within a minute his ass was asleep on the concrete.

Ezdehar calmly got back in the cab and made a call.

"That group text alert? Don't worry about that. I handled it," Ezdehar announced, suddenly in the mood to wrestle in a different kind of way with her husband. The thrill of choking that redneck and taking his shit, she wouldn't soon forget. After all, that thrill was one of the primary benefits of being a member of the River City Robinhoodz.

THE PILLBOX

BY CHRIS BARSANTI

Maplewood

You put three skinheads in a room, they'll form seven factions. It's incredible. You would think that in St. Louis, where there's at most a few dozen of us, we would stick together. But that's not how we are.

The rest of the world couldn't tell an Aryan Nation thug from a retro rude boy or straightedge. But among skinheads it's all purges and internecine strife. It didn't surprise me that there would eventually be a murder. I just wouldn't have thought there would be more than one. Or that I would be pulling the trigger.

Me, I've never been a joiner. I just liked the uniform and the music. It can be easier to strap on a premade identity in the morning than to figure out one for yourself. As idiotic as it sounds, I first shaved my head after I saw a picture of a band in *Maximum Rock'n'Roll*. Even on that black-and-white zine's smudgy pages, the skinhead singer looked like some aerodynamically designed vehicle for aggression. That was it. I was eighteen, already into punk rock, and breaking out of that hair metal and classic rock straitjacket happily worn by every guy I grew up with in the half-rural, half-suburban, nearly all white deadlands of St. Charles just across the Missouri River from St. Louis County.

I had anger. It had been building all my life and needed to explode somehow. So I showed up for class at St. Charles High one Monday with a bald head just as shiny bright as the new, black, twelve-eyelet Dr. Martens on my feet. I wanted to give a middle finger to everybody. It worked.

The first week my nose was broken by two black guys I used to be friendly with. The one throwing the most kicks said I was a fucking Nazi. I tried telling him that I had just been to a meeting of SHARP the night before. You know, Skinheads Against Racial Prejudice? But he couldn't hear me through the blood. Clips of that episode where the racist skinhead busted Geraldo's nose had been rebroadcast for months. My timing wasn't the best.

The second week my ex-friends started calling me "punk faggot." They painted *Randall eats dick* on my locker and looked for things to throw. Once a teacher's back turned, the erasers, food, books, and spit started flying. Anything to leave a stain or dent on my shiny head. I lasted almost a month.

It was April of senior year, so the school let me finish up with home study. They mailed my diploma and hinted that I had more exciting activities to enjoy than graduation or prom.

My mother had a less-friendly suggestion: "Get out."

My father had already split for Oklahoma with his praying mantis of a dietician girlfriend. But he left me his old gray Cutlass as a graduation present. So I threw everything I could into the trunk, popped my alarm clock on the dash, and sped down I-70 into the city, determined never to see St. Charles again.

I hit the places I thought punks would gather: Delmar, the Central West End. My newly acquired tribe was nowhere to be seen. So I squirreled myself away in dark corners of parking lots and alleys all over South City where a homeless eighteen-year-old could sleep without getting rousted or killed.

Having lost a lifetime's worth of friends and family, I

wasn't discerning about the company I kept. I hung around Vintage Vinyl, checked out the flyers, saw every band I could at Bernard's Pub and Cicero's basement, and tried to make conversation.

I made the acquaintance of a skinhead named Gene at a ska show in some rich kid's Great Gatsby mansion in University City. He was a lanky, genial, and none-too-bright military brat who had happily bailed on high school at sixteen, was booted out by his Air Force parents not long after, and now had more words to say than thoughts to back them up. Gene was twenty and at loose ends. He didn't just need a buddy. He wanted an accomplice.

I was happy to make any friend, especially once he invited me to move into his place. The Cutlass was getting rank after all those weeks of doubling as my apartment. Gene lived in a punk house on a shabby block of faded one- and two-story houses in Maplewood. It was one of those tree-shaded neighborhoods clustered where the city blurred into the county that looked idyllic enough for now but was forever on the knife's edge of white-flight collapse. The house was on one of the cheaper, rangier blocks close to I-44; plenty of space, and neighbors who didn't ask questions.

The guy whose name was actually on the lease called it the Pillbox because of the thick brick walls and the little crow's nest of a balcony above the front door. That was Anderson, the older art punk in the attic whose edge had blurred into a more general dissipation. Like most people on the verge of imploding, he had lost the desire to judge anything or anybody. He put up with Gene's monomania, and the peculiarities of all the other lost kids who floated in and out of the house.

Anderson slept beneath a sepulchral poster of William S. Burroughs and kept a Webley .38 under his pillow. Like Burroughs, Anderson received a monthly check from the family fortune and had a thing for guns. Earlier in the decade, before giving up on the local music scene, Anderson had imagined the house as an art collective. There were happenings in the garage and experimental movies projected onto a bedsheet in the backyard. He soundproofed the basement to record music. That dream died as the bands broke up and people got married or left for bigger, broader-minded cities where they wouldn't always perform to the same fifty people.

Now the basement was a shooting range. Anderson's arsenal was locked up down there in a towering gray metal gun safe. He liked to hang out at gun shows and certain kinds of sporting goods stores where records got lost and serial numbers were filed down to nothing. On shooting nights, we would blast the Necros and the Effigies while Anderson judged quick-draw pistol contests. I went with the Luger, while Gene favored the heavier .45 M1911. My favorite, though, was the long matte-black Mossberg 500 twelve-gauge shotgun. With the Mossberg kicking against my shoulder and its solid slugs ripping apart the old Rock Against Reagan flyers pinned to the piles of castoff wood we'd snaked from a nearby lumberyard, I didn't care how lost I was.

Anderson kept the utilities on and made sure there was always coffee. All the rest of us had to do was throw in a couple hundred a month for the rent and phone and take turns making sure the kitchen wasn't bare.

I had a mattress, a door with a lock, lights, and access to a shower. I got along with everybody, more or less. Even Wendy and Shana, the lesbian-separatist poets in the second-floor room next to mine.

In a month, the Pillbox felt more like home than anywhere I had ever known.

Gene and I would sit up all night in his upstairs room listening to records. 2 Tone ska bands, mostly. Tight rhythms, staccato and yet steady. Like his voice. I listened to him talk about the old days that he hadn't experienced and a once-proud British working-class subculture's fall from grace. The ideals of racial solidarity perverted by racist pricks, and all that.

Gene took me down to a copy shop on South Grand where Reggie, the night manager, was an old friend of Anderson's. He let all the zine kids and musicians print their flyers for half-off or even free sometimes. Reggie also made crisp and hard-to-spot fake IDs for bored kids like us.

We went to every hardcore and ska show there was—Crucifucks, the Meatmen, Ultraman, Drunks with Guns—but stayed out of the other skins' way. You never knew which lines you were going to cross.

Gene had a lot of beliefs. But they didn't include having a steady job. He was making five bucks an hour at the lumberyard a few blocks from the Pillbox. I got on there too. But our hours were thin and scattered. I was broke enough to start boosting boxes of cereal and pasta from the generic aisle at the ALDI supermarket.

We counted our pennies and donated plasma for twenty bucks a pop.

So when Tom and Drexel came up to us during an earthquake-loud set by the Urge in some yuppie bar down on Laclede's Landing and started talking about work, we listened. It was a cold December night outside. I'd spent my last five dollars at the door and I didn't know if I had enough gas to get us back home.

Tom was a lean, looming skin with a quick mouth but dead eyes that reminded me of Frankenstein. A onetime football star at Chaminade, he was another of those former jocks who had detoured into punk as an excuse for beating the shit out of people in the pit and claiming he was just slamming like everybody else.

Drexel was Tom's shadow, a paunchy, shit-kicking hoosier from some one-moonshine-distillery Ozark flyspeck who had joined the scene with a religious fervor that bored anybody who knew him for longer than five minutes.

I tried to keep my eyes on the Urge. It was more of that ska-funk thing the local bands were putting on that had purists like Gene steaming. But Tom kept talking. He talked about skinhead solidarity. He talked about how hard it was for a workingman to make it in modern America. He mentioned his friends from Chicago and the operation they had.

First Tuesday of the month there was a drop-off and a pickup at Ugly Debbie's, a well-past-rotten biker bar in the badlands of Sauget just over the river and south of East St. Louis. Pills were left behind and cash taken back to Chicago. Tom and Drexel had a circuit of 7-Elevens and fast-food joints they worked all around the county. Even with Chicago's cut, each of them were netting hundreds a week.

"The thing is," Tom said with a low urgency, "we need help. Trustworthy people. Chicago wants to expand. There's a lot of untapped territory."

Drexel, a foot shorter and wider than Tom, nodded enthusiastically at it all.

"You're one of us!" Drexel shouted over the thundering amps, as we shook on it. I briefly wanted to ask about the 4/20 tattoos on their knuckles. But I figured it was just more skinhead arcana and a question would paint me as ignorant. I went money-blind fast.

Much later, Gene admitted that he knew Tom and Drexel

192 // St. Louis Noir

were in with the Hammerskins. And that they were probably in the group that pounced the black skater kid on Delmar the year before and put him in a coma. That night, though, he didn't want to confuse the issue by bringing all that up. By the time I found out, it was too late.

That was eight months ago. Every first Tuesday, I drove over the river and through those eerie blank streets where nature fought a winning battle against what was left of East St. Louis. I'd flash my still-new ID at the doorman and stalk through the smell of spilled beer and peanut dust to the back office. I left one padded envelope and walked out with another.

It wasn't a cartel-worthy operation.

"Son of a bitch," the potbellied owner would say to me each time, spitting tobacco juice into his KSHE 95 mug as he eyeballed Chicago's cut of the month's cash. "You fellas do this a little bit longer and I can afford to shut this shithole down. Those East St. Louis niggers are driving off my business anyway. I'm thinking you skinboys have got them right."

I grinned in a friendly manner and said nothing. Like cowards do.

The selling was simpler. Whenever we plugged in the Christmas lights strung around the Pillbox's front porch's splintered white railing, the store was open. Customers (Gene insisted on calling them that) entered through a creaking gate in the chain-link fence cordoning off the backyard. We sat on the two avocado-green couches that took up most of the back porch. I played cashier. Gene was the dispenser, giving out the little round orange pills from the Ralston-Purina giveaway fanny pack he strapped on just for the occasion. He loved handling the merchandise, saying they reminded him of the go pills his dad used to talk about the Air Force giving pilots.

Anderson stood in between the couches, his hand on the

butt of the Luger sticking out of his jeans. He loved guard duty so much that he magically kept that let-me-tell-you-something mouth of his shut during business hours. I assumed he was trying to perfect his gunslinger glare.

We sold to the chatty punks who heard about us through that narrow, gossipy St. Louis grapevine. We sold to the darting-eyed preps who needed all the college-prep help that SLUH or Priory wasn't giving them. We sold to the occasional strung-out adults, those stringy-haired and pop-eyed wraiths who said they just needed something to get through the week. We sold to a hundred people who could have been undercovers and put us all away for decades

We should have been picked up in a month and would have been eventually. But we were white people selling to white people, and that will always give you an edge in St. Louis.

Within a week the house's name had a new meaning. Everybody was buzzing. Our teeth rattled in our heads. Sleep was just a memory. The lights never turned off.

I had enough money to start buying groceries, and from the brand-name aisles. The Cutlass wasn't always running on fumes.

I even had a girlfriend, of sorts.

Paul, for Pauline, was a vinegary spitfire still in her junior year but easily five years older than me intellectually. She had no patience for Gene's skinhead politics or our business.

"Hey, Curly 2," Paul would snap at Gene when walking into the Pillbox like she lived there. "Where's Curly 1?"

She called all skinheads Curly. I was number 1, so that was something.

Paul worked nights behind the counter at an old storefront diner up on Manchester. It had been forgotten by everybody in the world except for me, Gene, and the four crypt-ready old men who spent all day arguing about the Cardinals and how the city was going to hell. We liked the endless refills and cheap doughnuts. She read worn-out paperbacks I didn't recognize by Proust and Borges and did her best to ignore everyone else. I considered it a triumph when she said more than three words to me.

She was a careless beauty with keen blue eyes and angled birdlike features underneath her spiky ruff of hair which changed hues on a three-week rotation. I fell for her at a party in the Central West End thrown by some slumming art-collector friends of Anderson's who liked rough trade. In the middle of my desperate conversation-making ventures, she caught sight of a mohawk poseur shoving his girl to the floor. Paul stalked over and uncorked an uppercut at the guy like she had taken sparring lessons. We found his tooth in a fishbowl on the other side of the room. The applause rattled the glassware.

I loved that underneath the crust she was a diligent West County girl who went to St. Joseph's Academy and was going to get a full academic ride—somewhere with ivy-covered walls—without breaking a sweat. Once my pestering wore her down, I couldn't get enough.

She was angry like me. But at least she had reason. Paul told me one night about what happened to her friend, the one they found last year dumped in the River des Peres, that glorified concrete drainage ditch not far from the Pillbox. It had been a huge story, a St. Joe girl getting murdered like that. Nobody could remember such a thing happening. But the case eventually went cold and the news moved on to other horrors.

Paul told me about what she would do to her friend's killer. I didn't think it was just hyperbole. I knew that I would want her avenging me.

At least once a week we exploded in some argument or another. I'd suggest she go fuck herself. But then I'd tell her she was right and she'd cock an eyebrow at me: "Of course I'm fucking right, Curly. Are we going to keep listing obvious things all night?" After those fights, we'd end up in my bedroom at the Pillbox. But she never stayed long.

Paul had one year of school left; she was blowing town the second she was done. It was clear as the pain on her face. As was the fact that I wouldn't be going with her when she left. But that summer, we flew high and ran fast. I was nineteen and suddenly indestructible. It was 1989 and anything was possible.

Then it all changed.

The August pickup started as just another night in Sauget. Since my life in the criminal underground had begun, I had barely exchanged words with Tom. Just a nod and a back clap if we crossed paths at a show. I was fine with this arrangement; he always put me on edge. It was as though he was quietly expecting something from me that he never articulated. The packages came in and the money went out. That was all it needed to be.

But that night I arrived earlier than normal and saw Tom getting out of his red Ford pickup. Because of the heat, he'd taken his T-shirt off. I parked one row away in the mostly empty lot. I was fixing on my fakest grin and adjusting the thick packet of cash bulging out the front pocket of my gray Dickies when I got a look at Tom's bare chest. If I hadn't remembered the insignia from history class, I would know it from all the illustrated books Anderson left around the Pillbox.

The tattoo was over a foot wide, covering Tom's gym-inflated pectorals. The eagle's wings were unfurled in a stiff art deco flourish, its head perched to one side, with a swastika inside a circle at its feet. A Wehrmacht eagle.

Tom saw me looking at it and slid his T-shirt back over his head slowly, as though performing some horrific reverse striptease.

I kept my stupid grin on and walked up, meaning to keep on going toward the bar. He turned to stride beside me.

"Business is good?" he asked.

I kept my voice even: "I don't have much to compare it to, but yeah. Seems to be."

"Good. Chicago says they're happy. It's a good business. Nice and clean. No messing around, you know?"

"Absolutely."

"Randall . . ." He paused, and I felt a question coming that I would not want to answer. "Let me ask you this."

"What's that?"

"You know that the business is good. But it can't be just about business for us. I need to know something. Do you have Pride?"

He said it just like that. As though I should hear the capitalization in his voice.

I said, "Of course." As though I knew what he were talking about.

"Good," he said.

We showed IDs to the doorman, who couldn't have cared less. Tom put his arm around me as we walked inside; it felt heavy with muscle. His mouth was right at my ear.

"The white man needs all the help he can get these days."

I didn't say anything. We did our business in the back, the owner said what he always said, and Tom and I returned to our vehicles.

"Say hi to Gene for me," Tom said.

I nodded.

Tom's face tensed, as though he had just thought of something important. I steeled myself, not wanting to hear it. Instead, he flicked a Sieg Heil into the air. He waited, his arm stiff and his eyes wide in the dim, buzzing glow from the moth-shrouded lights mounted on the roof of Ugly Debby's.

I yanked open the Cutlass's long, heavy door and threw myself inside. The engine roared to life and I peeled away. Looking back in the rearview, I saw Tom still standing there watching me, his salute slowly dropping.

Gene put on a disturbed look when I told him what happened. But he didn't think we needed to do anything rash. I told him I was done and that he needed to be too.

Paul was the most furious I had ever seen her. She hadn't been above prevailing on us to slide a few oranges her way, especially those nights when we stayed up until dawn and she had to work a morning shift. But then she told me she wouldn't have taken a fucking one of them if she knew where they came from. I countered that she hadn't seemed too curious about the source at the time. She batted that line aside like it was a mosquito.

We were on the porch, trying to decide what to do. The house was empty for once and the Christmas lights were off for good.

Paul tore into me first for not thinking about who I was getting involved with. As a skinhead, how could I not have known that 4/20 stood for Hitler's birthday?

Then she turned on Gene: "You know that Tom tells everybody he knows Metzger, right? Don't you think they're in with some people who don't need an excuse to have a boot party?" She pointed at me. "This idiot is so green he doesn't even know what color laces to wear in his Docs. He doesn't *know* those guys. You do. What the fuck were you thinking?" She folded her arms and waited. No good answer was forthcoming and she knew it.

I said I would take care of it. We would sell our month's supply in bulk back to Tom and Drexel, take whatever kind of loss we needed to. Just to get rid of it.

Then it would be back to the lumberyard.

"No," Gene sighed, "I'll handle it. I hope you like working for a living."

Two nights later, Paul and I were sitting in the kitchen by the Pillbox's one operational phone. Gene was supposed to call after the hand-off. "Easy payday for them," he had assured us. "They'll find somebody else to do this in five minutes."

Paul fiddled with the black laces on the still-gleaming oxblood Docs I had bought her with last month's take. They were the most expensive present I had ever bought anybody. Now I was worried she was going to see them as tainted by blood money.

The wall-mounted phone rang. I jumped up and snatched the receiver. It wasn't Gene.

"Is that Randy?" Tom asked.

"It is," I answered. Paul watched me, her hands still. We both vibrated in the kitchen's dead air.

"Are you one of the mud people?" Tom asked.

There was a ringing in my ears. I couldn't comprehend why I was talking to him and not Gene.

"What?"

"I want to know, *Randall*, who your people are. Where do you come from?"

My mother was German-Irish. My father too, though he

always claimed to have some Apache blood. In his mind, that excused his "wild" behavior. "Why do you care?" I asked.

"Because I'm convinced that only somebody with mud in their veins would stoop to such betrayal. Like your mongrel friend. He admitted that he couldn't prove pure Aryan heritage. I think that was the last thing he said. Except for, *Please don't*, of course." He chuckled.

I gripped the receiver. Until that moment it hadn't occurred to me that I had just two friends to speak of in the world.

And now one of them was gone.

I was given instructions and directions, then the line went dead.

Paul stood and put her arms around me. She never did that. For a moment I imagined the two of us just leaving. Isn't that how stories about teenagers in love should end? With the lovesick couple escaping to the west and leaving all their troubles behind? One problem was that I hadn't said that I loved her yet. The other problem was that I had been told what would happen if I didn't follow instructions. To me. To her.

They told me to meet them at a parking lot downtown, just north of Washington Avenue. I looked around at Manchester as I passed through, taking my time at all the lights and scanning for police. I pulled in just after midnight. It was a perfectly dead place, just another blank concrete slab that had probably once been a row of tenements housing the Irish back in the nineteenth century and then the blacks who came up from the South early in the twentieth.

Tom's truck and Drexel's white police surplus Chevy Caprice were parked at a right angle to each other, their hoods almost touching.

I stepped out into the stifling, Mississippi-sodden August night air. Not far away in one of the warehouse clubs on

Washington, some band was making a painful-sounding noise. I couldn't see or hear a single car. There were no pedestrians, of course. Urban renewal at its finest.

No words were spoken. Tom was standing by the back of his truck, with Drexel to his side. Both looked casual and all too pleased with themselves. They were both dressed the part, with polished Docs, cuffed jeans, white T-shirts, and braces up. I walked over quickly to get it done with and looked at what lay underneath the tarpaulin in Tom's truck.

Even in the dim light cast by the city's few-and-far-between streetlights, I could see that Drexel and Tom's boots had done their work and then some. Gene's favorite T-shirt, the Specials, was covered in blood and gravel and tar after he had been kicked from one set of steel toes to the next. His face was stippled with bloody smears, swollen and dark like it had been injected with some purple liquid. I was only thankful his eyes were closed.

My fists clenched so viciously tight I thought my knuckles would snap.

"What do you think, Mud?" Tom said, flipping the heavy tarp back over Gene's stupid, trusting face.

I worked on keeping my face blank. I remembered Paul. "I think Gene panicked and did something stupid," I told him.

"You got that right," Drexel said, leaning back against the hood of his car with a grin.

"Yes, indeed," Tom said, leaning in close to me. His voice softened, as he shifted from intimidation mode to soothing. "There's no reason that business can't go on like before, is there?"

"Absolutely not."

"Good. And I hope we'll be seeing a lot more of you from here on out."

"I don't see why not." My molars were grinding together so hard now I was sure that both of them could hear the sound.

Tom smiled, his teeth like falling-over tombstones. "Well, get on with it, then. Just liked we talked about."

I nodded, walked back to the Cutlass, and popped the trunk. I put the keys back in my pocket and leaned down. I clocked the time.

What happened next was all Paul's idea.

After the call came from Tom, we had stood in the kitchen, unable to move. Our nerves were screaming. Disengaging her hug, Paul placed her hands on my shoulders and looked up at me. She was quiet for a few seconds. Then she told me what to do. I didn't make a sound until she was done. Then I repeated it back to her, twice.

Tom had told me I was responsible for disposing of Gene's body. To help make up for all this inconvenience.

So when I straightened up from the trunk, Tom and Drexel were expecting to see me with a blanket. They didn't look surprised by the heavy yellow work gloves I wore at the lumberyard. It was going to be a messy job, after all.

The Mossberg in my hands was more of a shock.

Drexel was farther away and so a bigger risk for escape; he went first. I fired from the hip, not trusting myself to get the shotgun up to my shoulder in time. The slug caught him in the chest. It tore a glistening fist-sized hole in his T-shirt and knocked him back over the hood of his car. The sound echoed back at me from the dark hulking buildings scattered one and two blocks away.

I had been shooting the thing for so long in the Pillbox basement, in the proper stance with ear guards on, that I wasn't prepared for the flat boom and savage recoil. I almost dropped the shotgun in surprise.

Tom was just as stunned as I was. That gave me time to shift the shotgun to one hand and pull the Luger out of the trunk.

I looked at Tom, remembering how he had just thrown the tarp back over Gene like he was covering up something disgusting, and wanted to pull the trigger right then. But I remembered what Paul made me repeat to her. I walked toward Drexel's Caprice, keeping the shotgun held high and pointed at Tom's face.

"Take it easy," I said to Tom, as I reached Drexel. "You don't need to panic."

I had never actually seen the blood drain from somebody's face.

"First time you've had a gun on you, right?" I asked him, standing at a slight angle between him and Drexel so he couldn't see what my left hand was doing.

He tilted his head in what I assumed was agreement.

I shrugged. "Well, I can't say I know how it feels. But I'm sure it's not pleasant."

The adrenaline surging through me was making every hair stand on end. There was a roaring sound in my ears. Time was tight. But still, I needed to say something.

"I didn't even like Gene that much, you know. We spent a lot of time together, but it wasn't necessarily by choice. In a different life, we wouldn't even have been friends."

"So, why?" Tom finally asked me, his heavy brow wrinkled in confusion.

"I should say that it was because he took me in, kept me from turning homeless, that I grew to appreciate him the more time we spent together. But that's not what this is about. I don't have a lot of friends to spare, you see. And you just murdered one of them. Beat him to death."

I had reams of words ready to go, more than I had ever said at one time. Then I realized it was enough; I had already said it all.

I pivoted to the side, bringing Drexel's right hand up with my left. My gloved finger barely fit over his underneath the trigger guard. But when I squeezed, the Luger cracked off a round all the same.

I didn't wait to see if the first one hit. Given the awkward angle and me using my bad hand, I couldn't take chances. I pulled three or four more times; to this day I couldn't tell you exactly how it all went. At least two hit.

One blew a hole into Tom's upper chest, just above his tattoo, that was probably nonfatal on its own. But another round sailed right through Tom's throat, spraying a scarlet mist behind him that seemed to hang in the air for a moment as his body crumpled.

I don't remember much of the rest, except for fitting the Mossberg into Tom's hand, racking another shell, aiming at the air over Drexel, and pulling the trigger one last time.

More echoes. My time limit was already past.

I tossed Tom's truck, finding the padded envelope of pills in a pile of flattened Budweiser cans and White Pride leaflets.

I didn't look at Gene again. I had three dead faces I would now be seeing for the rest of my life. I didn't want those memories to be any fresher.

When I pulled away, Drexel was still sprawled over the hood of his car like a piece of road kill. One of his boots dangling off the side kept twitching.

As I slid past, it stopped. I looked at my watch: it was just two minutes after I had popped the trunk. If I was lucky, nobody would have called in a report about hearing shots fired yet.

I drove west, as planned, keeping off the highways. Nice and steady, just below the speed limit. I flushed the pills down the toilet in a Denny's near Crestwood Mall and dropped the gloves and padded envelope in the dumpster of a strip-mall Chinese restaurant in Sunset Hills. I pulled over three times, first to vomit and then twice more to dry heave.

I knew our plan had more holes in it than plan. I didn't know if Tom and Drexel were right- or left-handed; how thorough the police would be with ballistics; or whether they would wonder why Gene had been beaten to death and the other two shot. I didn't even know if the two of them were actually dead; it's not as though I knew how to check for a pulse. I didn't read mysteries. But the police would be coming around the Pillbox soon, asking questions. Anderson had been briefed on what to say. After giving up the weaponry, he had professed total allegiance. Nobody else knew anything.

I was aware of all the ways it could go wrong, but prayed that it wouldn't. I had at best another ten months with Paul before she skipped town after graduation. Another ten months to love her, to thank her for giving me the vengeance she never had, to hope that I would stay free for all of it.

I had scanned the vicinity for witnesses once more before driving away. There were none to be seen, just mute buildings and weed-sprouted sidewalks. That didn't mean, of course, that nobody had seen three skinheads driving into the parking lot and one leaving.

But then, maybe it wouldn't matter even if they had.

People never can tell one skinhead from another.

THE BRICK WALL

BY JOHN LUTZ

Interstate 64

Eddie Delgado was running third in his 88 car, the one he called *Lucinda*, and so far he hadn't been touched. Ahead of him was the 57 car, trailing smoke out from under the hood. It was the 43 car that concerned Eddie. A driver like the one behind the wheel of 43 wasn't much more than a kid, wasn't actually going to finish ahead of Eddie Delgado. Letting the kid race at the track Eddie owned and managed was one thing. Letting him win was quite another.

Eddie's Speed-O-Rama was one of those dirt tracks found on the outskirts of a lot of cities, where future big-name drivers learned their trade and established their careers. The cars were held together with wire and duct tape, their doors welded shut so they wouldn't fly open in rolls or collisions. Drivers were belted in tight, like infants in those contraptions that made babies look like miniature astronauts. *Baby steps,* Eddie sometimes thought. But dangerous as hell.

The drivers didn't mind the danger. In fact, they fed on it. This was where they learned to survive, and then to win. Legends had raced at Eddie's Speed-O-Rama before becoming champions.

Eddie could have moved up to important tracks like nearby Wentzville, but he didn't want to. He liked being right where he was. Where he owned the track. Where he felt at home and in control. He liked to win.

Four laps to go. Time to thrill the crowd. Eddie let out a loud series of yips no one could hear over the roar of engines. The smell of high octane was carried on the clouds of dust and clots of mud, the result of keeping the track wetted down so dust wouldn't consume the oval and spectators. Eddie slapped the gearshift lever with the heel of his hand and *Lucinda* picked up speed. He wasn't like a lot of drivers, who jammed cotton or rubber plugs in their ears. This was Midwest muscle with RPMs, horsepower, and plenty of noise. Nobody looked at speedometers. They all read *fast!* And decibels were part of the deal.

This, by God, was what Eddie lived for.

Racing beat-to-hell stock cars—souped-up but within the parameters that were possible with cars people drove to and from work—wasn't for pussies. Eddie liked to demonstrate that to people on Friday nights, then brag about it afterward at the Eight Banger Lounge. That Eddie was part owner of the Eight Banger made his victories all the sweeter and more profitable.

Coming out of a skidding turn into the straightaway, Eddie mashed down hard on the accelerator and *Lucinda* responded. She was hot to go, and a surge of confidence flowed through Eddie. He'd felt it before. It was a sensation he never wanted to feel for the last time. He knew he was going to win.

As he moved up on 57, over a car length per lap, he couldn't hear the crowd over the engines, but he knew it must be roaring. Ahead of him and off to his right, he could see people standing up, rising like an ocean wave.

He did actually hear them roar when he used 57's back draft to help sling *Lucinda* around the vehicle.

And there he was, tied with the 43 car going into the final lap.

Tricky. But strategy wasn't everything. There was something more important: what Eddie thought of as *gut time*. That was what made a race-car driver.

Halfway around the track, the two cars remained tied. The east turn was coming up, with its brick barrier to protect anyone crossing to use restrooms or buy food and drinks. Eddie eased left and fell back slightly.

The 43 car took the bait. Eddie let mud from 43 splatter his windshield for a few seconds, giving the young driver false hope. Then he gunned *Lucinda* and suddenly dropped to the inside of the track. He loved to drive against inexperience.

Now it was *Lucinda* dishing the dirt. But 43 gradually pulled even, surprising Eddie.

As they roared into the turn, both cars went into their controlled skids. If one driver didn't make a move soon, either one might win. There could even be a tie. One of those kissing-your-sister races that satisfied no one.

Eddie didn't have a sister. He couldn't tolerate a tie. And second place was unacceptable.

Blasting out of the curve, he increased his speed as he eased right. The 57 car had gotten back into it. All three lead cars were close together now, almost wheel to wheel. The 43 car suddenly moved to the inside, controlling enough of the track to seize the race and the glory. *Gut time*. Whoever went into the next turn first would win, with clear track ahead to the checkered flag. Whoever hesitated would go into the wall.

Eddie went hard into the turn immediately, dropping low on the banked track. Mud clots flew in the corner of his vision. Someone was dangerously close. He knew that if the 43 car went straight it might hit him. He might be killed. The driver in 43 must know that too.

Lucinda was overheated and faltering. The 57 car emitted

streamers of black smoke and fell back, and the inside lane was open. Half the inside lane. Would the young driver of 43 risk his life by squeezing past Eddie and brushing the wall, possibly killing both of them?

For that not to happen, Eddie would have to give ground.

Gut time.

The kid in 43 decided to clip the wall and pray.

And win if he survived.

Eddie Delgado was born in Texas but grew up in St. Louis. St. Louis was where he began driving competitively, first the midget autos, then stock cars. His winnings increased exponentially, until the accident, when he'd run into another car's wheel that had broken loose. That was when he took the time to heal, and bought a local racetrack from a promoter down on his luck.

Eddie continued to race. He'd been a terror when he was younger, and even now, when he chose to pencil himself into a race, he was often the winner. That was one reason his dirt track still brought crowds: they knew there was a chance they were going to see hometown legend Eddie Delgado race his battered but famous stock car, *Lucinda*.

The human Lucinda had been the first woman Eddie laid, and he might have married her. But once she found out about him, got to know him really well, she moved all the way to somewhere in Canada, where he wouldn't find her.

"The truth is," Mickey Dolan said, now that the race was history, "you didn't have to block 43 on the turn."

Mickey was a short, muscular man, with bushy black hair beginning to gray and the features of a bulldog saddened and eager for trouble. Mickey and Eddie had met and been teenagers together in Dogtown, gone to the same St. Louis schools, gotten into the same kinds of trouble. Together they had gone on a streetlamp-breaking binge, attempted to climb a 200-foot TV tower, tried to blow up a tree with a jug of gasoline and a rag wick. The truth was, they had more nerve than sense. Mickey's father had been a St. Louis cop; otherwise, the boys probably would have spent time in juvenile detention.

After high school graduation, they both joined the Marines. That changed things.

This sweltering late afternoon the two men were in Mickey's backyard. It seemed isolated but was only about a hundred yards from Interstate 64, one of the main east-west highways leading to and from downtown St. Louis. Where Mickey and Eddie sat, at a round white metal table with a green umbrella over it to protect from the sun, the highway was invisible beyond some trees and a prefabricated fence that fit together like some oversized construction toy. The idea was to mute the sound of traffic, and it worked pretty well. Now and then a horn honked. Or an emergency vehicle with a siren passed. When the highway was crowded, like during rush hour or before or after a Cards or Rams game, you could smell the exhaust fumes that filtered through the trees. Both men enjoyed that.

"Are you saying I should have given 43 a break and lost the race so your son could notch a win?"

"You know I didn't mean that," Mickey said. "I simply meant you didn't have to block him. You could have given Alan a shot, seen if his car had it."

On the table were a couple of cork coasters and a blue vinyl cooler bag that held ice and six bottles of Schlafly beer. Mickey unzipped the cooler and shoved it over so Eddie could grab a bottle. Then he reached across the table, got one for himself, and removed the twist-top cap. These were veteran beer drinkers—neither man chose to use a glass.

Eddie took a long pull and wiped foam from his upper lip. "I own the racetrack, Mick. It's for stock car racing. Except for demolition derbies, that's what race cars do, try not to get passed."

"There are rules."

"Written and unwritten."

"It's a local dirt track," Mickey said. "Small time. It's not Indy or the Grand Prix."

Eddie shrugged. "A race is a race. And you might take a look behind you at your fine house, bought with prize money mostly won at Eddie's Speed-O-Rama. You're the one who decided it was time for your son to take on some of the competition."

"Alan was ready. He raced stock cars all over the country."

"Then he should have expected me to pass on the last turn. You might feel bad about it, and I don't blame you, but it's the life Alan chose to live, and, short though it was, he lived it."

With your approval hung in the air.

"The Marines made him think like that, like he could do any damn thing he tried."

"You and the Marines," Eddie said. "Alan thought he had the balls to break me on the track."

"You could have let him pass."

"It's not in my nature. Or in Alan's. Or in yours, Mick."

Unseen beyond the trees, the six-lane traffic on I-64 was building to a low, steady roar, reminding Mickey of the sea. He used to enjoy sitting at his outside table, drinking Schlafly, listening to that sound. He didn't like it so much anymore, now that Alan was gone. He tried to ignore the sound but couldn't.

It was almost rush hour, when all the yuppies and white-collar drones returned to their hives. It seemed they all drove I-64 to or from the western suburbs. Mickey thought sometimes it would be smart for them all to switch houses.

Eddie seemed not to notice the noise, even as the traffic increased. Maybe he'd spent too much time around race cars, listening to them howling and reaching for speed. Soon the noise would level off, as the cars slowed in heavy traffic until they were creeping for home. Sometimes, on burning-hot days like this, they would come to a complete stop. That was when the highway looked like nothing so much as a long parking lot.

Mickey sipped his beer and said, "It's true my son lived the kind of life he wanted, Eddie, maybe even died the death he would have chosen."

"So what's your complaint, Mick?"

"You hurried things along."

"He was good at his job," Eddie said, "and it *was* his job."

"So you got the checkered flag, and Alan got the brick wall."

Eddie planted his elbows on the table, but the metal was too hot so he quickly removed them and sat back. It was a typical July day, and there were crescents of perspiration beneath the armpits of his shirt. "There's nothing any of us can do about it now, Mick, except to say we're sorry."

"You're *sorry* you cut Alan off so it would be you or him at the wall?"

"There's a difference between sorry and guilty, Mick."

Mickey took a long sip of Schlafly and set the bottle on its coaster with exaggerated care, as if he might be afraid his hand would tremble. "Alan was moving up fast. You should have let him pass."

"That's not the way it works, Mick, letting people pass. That kind of thinking is how wars are lost. We're all sorry. To hear you say it, we're all guilty. You, your ex-wife, everyone."

"Don't forget yourself, Eddie. Alan chose to take a chance rather than let you win."

Eddie smiled. It wasn't a nice smile. In fact, there was something rapacious in it. "Like you taught him, Mick."

"We both taught him."

"Sooner or later we all make the choice he made, if we become winners. That's what it comes down to. We roll the dice in these beat-to-shit high-speed cars and take the ultimate and winning risk."

"You let him roll the dice and die, Eddie."

Eddie's face got flushed, then hard. "I treated him just the way I'd treat any other driver trying to take over my race." He finished his beer, then leaned across the table, looking hard at the other man. "What really bothers you, Mick, is that if you'd been in my place, you'd have given him the same choice. He could risk passing and maybe win, or maybe hit the wall. Or he could settle for second."

Eddie put down his empty bottle and stood up, scraping metal chair legs. He wiped perspiration from his forehead with the back of his wrist.

There was a series of chimes, and he wrestled his cell phone from his pocket. He said "Yes" four times, then broke the connection and laid the phone on the table. "I gotta take a piss."

"Go ahead," Mickey said. "The house is unlocked." He watched Eddie walk across the wide lawn to the house. He thought it was odd that, while he blamed Eddie Delgado for killing his son, he was sure the guy wouldn't steal anything from the house. Trust between longtime friends was a strange thing.

* * *

On the way out of the house, Eddie picked up a small crystal ashtray and slipped it into his pocket. He wasn't sure why.

Mickey didn't get up when Eddie returned, but he leaned back in his iron chair that looked too small for him.

"What they say is right," Eddie said. "We don't drink beer, only rent it." He propped his fists on his hips and made no move to sit down. "I got a business to run, Mick."

"It's hot out, and the traffic is thick this time of day." Mickey slid the vinyl cooler across the table. "You'll want this."

Eddie stared at him.

"A gift from me to you, Eddie," Mickey said with a smile.

Eddie was suspicious. *Was* this a gift? Or some kind of wise-ass comment? Had he somehow been seen pilfering the ashtray? Eddie played dumb and said, "The question is, why?"

Mickey shrugged. "The I-64 traffic is murder. You're gonna have a hot drive home. You got four more iced beers in there."

"Let's each have another before I leave," Eddie said.

"Sounds good."

Eddie removed two beers and handed one to Mickey. They wiped dampness from the bottles with their shirttails and twisted off the caps. Eddie raised his bottle in a casual toast to Mickey, who hesitated, then returned the gesture and took a long pull.

Within minutes, both bottles were empty.

"I'll get the cooler back to you," Eddie said, standing up. The beer, or something, was making him sweat as if he'd been out running in the summer heat.

"Whenever you think of it," Mickey replied.

Eddie was lowering himself into his silver Porsche, when

Mickey, standing at the wooden deck rail and looking down at him in the driveway, said, "There's one more thing, Eddie."

Eddie Delgado was about to start the Porsche's engine. Instead, he just sat there in the sleek convertible and looked up at Mickey. It was hot all right, here in the sun, and Eddie wanted to get the car moving so there was a breeze. He wasn't in a mood to put up with more of Mickey's bullshit. He kept his voice modulated, but the irritation came through: "What is it now, Mick?"

"I've got a shotgun here." Mickey held up a double-barreled twelve-gauge where it could be seen, then laid it on the rail. "If you move to start your engine or get outta the car, I'll use it."

Eddie didn't think Mickey had the balls to aim and fire a shotgun at him. On the other hand, he'd seen Mickey do some crazy things on the racetrack. That was why he was a winner. That was why they were friends. Or something like friends.

"Am I gonna get another speech, Mick?"

"Short one."

Eddie made himself smile. "Fire away."

"I thought about that," Mickey said. "Had a better idea. Fairer."

"Fairer to who?"

"Both of us. We're gonna let God decide, like He usually does in matters of life and death."

"Decide what?"

"Whether you murdered Alan just so you could win a race."

"Hurry it up then, Mick. I've gotta drive all the way into the city, and traffic is building up while we're here flapping our gums."

"You got a cooler on the seat next to you. Inside it, you got two unopened bottles and four empties."

Eddie thought back. Mick *had* put the empties, even their bottle caps, back into the cooler when the bottles were empty. Not like him to be so neat.

Unless he had a reason.

"So you and I each drank two beers," Mick said. "The kind with the twist-off caps."

"What's that got to do with it?"

"I opened one of the six bottles we started off with, added some poison, then replaced the cap. When I put that bottle in the cooler with the other five, I couldn't tell one from the other. I was careful of that."

"You can't put those twist-top caps back on a bottle."

"You can if you try," Mickey said. "Squeeze hard with a washrag and lean into them. And I only doctored the beer and replaced the cap on one bottle. Tried it on two or three, and finally got the hang of it so you can't tell one bottle from another."

Eddie's mind was working furiously, trying to put everything together, figure out what it meant.

"Either you or me," Mickey said, "already drank poison. Or there's poisoned beer in one of the two unopened bottles you still got in the cooler."

"What kind of poison we talking about, Mick?" Eddie could feel a tightening in his throat.

"I can't recall. It's tasteless and got a Latin name."

"Just like me, right, Mick?"

Mickey treated the question as rhetorical. "What'll happen is, once you drink this stuff, it's over for you. You— or I—won't feel any different for about half an hour after drinking the laced bottle, then it'll be harder and harder

216 // St. Louis Noir

for us to breathe. Then we won't be able to breathe at all."

Eddie realized he was soaked with sweat. "Which bottle is it in, Mick?"

"I honest-to-God don't know, Eddie. I put the six of them in without looking so I wouldn't be able to tell one from the other. Only God knows. In less than half an hour, one of us will be with Him and understand."

"I'm not gonna drink either beer," Eddie said.

"Your choice. Maybe you already downed the poisoned bottle. Or maybe I did."

"This isn't fair, Mick!"

"You still mad about that tasteless crack?"

"You damn well know what I mean!"

"It is fair, Eddie. We're starting even, like in a race, and only one of us will be alive when it's over. Time to take that chance."

"But I didn't agree to take *this* chance!"

"That's how it is with chances. I think Alan would have said death shouldn't be part of the learning curve."

"Mick! Please!"

"The nearest hospital is right off 64. There'll be an exit sign you can't miss. You might even have time to get your stomach pumped, just in case you already downed the poison."

"I know where the nearest hospital is! But in this traffic—"

Mickey aimed the shotgun.

Eddie started the engine. He raised the canvas top and turned on the air conditioner. Then he crammed the gearshift lever into reverse, backed up, and roared out of the driveway.

Eddie passed from sight, but Mickey stood and listened for a while as the Porsche accelerated. Rubber screeched on pavement. Eddie driving hard for a street that would lead to an

I-64 entrance ramp. The trouble was, I-64 was clogged with traffic this time of evening. Most of the vehicles weren't even moving.

Mickey went inside the house, leaned the shotgun behind the door, and sat in his usual armchair. He used the remote to switch on the TV and find the weather channel.

Five minutes of chatter into how St. Louis was suffering one of the worst heat waves in years, the traffic copter came on with a view west along I-64. The airborne announcer opined that traffic was so backed up that the scene below might as well be a photograph. Mickey leaned forward and squinted at the TV. He thought he might be able to spot Eddie's silver Porsche, but he couldn't.

Eddie zoomed around traffic until he found himself trapped on the shoulder by a stalled delivery van and a car with its hood up. He eased the Porsche back into the traffic lane, which immediately stopped moving.

His chest felt heavy, and he was having trouble inhaling. Or maybe it was his imagination. His dread.

He remembered his cell phone and discovered that it was damaged and not working. As if someone had stepped on the damned thing. Mickey! He must have broken the phone when Eddie went in the house to take a leak. Eddie felt another pocket and came up with the tiny crystal ashtray. Why had he picked it up in the house and slipped in into his pocket? He didn't even smoke.

Eddie turned off the engine to conserve gas, then walked from car to car until he found a woman who would let him borrow her cell phone. Standing there holding the sweat-slippery thing, he wasn't sure who to call. 911? The police? To report a murder? They'd laugh when he told them he was the victim. The woman was staring at him, her flushed face easy to read: she wanted her phone back before tomorrow. Eddie started to punch 911, then thought of an even faster way to get help in the creeping hell of traffic. He called information, then the Barnes-Jewish Hospital.

The woman he spoke with had an annoying, strictly-business tone. It was no way to talk to a dying man.

"You said you were the victim?" she said, seeming not at all impressed or curious about conversing with a doomed man.

"Yes, I've been poisoned."

"How do you know?"

"He told me."

"He?"

"My friend Mickey."

"He the one poisoned you?"

"Yes."

"Some friend."

"Listen, damnit!"

"Do you know what kind of poison?"

"No. And it's tasteless."

"Then how do you know you've taken it?"

"I don't! Not for sure. That's the point!"

"You know nothing about this poison?"

"No! *Yes!* It has a Latin name."

"Where are you located now, sir?"

"I'm on I-64, driving east toward McKnight. Or trying to drive."

"You're too ill to drive?"

"No, no! I'm fine. Other than being poisoned!"

"Continue as you are toward Kingshighway, then—"

"I know how to get there, but I can't! You don't understand. The goddamn traffic!"

"The Cardinals play the Cubs tonight, sir."

"I know *why* there's traffic. But the poison . . ."

"With the Latin name?"

"Yes! Yes!"

A nearby voice said, "I need to talk to my sister."

Eddie looked over and saw the woman who'd lent him the cell phone. She wanted it back. He raised his forefinger to beg for one more minute talking with the woman at the hospital. The woman who might save his life.

"My car can't move and is almost out of gas," he explained. "I haven't got anything safe to drink. I'm on a borrowed cell phone. POISON IS COURSING THROUGH MY VEINS!"

"I think you'd better get yourself right in here," the woman on the phone said. "Continue driving east toward Kingshighway—"

"Listen, damnit! I need someone to come get me in a chopper. That's the only way fast enough to save me. You have a helicopter, don't you?"

"You mean me personally?"

"No, I mean the hospital. If a person is dying, can't your helicopter—"

"Our helicopters are all in service, sir. In this terrible heat, people—"

"I know! I know! But . . ." Eddie thought he might be weeping. Or was it perspiration streaming down his face and burning the corners of his eyes?

"My phone!" the voice beside him demanded.

Eddie knew he had to give it back. One last thing to say: "Mickey Logan did this."

"Is Mr. Logan another victim?" the woman on the phone asked.

"Who the hell are you? Are you a nurse?"

"I'm not a nurse."

"I want to speak to someone with authority!"

"You got what you get. I'm a volunteer. I decided to help out because of the accident. A caravan of busses stopped too fast on the way to the ballpark and ran into each other. Front to back. *Bang! Bang! Bang!* Traffic folded up like an accordion. No one in the Cubs bus was hurt, because they were in last place."

"Is this a joke? Is this a goddamned *joke*?"

"Only if you're a Cub," the woman said.

"Listen! I was serious!"

"No ifs or buts," the woman beside Eddie said. She advanced on him in a way that suggested imminent combat. "I want my phone. Now! I was nice enough to lend it to you."

He handed her the phone. The heat seemed to shrivel him.

This is hell.

"You could say thank you," the woman told him.

But he didn't. He simply trudged back to his Porsche. It was a convertible. He could lower the top, get a little cool air that way. Also a lot of sun.

He knew that if he lowered the top he would fry like bacon.

Mickey leaned forward in his armchair for a better view of the traffic jam on TV. Some cars were pulled to the shoulder, overheated. Others were sitting still with their doors hanging open. A few drivers were out of their vehicles and walking around, trying to find shade.

Mickey knew there was no shade in hell. He looked carefully at the TV screen but didn't see a silver Porsche.

On the late news, however, it was reported that traffic had

been horrendous, especially in such withering heat. Three people had died, including a man in a Porsche on I-64.

Cause of death in all three cases had been heat exhaustion, even though the man driving the Porsche had a small cooler of beer in his car containing two unopened bottles, and could have remained hydrated.

Mickey turned the thermostat down a few degrees, then went to the refrigerator for a cold beer.

Wondering how things would have worked out if he'd actually put poison in one of the bottles.

PART IV

ACROSS THE RIVER

PART IV

Across the River

TELL THEM YOUR NAME IS BARBARA

By L.J. Smith

East St. Louis, IL

S itting on a plush barstool in my favorite watering hole—legs crossed, suited down in Armani, rich-bitch-litigator posture—I watch Dolly mix my Grey Goose martini with skills born of twenty years of bartending in the most prestigious bar in black St. Louis. As Dolly places the martini in front of me—her nineties neck-plunging Norma Kamali jumpsuit revealing cleavage and champagne-stopper nipples poking through skimpy spandex—I have to admit she still looks damn good.

Club owner Steve Charles, who fancies himself the black Sinatra, sings "Fly Me to the Moon." Every Thursday night Steve and the band, Jazz Classique, entertain his guests while Dolly keeps the drinks coming with smooth precision.

He works the room, singing into the cordless mic. He grabs one of the customers and starts swing dancing with her and the whole room is finger popping and slapping five as Steve puts on his show. Enjoying the view, I take a Dunhill from my sterling case. From behind me, Lance reaches around with a flame to light it, nestling his lips in the nape of my neck and moaning as he takes in my fragrance.

He whispers, "I see my money is keeping you lookin' and smellin' good. You smell so good, you givin' me a hard-on."

"Yeah, but I ain't the one, sweetheart," I inform him as I wipe his vapor off my neck. "If you would keep your ass out of trouble, I wouldn't have so much of your money, but what the hell. Keep doing what you're doing. I don't want to mess up my job security."

Lance, one of my oldest clients, can't see why he can't make a career distributing dope to street hustlers. The police can't get his employees to rat him out, out of fear for their lives and their families. Besides, the street hustlers don't care about getting locked up because Lance has some high-ranking police officials who manage to get evidence lost and cases dropped.

He slips a package into my jacket pocket. "This should make us even on what I owe you for court last week. Dolly, pour me a Rémy Martin straight up and put it on Kaycie's tab."

I call Michael. I love listening to Steve Charles, but I'm not about to sit here with all this dope in my pocket when I could be partying. I'm ready to get my freak on. Lance's drink is gone in two gulps.

"Give him another one on me, Dolly, and keep the change." I place a fifty on the bar and point my key fob toward where my Jaguar is parked.

"I'm on the way, baby," I purr into my cell, "but I have to stop by the office to pick up my works."

Kaycie Crawford—Attorney at Law, reads the brass sign on my storefront office in the Central West End. I enter through the security gate around back, close the blinds, and notice my phone blinking.

"Hello, hello! Ms. Crawford, this is Mr. Jacobsen from the Lindell Suites Condo Association. I need to talk to you about your

back HOA fees. Our lawyers are about to file to foreclose. Please call me so we can work out a payment arrangement."

I really don't want to hear this shit right now so I shut off the machine. I got clients who want to pay me in dope, jewelry, or hot clothing from Neiman Marcus. They know I like to look good and a few of them know I like to get high. I have to find some money from somewhere fast. My $5,000 monthly allowance from the family trust fund isn't due to hit my bank account for a couple of days. I can't let them white folks set me out on the street.

I decide to take a hit before I head over to Michael's. It won't take me but five minutes to get there from here. Just one more hit . . . then another . . .

My iPhone won't stop ringing and I'm frozen in the chair at my desk ignoring Michael's picture when it pops up . . . *Damn!* It's two hours later, and all the dope is gone.

"Kaycie, what's up, baby? It's twelve o'clock, I thought you would be here by now. Why didn't you answer the damn phone?"

I tell him I forgot where I put my pipe and left my phone in the car.

"Yeah, right! So why do you sound like you got rocks in your mouth? But that's okay, do me any kinda way. I've been sitting here waiting to get high with you, drink martinis, and have freaky sex, and you over there geekin' all by yourself!"

"I'll call Lance to bring me a sixteenth and then I'll be over."

"Forget it, Kaycie! I'm half-drunk, tired, and I'm going to bed. I'll talk to you later." *Click.*

Fuck him, then. Michael never has any money to put on a package anyway. I'm the one who buys the dope, and I bought that Grey Goose he got drunk on. Let me call Lance to see if he can bring me another one.

A half an hour passes and Lance hasn't answered his phone. I'd go back to Steve Charles's, but I know I look a mess after smoking a half-ounce of cocaine. In the office bathroom, I wash up and change into a turtleneck and jeans. I see the $2,000 leather coat I charged at Neiman's last week in my closet, tagged and still in the plastic. I tear the plastic and the tags off and put it on, forgetting that I intended to take it back to the store.

The back door opens and Jimmy and Jeremy enter, swooning and recapping the wedding. Jimmy looks like a black James Bond in his Yves Saint Laurent tuxedo and his bow tie untied, and Jeremy's in shirtsleeves with his jacket slung over his shoulder, both such beautiful men that a threesome fantasy flashes in, then out of my mind.

"Hey, Jimmy, what are you all doing here?" I ask, surprised.

"I left the directions to the East St. Louis after-party on my desk. How's tricks at Steve Charles's place?"

"Same old songs, but I like the vibe. I was just going to call you," I lied. "Do you know where I can get a nice package this time of night?"

Jeremy says he wouldn't mind having a little happy dust to take over to the party. Jimmy is aware of my habit and I know his extended family has connections, but this is the first time I've asked him about scoring any dope.

"I can take you over to my cousin's on West Bentley. How much you want to spend?"

"I got about five hundred on me. You all want to go in with me?"

Jimmy is hesitant but Jeremy reaches into his inside pocket and pulls out three hundred-dollar bills.

"Yeah, I'm game, we need a little pick-me-up since we're going over to the East Side."

The lovebirds pile into the backseat of my Jaguar and Jimmy directs me over to the 3900 block of West Bentley. It's one o'clock in the morning and the lounges are just closing. We park in front of a house with a dim porch light. The street is dark, the streetlight flickering, half-bare tree limbs hovering over the front yard in the early October chill.

"Didn't they used to call this neighborhood the Bucket of Blood?" asks Jeremy.

"That's when John's Canteen was still open," Jimmy says. "It used to be a lot of cuttin' and shootin' on this block. I haven't been over here since I finished school. I worked hard to get out of this neighborhood, but if my baby wants some happy dust . . ." Jimmy kisses Jeremy. "Okay, give me your money and I'll be right back."

"Wait a minute, Jimmy," I protest, "this is a lot of money we're talking about spending. I wanna see what I'm buying. You think we can get a couple of ounces for eight hundred?"

"Kaycie, this is a known crack house. You have too much to lose if you're caught transacting business here."

"I've got too much to lose just sitting out in the car too! Anyway, it's quiet."

"Yeah, it is. That's what scares me."

"Well, I'm staying in the car," says Jeremy. "I don't want to get my tux dirty."

"Jimmy, I'm comin' in," I insist.

"All right, all right, but don't tell them your real name. Tell them your name is . . . Barbara."

I follow Jimmy through the squeaking gate, a dog barking as it clangs shut. The front yard is devoid of vegetation except for a few tufts of weeds and fallen leaves. Loud music comes from inside and Jimmy knocks hard several times before the volume is lowered and a raspy voice bellows out, "Who is it?"

"It's Jimmy, Wanda, open the door!"

"Jimmy who? I don't know no damn Jimmy! What the fuck you want?"

"It's Jimmy Mack, your cousin, fool. Open the damn door, it's cold out here."

Two deadbolts turn, a chain drops, a metal bar slides away, and the door opens to a warm, cozy living room. Keith Sweat's "Make It Last Forever" plays in the background.

"Hey, Jimmy, what's up? Ain't seen you in a month of Sundays," Wanda says, turning one of the locks behind us. "You done got your education and stop comin' by to hang out with us . . . Look at you, all dressed up. Where you goin'?"

"I'm on my way to a wedding after-party and we want to get a nice package to take with us."

"Who is we?" she asks, peeping through the window shade on the front door. "This your woman?" she adds and snickers.

Wanda wears a bright yellow halter dress, a black silk flowered shawl, and a huge pistol grip sticks out of her cleavage. She's holding a pint of cheap vodka smeared with red on the bottle's mouth. A heavy-set, middle-aged woman, her hair's pulled back tight in a tiny ponytail, and her lips are slathered with red lipstick.

"That's Barbara. She's a good friend of mine and she wants to comp a couple of ounces. I know you still dealin' 'cause I see you still carrying Ole Ugly in your bosom."

"A .357 ain't no fashion accessory. I ain't got that kinda weight here, but I can call Kenny. He's just around the corner on Westbrook. You remember Kenny, don't you?"

"You talkin' about Little Kenny, Jackie's youngest boy?"

"Yep. Me and him work together as a team. He runs the

neighborhood." Wanda calls him on her cell phone, walks toward the hallway mumbling into it, then comes back into the living room.

"Kenny was a smart little boy," Jimmy comments, "I would have thought he'd be in college by now."

"He *is* in college, goddamnit—street college!"

I start laughing and Wanda invites us to sit down, turns the volume back up on the CD player, and starts swaying to the moanings of Keith Sweat. I can't stand Keith Sweat, but I bob my head to the music to act like I'm happy to be in this stuffy, quaintly decorated room.

"Is that your car, Jimmy?"

"It's mine."

"What kinda of car is that, uh . . . what's your name again?"

"Her name is Barbara," Jimmy answers, just in case I forgot.

"You look like money, Barbara. What you do for a livin'?"

Boom—boom, boom, boom, boom!

Before I can think of a lie, Wanda looks out the window of the front door and turns the deadlock. In walks Kenny, a tall, beautiful young man, well groomed, expensive cologne, solemn face. I can't stop looking at him.

"Who is that sitting outside in that Jaguar, Wanda? I told you about people sitting outside looking like they waiting to cop."

"Look, Killa, don't be comin' in here with that bullshit. He's with Jimmy and them!"

"What's up, Jimmy!" Kenny reaches out to slap him a manly handshake. "Ain't seen you in a long time."

"Yeah, well, I moved on to bigger and better things. I see you looking good, prosperous. How old are you now, nineteen, twenty?" Kenny doesn't answer. "How's your mama doin'?"

"She's on disability, works part time at Nelson's liquor store. She still lives around the corner."

Kenny looks over at me then turns to Jimmy. "So what's up?"

"You tell me. What's with this *Killa* shit?"

"That's what Wanda calls me. It keeps the scallywags in line."

"We want to get a couple ounces, man . . . for eight bills."

Kenny takes a long look at Jimmy with a smirk on his face. "All right, man, since you spending that kinda cash, come on to the back."

As I stand up to follow them, Kenny pauses and turns to Jimmy: "Who is this?"

"That's Barbara. She's cool. She's the one with the money."

"Is that your Jag out there?"

"Yeah, it is."

In the kitchen he lays down two large plastic sacks of powder on the glass table. I pick them up, open one, dampen my pinky with my tongue, and taste the product. I nod approval and count out eight hundred-dollar bills on the table. Kenny picks them up quickly, walks down the hallway, and exits, slamming the door. Wanda locks it behind him and comes back to the kitchen.

"Uh, what's up, Jimmy?"

He knows exactly what she's expecting. He opens his package, pulls one of his business cards from his inside jacket pocket, and scoops out a hefty portion of powder.

I see Wanda has baking soda sitting on the counter. "You mind if I rock this powder up?" I ask.

Wanda grabs a cigarette out of her pocket and lights it as she ponders the request. "So you one of those high-society crackheads who knows how to cook dope?"

"Don't let my looks fool you, Wanda," I answer. "I know my way around this shit."

Jimmy balks and gives me an *I'm not about to stay here* look. "Wanda, let me talk to Barbara for a minute."

Wanda leaves the room.

"Look, Kaycie. Me and Jeremy use powder, we don't smoke that shit. How about you stay here to do what you got to do and I'll take your car to the after-party. You can catch a cab home. Let me talk to Wanda. She's cool. She ain't gonna do nothing to you."

I'm so eager for another hit, I don't protest. Jimmy goes to the front room to talk to Wanda and soon they both come back to the kitchen.

"Jimmy, be careful with my car, hear? Let me have thirty dollars for cab fare and you can drop my car off at work."

"Wanda, is that cool with you?" Jimmy asks.

"Yeah, it's cool. I like your style, Barbara. You got class."

My plan was to cook up the powder, leave some with Wanda, and catch a cab to Michael's, but after listening to music, talking about our love lives, and drinking a fifth of rot-gut vodka, it's four o'clock in the morning before I call a cab. I arrive home, shower, and get four hours of sleep before waking up. I call a cab to take me to the courthouse.

When I arrive there's a long line of people waiting to be scanned for weapons and contraband. I stand in line with eight other lawyers with motions for continuances. At eleven thirty, I'm out of there and I call Jimmy to check who's called.

"Lance returned your call this morning and a cashier's check for ten thousand came from the Jeffersons for their son's armed burglary case."

"Thanks, Jimmy. I'll be there in a few minutes."

I usually bank the legal fees but right now I have to use it to keep afloat because of my recreational activities. Luckily, it's enough to stop the foreclosure proceedings on my condo. Before I leave I get a call from Lance.

"Kaycie, one of my boys, Kenny Rollins, has been locked up for murder. He's downtown and needs a lawyer."

"I'm on the way," I tell him, and then I ask Lance about Kenny.

"I've been knowing him since he was a little boy. His mother has been struggling with drugs just about all his life. Kenny has to pay her rent and bills to keep her from getting kicked out. He's been trying to beat a case where he claims a detective name Lakewood planted a bag of crack in his pocket when he couldn't find any other reason to detain him during what the detective called a 'routine traffic stop.'"

An hour later I'm led into the holding cell. Kenny's perfectly featured face is scratched, swollen with dried blood in the corners of his mouth, and oily sweat stains smear both sides of his face. He looks like a defeated pit bull, hunched over, elbows resting on his knees, his hands cuffed. He glances up when the guard opens the cell and stares at me, stunned.

"Hey, Kenny. I'm Kaycie Crawford. Lance called me to represent you. What happened to your face?"

"Don't worry about it, Barbara—or whatever the hell your name is. I sure don't need a motherfucking crackhead for a lawyer."

"You'd be surprised how many crackhead police, lawyers, and judges are out there. One thing for certain, you're the one caught up in jail, not me. Now, do you want me to help you or not?"

Kenny looks at me again, humbled at the possibility of being sent up. "I guess you must be okay if Lance called you."

"Lance is one of my oldest clients. You see, he hasn't been convicted of anything yet. So talk to me."

"The police found one of my customers dead in the gangway in the 3900 block of Westbrook. Her name is Maxine Robinson and her husband, Grady, is one of my associates."

"How did she pay for her dope?"

"She was a substitute teacher over at the Delmar Middle School by day and a dope fiend by night. Grady is a good shade-tree mechanic, but he can't keep a job in a shop very long."

"Why is that?"

"Grady works on the hustlers' cars in the alley, sometimes for cash, sometimes for hits, sometimes to pay his dope bills. Maxine was the one with the steady income."

"How did she die?"

"She was beat to death. The police showed me a picture with her face bashed in and her body all twisted. They say they found my fingerprints on her purse there on the ground."

"How did your fingerprints wind up on her purse?"

"The goddamn police is lying! They ain't found my fingerprints. They just trying to set me up because they ain't never caught me ridin' or walkin' dirty."

"What do you mean, *riding or walking dirty?*"

"They've been trying to catch me slinging dope for the past year. I don't walk around with that shit on me. I don't carry it when I drive my car or when I'm hangin' out on the block."

"So you're telling me they manufactured fingerprints to put on her purse? Come on now, stop lying. Out of all the folks who hang out in that neighborhood, how did they pick you out? Have you ever been arrested before?"

"Nope. For the longest time they didn't even know what I

looked like, they just knew the name Kenny, nicknamed Killa. It wasn't until that narc Lakewood pulled me over and planted that dope on me that he found out who I was. They booked me in night court, locked me up."

"You still haven't told me how your fingerprints got on Maxine's purse."

"Maxine owed me a hundred dollars and she was ducking and dodging me for a week. She got paid last Friday. When I caught up with her ass Friday afternoon, she come talkin' 'bout she ain't got it. She was higher than a jet pilot. She had just got off work, it wasn't even four o'clock yet. I slapped the shit out of her ass and snatched her purse and emptied it out on the ground, picked up her wallet, and took out her debit card. I hauled her ass to the ATM around the corner at the liquor store and I got my money."

"So Kenny, where did you take her then?"

"Nowhere. I left her ass in the parking lot and drove off. They got cameras, they'll show that I drove off. Once I got my money, I was through with her ass. I got no reason to kill her. She's still one of my best customers. Hell, she got a job."

"How hard did you hit her, Kenny? Was she bleeding?"

"Yeah, she was bleeding and her lip swelled up, but I didn't care. The customers saw me dragging her to the cash machine, but they looked away, minding their own business."

"Well, now you got a witnesses who saw you dragging a women into the store bleeding and swollen around the mouth. That's not good at all. The police say she was killed late Friday night or early this morning. Where were you?"

"I spent the night at my baby mama's house."

"What's her name and where does she live?"

"Her name is Fulani James. She lives in the Ville on St. Louis Avenue."

"Kenny, I charge $2,500 for a retainer and $1,000 per day. Can you handle that?"

"I'll get you your money. Just don't you smoke it up."

Just then, a deputy sheriff arrives to take him to his arraignment, and so I miss my chance to tell Kenny to go fuck himself.

Kenny is remanded. Lance is in the courtroom and suggests I go home with him so that we can talk more about the case.

When we get to Lance's loft, he goes into his bedroom, comes out counting thirty-five hundred-dollar bills on the spot, and lays them on the kitchen counter.

"Kenny's pretty face and good manners fool a lot of people. He can be treacherous," Lance says. "He tells me he wants to get into the real estate business."

"Do you think he's innocent?"

"Kaycie, that's not my concern. My concern is that you win this case. I am fond of Kenny and I want to see him make something of himself."

Jaimie Brown is a private investigator. I still owe her $2,000 for my last case and she won't answer my calls. I leave a message telling her I have her money and after thirty minutes she calls me back.

"Okay, so you have the two grand you owe me, but I want my fee for this case up front. So what's up?"

I fill her in on the case. "The police report shows that an old drunk named Leroy saw Kenny slapping Maxine Robinson in the alley Friday afternoon. Jimmy's cousin Wanda lives around the corner. She may know something."

The street doesn't look so scary in the daylight. Wanda's sitting on her porch with an older woman, both of them drinking beer and looking upset.

Jaimie pulls up on her black motorcycle, clad in black leather from head to toe with a black helmet featuring a Black Power logo on the back. She removes her helmet to reveal her bushed hair in all its glory.

"Hey, what's up, Barbie Doll?" chimes Wanda. "Mama, that's Barbara, the one I was telling you about."

Jaimie drops her head to hide her snickering. She knows that I've been over here getting high.

Wanda introduces her mother as Ms. Connor and we cordially greet each other. "We haven't seen or heard from Kenny in a couple of days," she says, assuming I'm there to score more dope.

"Wanda, my name isn't Barbara, it's Kaycie, Kaycie Crawford.

"What you mean your name ain't Barbara? So what the hell? You the police?"

"Kenny is locked up for killing Maxine Robinson. I'm his lawyer and this is my investigator, Jaimie Hunter. Did you know Maxine Robinson?"

"Yeah. She's dead. They found her beat to death in the gangway on Westbrook."

"They think Kenny killed her."

"Kenny didn't kill Maxine! Anybody coulda killed her. She was always getting high in the alley hiding from her no-good, greasy-ass husband, Grady."

"Be quiet, Wanda! You talk too much," her mother says.

Wanda continues: "That narc Lakewood's been terrorizing all the women in the neighborhood, taking their dope and pushing them around, trying to get them to rat Kenny out. He coulda killed Maxine."

"Wanda, you need to shut up telling everybody's business in the neighborhood," Ms. Connor says. "Whoever killed her won't appreciate you running your mouth." She gets up from her seat on the porch and goes into the house.

As Wanda speculates to Jaimie about Grady and everyone else who lives in the neighborhood, I follow Ms. Connor into the shotgun house, peer into the empty living room, and hear noise coming from the next room. Quietly, I ease down the hall to the adjacent room to find Ms. Connor ransacking a bedroom. The bed is disheveled, dresser drawers open with contents tossed.

"Can I help your find something, Ms. Connor?" I ask, startling her.

"You can get yourself hurt sneakin' up on people, young lady!"

Jaimie follows Wanda into the house as she promises to kill anybody who says Kenny murdered Maxine. Seeing her bedroom torn up she turns to me, exposing the pistol grip in her bosom.

"What the hell are you doing in my room?" She reaches to pull out Ole Ugly but hesitates when Jaimie opens her leather jacket to expose a holstered .50-caliber revolver—silver with a black waffle-textured grip.

"Relax, baby. I got a license for mine," Jaimie says.

"I came in and found your mother tossing your bedroom," I tell her. "What do you suppose she's looking for—Kenny's stash?"

"All right, Barbara, or whatever your name is, you can get the fuck outta my house. Biker bitch, get her ass outta here."

"Jaimie, why don't we go around the corner on Westbrook to see if anybody heard or seen anything Friday night."

Jaimie glides past Wanda, winks at her, then walks to the curb and starts her motorcycle, revving it up loud as she makes a U-turn toward the corner.

"I'll kill that bitch," Wanda mumbles under her breath.

"You'll answer to Lance if you try. You know who Lance is, don't you?"

Surprised that I know the man, Wanda cautiously replies, "Yeah, I know who he is."

I join Jaimie around the corner and we talk to the neighbors and folks sitting out on their porches. Nobody claims to have seen anything.

An elderly man dressed in three layers of clothing with the smell of coal oil is collecting cans along the curb in front of a boarded-up house. I approach him with a flirtatious demeanor.

"Hey, how you doin'? My name is Kaycie. You live around here?"

"Sometimes I sleep in there," he says, pointing to the empty structure. "I got it set up all nice and cozy and warm. You wanna come in?"

"Maybe next time. I heard Maxine Robinson got killed around back last night. Did you happen to see or hear anybody getting beat up?"

He looks over both shoulders and sees that the neighbors are watching him. "I ain't seen or heard nothing!" he shouts, shaking his head.

"Do you know where Grady Robinson lives?"

"He lives in Miss Freddie's house down there on this side of the street, way up on a hill with the white porch."

When we pull up in front of the Robinsons' house, children with no coats and runny noses play in the front yard. We climb the steep steps and the kids run into the house. I ring the bell and a voice yells that the door is open, and we enter the hallway.

There are folks in the front room playing spades. The players are slapping their cards down and talking shit. The air is thick with tobacco, marijuana smoke, and stale beer, while Johnnie Taylor's "Last Two Dollars" plays on the radio.

When Jaimie asks if anybody's heard or seen anything, they shake their heads, barely paying her any attention.

Grady walks up behind me in the room's doorway, too close for comfort. I stand my ground.

"Hello, sexy. I hear you're looking for me." Then he turns to Jaimie and says, "I can tell by the way you're dressed that that's your bike out there."

"I'm Kaycie Crawford, attorney at law. Where were you last Friday night, early Saturday morning?" I ask.

He takes a few steps back and his flirtatious body language turns defensive. "I was in the house asleep by ten o'clock Friday night after a long day working on cars."

"When was the last time you saw Maxine?"

"I saw her when she left for work Friday morning, but I didn't see her after that and I wasn't looking for her because I knew she was probably out in the alley somewhere geekin' like she always do. I didn't know what happened until the police came knocking on the door early this morning."

"Grady. Grady, come here," his bedridden mother calls from the next room. "Who is that out in the hallway? Tell her to come in."

In the bedroom I tell Ms. Freddie we're in the neighborhood investigating Maxine's murder. She orders Grady out of the room and invites me to sit. The only chair in the room is her wheelchair. She tells me to come close because she knows her son is eavesdropping.

Ms. Freddie says, "There's a saying around here: what goes on in this neighborhood stays in this neighborhood. But that ain't right when it comes to somebody getting killed. I heard some loud talking in the alley behind the house last night 'cause I like to have my window cracked open to let some cool air in.

"I heard some men fussing about somebody talking to the police about Kenny. I think I heard Maxine's voice screaming that she didn't say nothin' to nobody but they kept on hollering and then there were sounds like cans and bottles falling and banging on the dumpsters. Soon after, I can hear moaning and I think that was when Maxine was getting killed."

"Were you able to see who it was?"

"No. I can't get up out of the bed without help. I have to call Grady or one of the kids when I need to go to the bathroom. When it got quiet, I heard some noise in the gangway, but I didn't think nothing of it. Sometimes, it's just Maxine back there smoking her dope.

"One thing I know for sure: Ms. Connor, who lives around the corner on West Bentley, sold Grady a $100,000 insurance policy on Maxine six months ago, and I'm just hoping that Grady hasn't done anything stupid."

When Jaimie and I return to Wanda's house we find Ms. Connor in the front yard barbecuing. "Ms. Connor, I know you sold Grady a life-insurance policy on Maxine. Why didn't you want to tell us that? Don't you know that makes Grady a prime suspect?"

"It don't necessarily," she counters. "Grady owes me $5,000 I loaned him for his car repair business. He smoked some of it and invested some with Kenny to buy cocaine. I thought Kenny would make up for Grady's loss. That didn't happen. So no, I don't give a shit about helping Kenny because in my mind, he owes me too."

"You and Grady have more to gain from Maxine's death

than Kenny," says Jaimie. "You know we will subpoena you to testify about the insurance."

"You can go to hell. I ain't testifying about shit and you need to leave my yard before Wanda gets back. Folks who get hurt in this neighborhood end up in a dumpster out in the alley."

Back at the office Jimmy hands me the police files and the coroner's report. Maxine was bludgeoned with a baseball bat and at least two people stomped and kicked her body until it was a sack of bones. The report also states that she was killed in the alley and dragged into the gangway between the Robinsons' house and the vacant house next door.

If Kenny says that he left her at the gas station then we've got to figure out where she went from there and who was the last person to see her alive. The time of death is estimated between eleven p.m. and two a.m. Saturday morning. Jaimie stops examining the crime scene photos and speaks.

"First of all, Kaycie, before I say anything about this stuff, I want my two grand plus my daily rate. That comes out to $2,150."

I hand her an envelope of cash.

"Thank you." She shakes her head. "They are crazy over there on Westbrook. They act like they don't care about Maxine. And that Grady looked me up and down like he wanted to lick the leather off my body."

"He's not that bad looking if he wasn't so dirty," I say. "For all we know, Grady could be thinking he's going to collect the money, not realizing that he may be the next one they find dead. He could pay back what he owes Ms. Connor when the policy pays out in six months, but I can't see her being satisfied with a repayment of a measly five grand, even with 100 percent interest."

Sunday, I go to visit Kenny. He doesn't look so good. His face has been cleaned up, but he's tired and haggard.

"Kenny, what do you know about Ms. Connor writing a $100,000 insurance policy on Maxine for Grady?"

"She's got her broker's license, and she's written insurance policies for a lot of folks in the neighborhood."

"It doesn't seem like Grady is responsible enough to keep up with the monthly premiums."

"Ms. Connor pays the premiums for him and he gives her money every now and then when she sees that he's been working steady," Kenny replies. "I wouldn't be surprised if she was plotting on Grady and Maxine, or even me, for that matter, since I owe her about two thousand."

"Why would you owe her any money?"

"Sometimes she fronts me money to buy dope when I'm short on cash. She's been hounding me about it and I think she ratted me out to the narc."

"Lakewood?"

"Right. He hassles the prostitutes, takes their dope, and forces them to do things in exchange for not locking them up. Ms. Connor is behind on protection payments to him. There have been so many police calls from her tenants, she can't afford any more trouble."

"How does Wanda fit into all this drama?"

"Wanda has no income other than selling dope for me. She either smokes it up or gives it away to the hookers when they come by the house late at night. I slapped her around a few times, but it doesn't seem to matter. I figure that Ms. Connor should be responsible for Wanda's debt."

Back at the office I call Lance and tell him I need to see Kenny's girlfriend.

When Fulani James arrives, she's tastefully dressed in a sharp leather jacket and a black wool dress with a leather belt. Kenny Jr., about five years old, is looking handsome in a wool tweed sports jacket with a turtleneck and khakis.

"Is this Kenny Jr.?"

"Yeah, this is me!" the boy replies.

"You both look really nice. Have you all been to church?"

"Thank you. Yes," she answers. "I'm worried about Kenny getting convicted. My baby needs his daddy."

"Do you believe he's innocent, Ms. James?"

"You can call me Fulani, Miss Kaycie. Yeah, I believe he's innocent, but I also know he's got a temper. I told him if he ever hit me, I'll shoot his ass, and he knows I'm not playing."

"Fulani, where do you work?"

"The gas company. I'm going to St. Louis U, majoring in business administration. I've been trying to convince Kenny to stop this dope slinging and enroll in school. He has a good head for business. And he's a good father."

"Fulani, can you prove that you were with Kenny last Saturday night?"

"Yeah. We took Little Kenny to see a movie downtown after dinner at the Bread Company. Afterward, we came home and Kenny stayed until the next morning."

"Do you have any receipts?"

"Nope. Kenny paid cash and I didn't keep any receipts or ticket stubs." Fulani is beginning to sound discouraged. I ask her if she has a family photo and she hands one over.

"Fulani, I'm going to have my investigator show your picture to the employees at the cinema. Somebody will remember you all."

When they're gone I call Jaimie so she can get the photo and find witnesses at the movie theater.

Later that afternoon I drive to Westbrook with Lance. We pull up around the corner on Davenport and Lance sees one of his "sales reps."

"What's up, Big Rush? What's been happening around here?"

"Running from Lakewood. He's been hassling folks more than usual lately. I thought you and him were cool."

"We were until he tried to raise his price. I warned his ass I could have his job at any time, but he don't believe it."

I butt in. "Hey, Big Rush, have you noticed anybody in the neighborhood spending more money than usual lately?"

Lance looks at me sideways. "Big Rush, this is Kaycie Crawford, Kenny's lawyer."

"Now that you mention it, Troy and Tyrone have been buying dope, drinking cognac, and partying on Vandalia up over the doughnut shop the past few days. They're both usually begging to run errands for us so we can give them a hit or two. Troy told me he won the lottery."

We drive over two blocks to the corner building. The doughnut shop is closed. Lance knocks hard on the door, then he looks up at the window to see somebody peeking through the crooked blinds. He knocks again, turns the doorknob—the door is unlocked. We climb the stairs and find Troy sprawled out asleep across the bed with a topless woman sitting at a table smoking crack while roaches crawl up and down the wall next to her.

"Troy, wake your ass up!" Lance snaps, then turns to the woman. "And you—get your ass out!"

Dumbstruck, she throws on her coat, grabs her pipe, scrapes some crumbs into her hand, and runs down the steps, slamming the door on the way out. I look on the table to see if there's anything left.

Lance grabs Troy by his dirty sagging jeans and pulls him off the bed. "Troy, I said wake your ass up!"

Troy, still half-dazed, answers, "Wha . . . what . . . ? What you want, Lance? How the hell you get into my house?"

"Where's Tyrone? Where in the hell y'all get all this money you've been spending?"

"I hit the lottery, man!"

"Oh yeah? What were your numbers?"

When Troy starts stuttering, Lance grabs him by the throat. "You lying, Troy. What you know about what happen to Maxine?"

"How the fuck I know? That crazy fool is always hidin' in the alley smokin' her dope. She don't ever share. I'm glad her ass is dead."

The downstairs door opens and slams and Tyrone runs upstairs only to find Lance waiting for him next to the doorway. Lance throws him down on the floor next to Troy and pulls out his nine millimeter.

"Tyrone, where Troy get all this money?"

Tyrone doesn't respond, glancing over at Troy as if he might answer for him.

"Tyrone, I'm going to ask you one more time: where did all the money come from?" Then Lance fires his gun into the dirty mattress and they both start hollering. I damn near scream, but I don't dare.

Tyrone yells, "Ms. Connor gave us the money!"

"Shut the hell up, Tyrone," says Troy.

"Fuck you, Troy. I ain't about to get shot covering for your mama. If I go to jail, I'll still be alive. It ain't like I ain't never been in jail. Look here, Lance, Ms. Connor gave us five hundred apiece if we take down Maxine. Troy hit her in the head with the bat and we both stomped her ass and dragged her into Grady's gangway."

"Lance, call your contacts on the force and tell them to pick these two up."

Kenny is released after a week, his bail still pending on the drug charge that Lakewood trapped him on. When Kenny comes out of the elevator into the lobby, he hugs Lance. He grabs me and kisses me on the lips and softly says, "Thank you," then runs out the door to where Fulani and Kenny Jr. wait outside.

"Kaycie, you should pay *me* for cracking your case. Jaimie wasn't nowhere around."

"Man, you need to quit," says Jaimie. "You know I talked to some of those dudes over there on Westbrook and all they wanted to do was grab me until they saw I was strapped. By the way, Kaycie, I will be sending you my bill."

"I'll need your help with Kenny on this drug charge. Let's go to Steve Charles's for dinner and drinks to celebrate—my treat. The sky's the limit."

After a sumptuous steak dinner accompanied by several martinis, Rémy Martins, and an endless glass of club soda with lime for Jaimie, we all go our separate ways, Lance to his loft apartment, Jaimie to her boyfriend's house.

And me, I start to call Michael but hang up instead. Then I head over to Wanda's on West Bentley and knock on the door. I can hear that damn Keith Sweat moaning and groaning. I knock harder.

"Who is it?" Wanda screams in her deep raspy voice.

"It's me, Barbara."

ONE LITTLE GODDAMN THING

BY SCOTT PHILLIPS

Sauget, Illinois

Commercial St. Louis looks like it was razed entirely and replaced by a different city on the same grid. The grocery stores, banks, drugstores I knew are all gone, replaced by new ones in the wrong places. Chain stores, all of them, the same as I've been seeing in Kansas City the last six months. Right now I'm sitting in front of a bar on Maplewood just west of McCausland, or rather the space where the bar used to be. Now it's a sandwich shop. Even after thirty years of prison food those chain-store sandwiches taste like shit to me. I got my first blow job in that bar's parking lot, from a friend of my sister Kathie's by the name of Cheryl Krieger. The same Cheryl who ended up testifying against me; I certainly don't blame her for it, but I can't pretend it didn't hurt at the time.

But that first night, years before, Cheryl and I had been at the bar for a couple of hours, drinking beer served up by an elderly bartender with a pocked, purplish nose, spectacularly bushy white eyebrows, and no apparent compunctions about serving underage kids. Cheryl put her hand on my thigh and whispered in my ear that we should go outside to my car. There, on the squeaking vinyl upholstery of my '78 Isuzu, she swabbed my virgin knob, and the look of proud satisfaction on her face as she wiped her lips clean with the back of her forearm afterward remains as vivid in my mind as any memory I can lay claim to. While I'm trying to remember exactly which space it was where this happened, it occurs to me that sweet lusty Cheryl could be a grandmother by now.

Thirty years I've been gone, almost. One pass through town, just to satisfy my curiosity about a few things, and then I'll be gone again for good. I'm not very sentimental by nature; that fondly remembered blow job is about as close as I'm going to get to nostalgia.

I won't be seeing my sister Kathie, except maybe from a distance if things go right; just a brief, tangible reminder that I pissed my youth away for a good reason. My last contact with her consisted of this charming letter, addressed to me shortly after the start of my Irish vacation:

> *Dear brother Tony,*
>
> *It pains me to write this sad missive but you will understand that with Mother and Father gone and you in prison I am now the head of our family.*
>
> *Douglas and I are attempting to bring up the children in a good Catholic manner and they must not know that their beloved uncle is a "jailbird" or convict and so I have told them that you were unfortunately killed in a motorcycle crash involving one of those big trucks one sees on the highway. Do not worry, I informed them that your tragic death was quick and painless but that you had time to tell the highway patrolman that you sure loved your nieces and nephew.*

(I imagine the kids still think I'm dead. I'd love to show up at Thanksgiving dinner and surprise them with the truth, have a look at my various nieces and nephews, but that wouldn't be fair to Kathie. As far as she knew—and according to her own husband and the state of Missouri—I was the kind of person you didn't want influencing your kids.)

> *Douglas is especially real disappointed in you. He has always looked up to you and considered you at one time like a real brother. Don't worry about me for he is starting up his own construction business and will be a good breadwinner for the children and me.*
>
> *Affectionate goodbye,*
> *Kathie*

All I'd asked in return for twenty-eight years of my life was for Doug to do right by her. I get back into the car and drive over to McCarran Construction, not certain exactly what my intentions are. It's ten minutes to noon when old Dougie comes out, looking hale and hearty, a little gray but still a big man with a straight carriage and a purposeful stride. He always did have that gift of looking like a straight arrow; when we set our shop teacher's garage on fire in seventh grade he was caught a block away and talked his way out of the whole scrape, throwing suspicion on a pair of nonexistent black guys in a gold Lincoln Continental. I had a bit of the same gift— maybe that's why we were such good pals. Together we were able to get away with misdeeds that children of more sinister mien would have gone down for, and hard.

Besides the gray at the temples, his only concession to the passage of time is a pair of steel-rimmed eyeglasses that make him look like an engineer or an architect. He gets into a Caddy, recognizable as such to my eyes only by the familiar logo on the rear hatch. My own car—the property of my wife Paula, in fact—is an older and considerably more modest model; even so, there are components that I find unnecessary, distracting, or confusing. The first time I drove it in the rain, Paula had to explain to me where the windshield wiper controls were, and at that moment I knew that without her help I'd be 100 percent fucked on the outside.

The Cadillac's bumper is festooned with all manner of information on the fancy private schools the kids attend and not-so-subtle hints at Doug's politics, about which I don't give a shit. One reading *EQUAL RIGHTS FOR UNBORN WOMEN*, though, makes me wonder whether Doug has ever ratted me out to my sister about Cheryl's abortion. Doug didn't approve at all back then, yelled at us both and called it murder, asking me what was I going to say in confession. When I told him I didn't go to confession anymore, didn't even consider myself a Catholic anymore, it was about as close as our friendship ever came to collapsing. But he stopped talking about it, and I assumed he must have gotten over it eventually.

The Caddy turns onto Kingshighway. I don't know whether Doug is going home or to a restaurant for lunch, but on the off chance it's the former I want to find out where they live; if it's the latter I'll drive on.

At I-44, Doug takes the on-ramp, heading east toward Illinois. I don't know that side of the river well but maybe there are some nice towns within commuting distance. I never saw or heard of one, but still.

It should have been simple. Cheryl used to work there, and in fact the reason she quit was a fear of getting robbed. A lack of attention paid to security, cash lying in a safe left unlocked half the time. She told me about the elderly proprietor, superstitious about hiring a guard, so set in his ways the nightly routine hadn't varied since the late 1950s, according to the old lady who worked with her. If I hadn't gotten my name into the papers, Cheryl never would have known she'd had any part in it. Listening to her testify, I understood the degree of guilt she felt for having innocently tipped me to it. I understood it because I felt the same guilt, because I'd been the one to get Doug involved. The proceeds were supposed to get the construction firm up and running. I even told myself we'd pay the old man back once the money started rolling in.

Across the river the Caddy pulls off at the miserable, barren village of Sauget. I maintain a discreet distance and when it pulls into a large parking lot, freshly paved and serving a number of businesses, I keep driving. He parks a good distance from any of the buildings, and the Caddy's windows are tinted so I can't see what he's up to, but based on my observations of nearly everyone I've met since getting out, I imagine my brother-in-law is checking one pointless fucking thing or another on his phone.

I pull into the lot of a restaurant on the opposite corner of the intersection. Inside I get a table next to the window and order a cheeseburger with fries. I'm almost done eating when Doug finally steps down out of the giant jeep-like vehicle—another ubiquitous aspect of modern American life that makes me feel like a time traveler—and strides toward one of the buildings that border the western and northern edges of the big lot. He's not headed for the furniture liquidators, nor to the used-kitchen supply warehouse, nor to any of the various storage bays. As he passes a parked county sheriff's car, he gives the deputy a friendly, familiar wave which the officer returns with crisp military élan, and he then disappears inside a building marked with a giant neon sign reading, *CINNAMON BUNZZ: A Gentleman's Club.* Silhouettes of chesty women recline atop and lean onto the sides of the sign, and I wonder what Doug could possibly be doing in such a place. The old Doug wouldn't have considered doing business with any sort of establishment of an immoral nature; I once had to hire a couple of near-strangers to help me tuck-point a massage parlor in St. Charles County because Doug wouldn't have anything to do with it. Maybe the experience of running a big construction company all these years has made him look at money differently.

I'm not particularly hungry anymore but I order a slice of peach pie and drink some more coffee and wait for Doug to come out. When I'm finished the waitress keeps coming over to warm my coffee up, but I'm getting self-conscious sitting there for such a long time. I'm about to get up and walk to my car when Doug finally comes out the front door and heads for his car, smiling and nodding at the deputy. I leave a twenty on a fifteen-dollar tab and thank the waitress as I pass by her on my way out the door.

Following the freak Caddy back into town, I try to guess where Doug and Kathie will have ended up. He's done well, by the looks of things. Maybe Ladue? Creve Coeur? On the back of the Caddy there's a sticker for a radio station, and I feel a sudden desire to hear music. Knowing Doug, I assume that 99.1 JOY!FM is a rock station, but what comes over my speakers is treacly, weak-kneed Jesus pop. I've got nothing against religious people, but I had a cellie awhile back who used to listen to that Christ elevator music and it fucking scarred me. I listen for a couple of minutes, wondering if maybe the Caddy isn't actually Kathie's car. Surely Doug is up there rocking to Foghat and AC/DC on KSHE, but it strikes me that this crap, if not explicitly Protestant, is certainly not Catholic enough for the likes of Mary Kathleen Gillihan McCarran.

We pass the exits for Ladue. Then we pass 270, which by my lights is the best way to get to Creve Coeur. Once again I'm struck by how little I know my hometown anymore; there might be new freeways or underground tunnels leading to all the suburbs for all I know. Finally we arrive in Chester-field, now built up to an astonishing degree, outlet malls and upscale hotels and shopping centers as opposed to the open farmland I remember. We take an exit I'm pretty sure didn't exist in my day and I consider slowing down in case Doug is watching, but I know perfectly well he doesn't think that way, and I stay within an eighth of a mile of his ass-ugly Caddy.

When Doug pulls into a cul-de-sac I keep driving. Half an hour later I return. The Caddy sits parked in the circular drive of a three-story mansion, gabled and mansarded and look-ing like something out of a movie. The notion that my sister might live in such a house is completely foreign to me, but I feel a quiet pride that my sacrifice has allowed her and her kids to live out their lives in luxury.

And then, heading back to I-64, I find myself wondering why there are school stickers on Doug's car, which appears brand new. Twenty-eight years ago my littlest niece was not quite two years old. Must be grandkids.

Mrs. *Floyd Willis* was how the *Post-Dispatch* identified the bookkeeper in the morning, though it was long past the time when the papers named women as though they didn't have first names of their own. I suppose that was all the informa-tion they'd dug up by press time. The next morning she was Mrs. *Nina Willis* and the next day there was a note that it was pronounced *Nine-uh*. She wasn't supposed to be there when we came in at closing time, should have been at home with Floyd watching *Magnum, P.I.* or *T.J. Hooker* or *The Cosby*

Show. When we bumrushed the old man into the back room and Doug saw her, he freaked out. He shot her in the face and then shot the old man. Nobody was supposed to get shot. Nobody was even supposed to have live ammo, especially not Doug.

Back at the motel, I call Paula and tell her about my day. She's worried, doesn't think I should be there. "You're not safe out there in the world. Come on back to KC, sweetie."

"It's just another day or two."

"Be careful and don't do anything foolish."

I did my full stretch. I have no parole officer to answer to, no restrictions on my travel, but she's still afraid I'm going to break some law and go back to prison. I remember meeting her in the visitation room, coming to see her own no-good burglar brother, how sad she was about him and where his dumbassery had landed him. "I won't do anything stupid, sugar. I'm coming back to you."

She's the only person I ever told the truth to about August of '87. Since it's safe to assume Doug never came clean to anyone, it's a secret only we three know. She swears she's never told her kids or the rest of the extended family, who all treat me fine, considering their beloved mother—aunt, sister, grandmother, etcetera—married a convicted murderer while he was still incarcerated. She's smart and pretty and if it weren't for her I'd be flopping somewhere, maybe in a shelter, maybe planning something nonviolent that would get me sent back to the relatively uncomplicated existence I knew in the joint. So do I consider myself lucky? Yes, officer, I most certainly do.

At one thirty in the morning I walk over to the parking lot of

258 // St. Louis Noir

a bar near the motel and make a quick round looking for a vehicle with the keys inside, belonging to someone who showed up late and already drunk, someone who might even be too drunk to realize they've had their vehicle stolen when they come out at closing time. Thirty years ago I might have hot-wired one, but I have no idea whether this is even possible anymore. And good fortune is with me tonight. A recent-model Ford, a small, ugly thing with Illinois plates, sits there with its door ajar and dome light burning, a set of keys lying there on the asphalt. I pick them up in a latex-gloved hand and tell myself I'm doing the owner a favor; he won't get shot through the windshield driving home plastered, and tomorrow he'll get his car back, with a functioning battery to boot.

I park down the street from Doug's house and, despite myself, drift off to sleep in the driver's seat. At four forty-five I awaken to a rap at the window. I squint at a flashlight carried by a short, thickset woman in uniform, and I pick up one of the latex gloves as a shield between my fingers and the crank before fumbling with the window.

"May I ask what you're doing out here this time of night, sir?" She looks to be in her late forties, with a shiny, round face, and she lacks the belligerence some rent-a-cops have.

I'm dressed in a nice, clean shirt, my haircut is a mere three days old, and I made a point of shaving before leaving the motel. Two-thirds of a lifetime spent in custody have made me slick when dealing with authority. "I'm sorry, officer. I was making a surprise visit to my baby sister and brother-in-law, they live right there. I drove in from Springfield, didn't get in until about two, and didn't want to wake them up. Like I said, they're not expecting me."

She shines the flashlight into the car and sees nothing of particular interest, and I note that her uniform is that of a neighborhood security patrol, so she probably doesn't have the means to run my plates. "What's the matter with a hotel?" she asks.

"I'm fine sleeping in the car. Doug's an early riser, so's my sister. If you don't want me on the street, I can clear out."

When she looks at me as though trying to judge my character via my physiognomy, I know I've won. My face has always been as sweet and honest as a toddler's.

I wake again with the dawn. I turn the radio on low and wait. Doug eventually comes out fully dressed and drives the Caddy away. The house has what looks to me like a three-car garage; what the hell are he and Kathie storing in there, anyway?

Another half hour and the passage of time starts making me antsy. If Kathie doesn't walk out the door in another fifteen minutes, I'll abandon the car in the parking lot of the outlet mall and call a cab. When the front door opens, it's not Kathie. It's a woman in her late thirties or early forties with luxuriant, shoulder-length blond hair, tottering on three-inch heels, made up so elaborately that it's hard—though not impossible—to make out the look of frustration and resentment on her face. Looking closer, I think she may have had some sort of plastic surgery or neurological event that froze her face that way. She grabs the *Post-Dispatch* off the driveway and reenters the house. A niece? The oldest might be that age. The younger one? Maybe. I try to remember exactly what their ages would be and after a minute I give up.

I'm about to leave when the garage door opens. There are three cars inside, all of them monstrosities like Doug's Caddy. I wonder which one is Kathie's. A giant black vehicle pulls out, the blonde at the wheel, and I give it a minute to get down the street before starting my engine and following.

She takes 64 all the way into town and gets off at McCausland. Waiting at the off-ramp stoplight I see a pink cursive monogram on the rear windshield: *TML*. That puzzles me for a moment until I realize that the M in the middle is the largest letter, and that the initials are actually *TLM*, and as I follow her turning left toward the park, I try to think what the *TL* could stand for. Little Teresa's middle name, I'm pretty sure, was Jane, after my mom, and the other niece's first name—all I can call forth from my memory—was Marie. Maybe this is little Mikey's wife.

I follow her to a school and drive on by when she turns into the parking lot. This is starting to get confusing, and I turn back to the freeway to drop the car off someplace where my taxi bill back to the Wentzville motel won't be ruinous.

"Can you help me with some of this Internet business?" I ask Paula.

"Well, that's a first."

I explain the situation to her, leaving out the stolen car. "Can you get on there and find out if my little nephew Mikey's married?"

"Probably. What's his last name?"

"McCarran."

"Born when?"

"Seventy-nine, maybe '80?"

"Middle name?"

"John? James? Something with a J."

"That's real helpful."

I watch the television for a while, a *Columbo* rerun, and right before Peter Falk gets that look in his one real eye and starts dismantling the killer's story, the little phone trills. I'm still not accustomed to the fucking thing and the ringtone makes me jump.

"Hello."

"Your nephew's married, but he lives in Florida. Another thing you're not going to like much."

"Okay."

"Your brother-in-law's got a Facebook account."

"I thought everybody did now."

"It's what's on it. That lady who dropped off the kids at the middle school, that's his wife, Tamara, and they have four kids."

I feel nauseous. My throat constricts, and though I'm alone in the room, I'm still embarrassed that tears are welling in my eyes. "Kathie's dead?"

"No, sweetie, she's alive. She's got her own page."

"That's impossible. Neither one of them would ever get divorced. They're more Catholic than the pope."

"Well, they are, and from the looks of it, Doug is a pretty active member of some megachurch out there in Chesterfield, so I'd say he left the whole Catholic thing behind with your sister. Sorry."

"I can't believe she'd allow that."

"It only takes one to make a divorce. I Googled *Douglas McCarran St. Louis* and got all kinds of responses. News articles about the construction firm, charity stuff, that megachurch. Looks like he's a big swinging dick in your hometown, hon. Also, there's rumors he's planning to run for lieutenant governor."

Dougie? Dim Doug? Douglas McCarran the panicky impulse killer, lieutenant governor of the State of Missouri? It sounds about right, actually. "Find out where Kathie lives, would you?"

262 // St. Louis Noir

Late in the afternoon I'm in Dogtown, parked on a residential street not far from Doug's construction company. Kathie's house is smaller than the one she and Doug lived in back when. The aluminum frame of her screen door is twisted out of position, as though someone very drunk tried to break in, and the grass is high enough she's likely to get a citation before long. Shame on Mikey for going down to Florida. I'll have to get Paula to find out where my nieces are, see if they have husbands who can step up to the plate like men.

Twenty minutes after five she pulls up in a little Asian car, one of those makes that didn't exist when I was free, and parks in front of the house. She's shorter than I remember, getting fat, and she limps as she carries a bag of groceries up the steps. It seems to me that she's aged more than I have since the last time I saw her; she could be my older sister. Hell, she looks like she could be our mom's older sister.

Next day I have lunch again at the Sauget restaurant and wait for the big ugly Caddy to show in the strip club lot. One good thing about working with Doug was how reliable he was. A creature of habit, you might say, predictable as the phases of the moon. Now I have an idea Dougie Boy might be a regular at Cinnamon Bunzz; the question is, how regular? Once a week, twice? Five times?

And at 12:27 he pulls into the lot and parks in damn near the same spot as a couple days earlier. That's all I need for today, and I finish my burger and leave without waiting for Doug to get out of his vehicle, careful nonetheless not to let him see me going to my car.

I call Paula that night and reassure her that nothing bad is going to happen, that I'll be back as soon as I can be. That might be tomorrow night or it might not. When I get off the phone I head over to the tavern from whose lot I borrowed my wheels the other evening, and find the recovered vehicle sitting there, presumably locked this time. At the bar I nurse a beer and listen to a sad, hollow-cheeked man telling a friend about the difficulties involved in getting his stolen car back from the impound. I feel like buying him and his friend a round as compensation but resist the temptation.

Unlike her unfortunate employer, Mrs. Floyd Willis—Nina—survived the bullet to her brain, though not without sustaining some serious intellectual deficits, as the doctors called them. At trial she testified that I had acted alone, and that she'd remember my face anywhere. In fact, Doug and I had both been wearing rubber, over-the-head Ronald Reagan masks, which we'd thought would be hilarious. I didn't contradict anything in her testimony, since the notion that I'd acted alone served my purposes well. I had a real bleeding-heart judge—not many of those around anymore, not in Missouri—and though I declined to reveal where I'd hidden the proceeds of the robbery, he sentenced me to twenty-eight years. Every time I had a shot at parole they'd ask where I'd stashed the money and I'd tell them I couldn't rightly remember. But it all went into Doug's construction business, which was supposed to be mine as well.

Which is just the way the shit happened to stick to the wall that time.

At eleven thirty the next morning I park my car in back of Cinnamon Bunzz next to what I hope and presume is an emergency exit and walk around the corner to the front. Though the presence of the cop car fills me with dread, as a test of will I give the deputy a friendly salute when I pass. He returns it with a friendly grin.

Inside, I take a seat at the bar and order a Wiedemann's, which the bartender has never heard of. "They still make Old Style?" I ask.

"I got Bud, Bud Lite, and that's it on tap. In a bottle I got Corona."

"Is that A-B?"

"They distribute it." Her hair is cut in a sort of shag, with gradations of color ranging from platinum to black, and her tank top is so tight it looks like it must hurt.

"I got an old grudge. Got fired from there over a fight with my supervisor back in '82."

"Shouldn't argue with the boss."

"Wasn't that kind of fight. I cut off a piece of his left ear."

"Hah. Like Johnny Cash."

"All right, I guess I can forgive them after all this time. Bud it is."

She must be about thirty, and I suppose that's considered old in this place. She pulls a draft, sets it in front of me, and gives me a curious, crooked-toothed smile. "What's your name, sugar?"

"Luther," I say, in honor of an old, dead cellmate.

"Well, Luther, I'm Noodles, if you need anything you let me know. Got Salty Taffee and Cinderella up on stages one and three and there's lap dances in the back."

At 12:32 Doug walks in and shouts a big hearty hello to Noodles, who waves back at him with a smile as insincere as I've ever seen outside of a jailhouse preacher's face. It's funny hearing his voice. It hasn't changed much, a little croakier than before but still full of the joyous conviction that

the whole damned world loves him. He heads straight for a
back room, snapping his fingers and shouting out for a certain
Cherry Vanilla to join him.

"Not a particular fan of old Dougie's?" I ask Noodles,
seeing her as a potential ally.

"That cocksucker. You know him?"

"Used to. Not an admirer myself. What's your beef? He a
bad tipper?"

"Nothing like that. Let's just say he has a cavalier attitude
and leave it at that."

"That's what I hear."

"And in a place like this, the competition is pretty fierce."

I wait for five minutes. I don't know how long a lap dance
is supposed to take, but if Doug's a quick finisher it's time to
intervene. I leave a twenty on the bar and wink at Noodles.

"Time to renew that acquaintance," I tell her, jerking my
thumb toward the door behind which Doug disappeared with
Cherry Vanilla.

"You can't go back there, Luther," she says.

"It's okay, I'm just poking my head in."

She starts to say something else, then stops. Surely her job
is to stop me, or to call the muscle and have them do it, but
she cocks her head and looks amused.

Cherry Vanilla is a remarkable fit young woman, her back
muscles and quads as well developed as any obsessive peni-
tentiary body builder's, and as I quietly push the door open
she's gyrating her pelvis just above Doug's own to the tune of
"Dream On," his cock in his hand and his eyes fixed on her
finely trimmed blond bush, a harsh grimace of concentration
on his mouth. Their skin shines purple in the lurid glow of a
black light.

266 // St. Louis Noir

"Hiya, Dougie, funny seeing you here," I say, and, startled, he stands, sending Cherry Vanilla tumbling to the ground.

"Jesus, Doug!" she yells, then turns to face me. "You get the shit out! You want a lap dance, you ask at the fucking bar."

Meanwhile Doug's looking at me, completely baffled, mouth open like he's about to venture a guess as to who I might be, cock still engorged in his hand. He looks as dumb as I've ever seen him look.

I pull the filleting knife out of my inside jacket pocket and Cherry Vanilla screams. The music is loud enough that I can at least entertain the notion that the security guard didn't hear. I lunge forward and get a good swipe at Doug's dick. I get his hand instead, and when he jerks it away I slice his swollen dick. It's not completely severed, but it dangles by a fleshy thread, and Doug and Cherry Vanilla are both yelling. They're so loud I have to get right up on top of Doug, who's writhing on the floor and sobbing.

He looks up at me in horrified recognition, tries to say something but can't manage to form the words.

"Remember, no statute of limitations for murder, Mr. Lieutenant Governor," I tell him.

He's looking in horror at the bloody shreds of his member, keening in pain and sorrow.

"I asked you to do one thing," I tell him. "One little goddamn thing."

I run out to find the security man, a potbellied, mustachioed goofball in a stained Cinnamon Bunzz polo shirt, huffing toward the back. "For Christ's sake, he stabbed her!" I call out to him. "Call an ambulance, call the cops!"

Not being a very good security man, he runs right past me

toward the screams. Before I walk out the emergency exit to my car, I wave at Noodles and give her a thumbs-up.

This morning I bought what I understand is called a burner phone, since I don't want this call traced to Paula. As I drive away, I dial the first of a pair of numbers I programmed into it this morning. "KSDK TV," a voice says. "How can I direct your call?"

"Newsroom," I say.

After I'm confident I've convinced the initially skeptical reporter, I call the *Post-Dispatch* and give them the same tip. By that time I've made it from 55 north onto 70 west, and I figure it will take me a good five hours to get to KC and Paula. I don't intend to go so much as a mile per hour above the posted limit, don't intend to ever commit so much as a misdemeanor ever again.

By the time I hit Wentzville I'm feeling pretty good. I put on KSHE and I take it as a good omen that they're playing Foghat.

ABOUT THE CONTRIBUTORS

J. Ayres

JEDIDIAH AYRES is a preacher's kid, high school graduate, and the author of some books. No awards, no convictions.

Chris Barsanti

CHRIS BARSANTI is the author of *Filmology*, *The Sci-Fi Movie Guide*, and the *Eyes Wide Open* film guide series, and a contributor to *Punk Rock Warlord: The Life and Works of Joe Strummer*. His writing has appeared in the *Chicago Tribune*, *Playboy*, the *Millions*, *PopMatters*, *Virginia Quarterly Review*, and *Film Journal*. He is partial to Schlafly Pale Ale.

Jay Fram

LAURA BENEDICT is the author of five novels of dark suspense, including *Charlotte's Story* and *Bliss House*, the first books of the Bliss House trilogy. Her work has also appeared in *Ellery Queen Mystery Magazine*, *PANK*, and numerous anthologies like *The Lineup: 20 Provocative Women Writers*. She lives with her family in Southern Illinois. For more information, visit laurabenedict.com.

Ros Crenshaw

MICHAEL CASTRO, called "a legend in St. Louis poetry" by Charles Guenther in the *St. Louis Post-Dispatch*, is a widely published poet and translator. *How Things Stack Up* is his fifteenth book. Castro is the recipient of the Guardian Angel of St. Louis Poetry Award from River Styx and the Warrior Poet Award from Word in Motion, both for lifetime achievement. In 2015, he was named St. Louis's first poet laureate.

Ray Flanary

S.L CONEY, whose formative years were spent bouncing around the United States, is proud to call St. Louis home. Coney's short story "Dead By Dawn" appeared in *Noir at the Bar, Volume 2*.

Ryan Frank

UMAR LEE is a St. Louis–based writer, activist, cabbie, wrestling enthusiast, and father of two. He has previously published two novels, *Tea Party Twelver and the Muslim Brothers* and *Dunya Dust*. His work has also appeared in the *Guardian*, *Politico*, and *Quartz*, amongst other publications. He appeared frequently on MSNBC, Al Jazeera, and Press TV discussing the Ferguson protests after the murder of Michael Brown. Presently he's a candidate for mayor of St. Louis.

Jennifer Lutz-Bauer

JOHN LUTZ is the author of more than forty-five novels and 225 short stories. His thriller *Single White Female* was made into the movie of the same title, starring Bridget Fonda and Jennifer Jason Leigh. He has received an Edgar Award and two Shamus Awards, as well as the Private Eye Writers of America Lifetime Achievement Award. Lutz and his wife Barbara split their time between St. Louis, Missouri and Sarasota, Florida.

Kristina Blank

JASON MAKANSI'S short stories have appeared in the *Dos Passos Review*, *Big Muddy: A Journal of the Mississippi River Valley*, *Marginalia*, *Mizna: Prose, Poetry, and Art Exploring Arab America*, *Rainbow Curve*, *Arabesques*, *Noir at the Bar 2*, and other publications. He is an associate editor for *December* literary magazine and cofounded Blank Slate Press (now Amphorae Publishing Group). He recently completed his first novel, *The Moment Before*.

Amy Marks

PAUL D. MARKS is the author of the Shamus Award–winning noir mystery-thriller *White Heat*. His story "Howling at the Moon" was short-listed for both the 2015 Anthony and Macavity awards for Best Short Story. *Midwest Review* calls Marks's noir novella *Vortex* "a nonstop staccato action noir." He also coedited the anthology *Coast to Coast: Murder from Sea to Shining Sea*.

Ingrid Pape Sheldon

COLLEEN J. MCELROY is the winner of the Before Columbus American Book Award for her book *Queen of the Ebony Isles*. Her most recent collection of poems, *Sleeping with the Moon*, received a 2008 PEN/Oakland National Literary Award, and *Here I Throw Down My Heart* was a finalist for the Binghamton University Milt Kessler Book Award, the Walt Whitman Award, the Phyllis Wheatley Award, and the Washington State Governor's Book Award. She lives in Seattle, Washington.

Tex Lebeauf

SCOTT PHILLIPS was born in Wichita, Kansas, and lived for many years in Paris (France) and Southern California. In the early 2000s he moved to St. Louis. He is the author of seven novels and a collection of short stories, and his novel *The Ice Harvest* was made into a film in 2005, directed by Harold Ramis and starring John Cusack, Billy Bob Thornton, and Connie Nielsen.

Linda Smith

L.J. SMITH is a writer and producer of theatrical and community affairs productions. She is the founder and executive director of A Call to Conscience, Inc., a theater collective that dramatizes historical themes dealing with the struggles of the oppressed. Smith has had poetry published in *Sisters-Nineties Literary Magazine*, and *Drumvoices Revue*. Her poem "City of the Century" was selected for inclusion in the 2009 Metro Arts in Transit's Poetry in Motion program.

Jeigb Singleton

LAVELLE WILKINS-CHINN, a native of St. Louis, is the dramaturge for A Call to Conscience (c2c), a St. Louis–based theater collective, and has performed with several theater companies including the St. Louis Black Repertory Company and Pamoja Theatre Workshop. Her fiction has been included in *The Hoot and Holler of the Owls*, a Hurston-Wright anthology, *Arts Today*, an online St. Louis e-zine, and her poetry has been featured in *Drum Voices Revue*, a multicultural arts periodical.

Calvin Wilson

CALVIN WILSON is an arts and entertainment writer who has worked at the *Kansas City Star* and, currently, at the *St. Louis Post-Dispatch*. Wilson is also creator and host of *Somethin' Else*, a jazz program on the Radio Arts Foundation radio station in St. Louis.

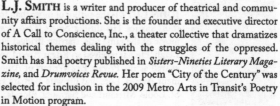